# CURSE OF WINGS AND DARKNESS

## AMY PROKOPIS

Amy Prokopis

Cover image by Amy Prokopis

Edited by Lucia Ferrara

Published by Amy Prokopis

First printing edition October 1, 2024

www.amyprokopis.com

For those who needed an Angel and didn't have one.

# DISCLAIMER

This book discusses mental health, sexual assault, and contains sexual content. There is also mention of homophobic behavior among family members.

# CHAPTER 1

"Our final is the same time next week," Dr. Bartlett said as everyone finished gathering their things in the lecture hall. "Don't forget to buy a blue book from the student store for the essay portion."

I zipped up my backpack and grabbed my water bottle, holding it between both of my hands as I waited for the rest of my row to file toward the exit ahead of me. I let out a deep breath, then another, then another. The longer I waited, the more I worried that I would be stuck in the lecture hall with our professor who'd told me last week that my essay was trash. I stuffed the paper in my notebook before I had even gotten to the end of it. It was that bad. I was having nightmares that ended with red letters, making it hard to even make the walk here for class without feeling like my heart was going to burst from my chest.

I caught Dr. Bartlett's eye, quickly averting my gaze and squeezing past the last two girls at the end of the row.

"Sorry. I need to... I have a thing," I said as I nearly tripped over their feet to get to the aisle. I hurried up the last of the steps and out the back door. Four steps exactly and I was outside the building, the cool air making my lungs contract when I breathed it in. Still, it was better than being in that tight lecture hall.

It wasn't until my heart slowed that I realized I'd started walking in the opposite direction and I turned to make my way north toward my apartment. Thank God this was my last class of the week. Pre-finals week was hell. You'd think it would get easier by your third semester, but I was a nervous wreck the entire week the same way I was freshman year.

When I turned around, I noticed a boy leaning against the wall of the building. He was hot. He had curly blond hair and blue eyes that I thought pierced my soul even from six feet away. I felt my face flush the minute I realized he was staring right at me, silencing the panic that raced through my heart moments before and igniting a new kind of flame I was sure was obvious in my red face. He straightened up and smiled.

"Hey," he said. "You have a class in there, right? I've seen you get out at eight every Monday, Wednesday, and Friday."

I nodded, a weird sound of approval coming out.

"Damn. I didn't mean it like... I'm not like watching you or anything. I have a class in this building that gets out at the same time," he said and gestured toward the building he'd been leaning against before. "Are you a film, English, drama...?"

"Music," I said and cleared my throat. "I'm a music major. Cello."

He nodded as though considering what the words meant.

"Very cool. What's your name?" he asked.

"Um, Lily," I said, my heart starting to pick up pace again.

"Good to meet you," he said and extended his hand. When I took it to give it a shake, he stepped forward, close enough now that I could smell him. I couldn't place the smell, but it was the best thing I'd smelled in a long time. It was like the sweetest pastry, comforting.

"G-good to meet you too," I said and backed away, placing my hand on my water bottle and turning it between my hands.

"I'll see you around. Maybe next week. Hopefully sooner."

The way he said it paired with the way his eyes roved over me before he turned and left had me a blushing mess. I was a puddle. I melted right there and anyone and everyone could probably see that I was having a nervous breakdown over a boy I didn't know. Even now that he was halfway across the courtyard, I was struggling to calm myself. I didn't even know his name. What was wrong with me? Why didn't I think to ask his name?

I walked in the direction of my apartment, walking faster than I had planned just to try matching the rhythm of my heart. Exercise was good for anxiety. I knew that from therapy. Exercise always helped me to get a grip and clear my head. So, I walked fast until I was at the front entrance to the apartment. I scanned my card and walked into the lobby, walking right past the front desk like normal and went to the elevator.

My apartment was at the top, so I had a while in the elevator to decompress. I felt tears well in my eyes before I slowed my breathing, using a breathing technique I'd learned from my Intro to Psychology class. When the elevator dinged and the door slid open, I felt much calmer as I walked down the hall. My unit was at the end of the hall, the last room. It meant that my bedroom had a window that looked over the street and the city lights.

I turned my key in the lock and walked in, finding Anne at the stove making dinner like she normally did.

"Hey," she greeted and tucked a loose strand of dark hair behind her ear. "How was class?"

"Good," I said and passed her on the way to my bedroom.

Just past the tiny kitchen was a shared living room with a wall of windows that opened onto the balcony. To the left was Anne's room and to the right was mine. Hers had strings of blue Christmas lights hanging around the perimeter and mine had magenta lights. I went to my room and sat my backpack on the desk chair, stepping out of my tennis shoes and tossing my socks toward the hamper where one bounced off the plastic and settled on the hardwood floor.

"I have ramen ready," Anne called.

It was a Friday tradition. Anne made ramen and I came home from class to eat it with her. Each week was a different kind of ramen, but it was always ramen. Most Friday nights, we would go out in the city. Her favorite spot was a club just down the street that was frequented by other NYU students.

We ate in silence at our small kitchen table for a long time. I finished most of my dish, with only some of the warm broth left, before we moved to the living room to watch TV. Anne pulled up an old episode of Ru Paul's Drag Race, from one of our favorite seasons. I sipped the broth from the bowl as she finished her helping and set it aside, eager to make conversation judging by the way she sat forward on the couch.

"We should go to the club tonight," she said.

I knew that what she really meant was that we should go out and find people to hook up with. I was still figuring out how to navigate that arena. It wasn't like I was a novice or anything. I'd had sex. It was horrible, but I did it. I just shook it off and told myself that everyone's first time was terrible. Still though, did it really count if you just lay there because you didn't know what to do and the guy figured out after a few thrusts that you were a virgin? Did it really count if he changed his mind halfway in and left?

"Sure," I said, more to please her than anything. I'd do what I usually did. We would go to the club together and dance, which was always fun. I'd have a few drinks, which would ease the anxiety. I would loosen up. I might even talk to someone while she ran her usual plays and won over some girl, buying her a drink, and then I wouldn't see her until they turned up at our apartment well after I'd gotten ready for bed and sat down to enjoy some tea and a sappy romcom.

"Good. This time, some guy is buying *you* a drink. I swear. I'll make it happen," she said and bounced toward her room to get ready.

She'd been my best friend all through school. We started at the same intermediate Catholic school before moving up to the all-girl's school down the road. My parents sent me there because it was a prestigious school and it was the most expensive in the state, if not the whole country. I loved it because my orchestra teacher was amazing and having played the cello himself for years with the New York Phil, I was starstruck every day fourth period.

Anne came out to me during junior year, though she didn't really need to. I had an idea. She didn't care when we had the yearly ball with the boy's school, basically the Catholic school version of prom done on an even larger scale considering we all came from rich families. She even skipped it our senior year when one of our teachers was appalled at the idea that she was even considering wearing a pantsuit. College had been freeing for us both in a sense. She was living openly as a lesbian and bounced from relationship to relationship, always the social butterfly, and I explored the world of music I really craved to learn. It was perfect, though no one from home knew about it. They would all die if they knew what either of us were doing with our free time.

Anne had always been the adventurous one and introduced me to so many things since we met. I went all of freshman year thinking that her interest in CNC was some kind of engineering thing.

In case you didn't know, like me, CNC is not an engineering thing. At least, it wasn't where she was concerned.

"Take your hair down, it looks sexy!" she yelled from her room. "Wear dark clothes They look better under the club lights, and they make you look slim. And wear heels because they make your ass look so much better. It's basically instant butt-lift. Make sure to go heavier on the eyeshadow to show off your eyes. But don't wear anything on your lips. It just smudges on the drinks and if we find you some guy for the night, it will definitely end up all over him!" she yelled from her room.

She was right. She always was. What's more, when you were a lesbian, you paid a lot of attention to the way women looked and she knew how to make my natural assets look better.

"So, my black dress then?" I asked. I only had one and I only wore it out to the club.

"Yes!" Anne yelled as though it was the obvious answer.

I took my bowl to the kitchen sink and went to my bedroom. I pulled out a pair of chunky black heels and my black dress. It was the shortest dress I owned, barely covering my ass, but it was a perfect fit. It was the kind of bodycon dress that didn't move unless you wanted it to and hugged all the right places. The back was open aside from the criss-cross strap. I stripped off my T-shirt and leggings and pulled on the dress. I'd freeze on the walk there, but Anne said that the way I looked in that dress was worth the fifteen minutes of discomfort.

It took me an hour to get ready. I let my blonde hair hang loose around my shoulders, taking extra care with my eye makeup until Anne joined me in the bathroom to nag me about my curls and my basic makeup. I curled the ends of my long hair. It was my favorite way to wear it and even my mom had approved of the ultra-feminine style. I put more eye shadow on than normal like Anne told me too, feeling a little too sexy by the time I was done.

"That's perfect," Anne told me when I stepped back into the living room.

"Are you sure it's not too much?"

"Absolutely not."

Anne was dressed in a sparkly pair of pants with a matching halter top and wore her hair straight.

"You promise that you'll stay with me?" I asked. If the goal of tonight was finding me someone to hook up with, I didn't want to do it all alone. The last time proved that I was crap at all of this. I always second-guessed myself. I went for the wrong guys and I always ended up with someone that Anne said was a walking red flag, someone that liked the whole doe-eyed good girl act even though mine was an honest naivety and not an act at all. Anne was great at calling people's bullshit, but depending on the goal of the night she didn't always stick by my side to the end.

"Yes," she said. "Why are you so nervous?"

"Because I'm a half-virgin and I look more like a baby playing dress up than a twenty-one-year-old," I moaned and stomped my foot.

"Half-virgin? Girl, please," she said and left me standing in the living room to go to the kitchen. She pulled down two shot glasses and a bottle of tequila. "Come here."

I met her at the center island as she poured the shots, sliding one toward me.

"This one," she said and raised her glass "is because we both look hot as hell."

I clinked my glass against hers, tapped it once on the counter, and drained the entire thing with a grimace. When I sat the glass down, she filled it for a second time.

"I don't know," I said. "Finals are next week, and I have two papers due *and* a recital."

"Which is what this one is for," Anne said and slid the glass back to me. I picked it up and raised it in the air, mirroring her. "This one is for the end of the term. This time next week, we both will have crushed all our final exams and have two years of college behind us. That's a reason to celebrate and that's exactly what we are going to do tonight."

I downed the second shot after she did, taking a moment to recover as she let out a cheer.

We watched a few more episodes of Drag Race, making plans for the night, before we gathered our things and left. The club was a popular spot among NYU students, so when we got there at ten-thirty it was packed with people in their twenties. We were lucky enough to get in before it got too busy, walking past the bouncer and into the room. We were immediately bathed in red and purple lights, and loud pop music vibrating the floor under my heels.

Anne led the way to the crowded bar, pulling me through the crowd by my hand. We waited a few minutes before we were able to flag a bartender and order two house margaritas. I sipped from mine as we turned to look over the dance floor. Bodies meshed like they were all a part of the same choreographed dance. I was halfway into my drink when I noticed a pair of piercing blue eyes.

The boy from the courtyard.

My breath hitched in my chest as he started toward us.

"Oh God," I said and pulled on Anne's arm. "He's coming over."

"Who?" she asked and looked away from a group of girls. "The blond guy?"

"He's from campus. I talked to him today," I said in her ear.

Anne gave me an interested look, but clearly not interested enough to stick around. She took a few steps away and before I could stop her, the boy reached out to touch my arm.

"Hey," he shouted over the noise. "How about I buy you another drink and we get to know each other more, Music Major?"

Cheers erupted as the song ended, loud enough to keep me from speaking. Maybe it was for the best, one less embarrassing thing I could do. I nodded and let him lead me toward the bar, calling to the bartender until he got her attention. He motioned toward my drink and that was enough for her as she turned to make another margarita.

"What's your name?" I asked, remembering that I'd forgotten that little detail earlier.

He lowered his glass from his lips before he could take a drink, smiling.

"Aaron," he said. "I hoped I'd see you before next week, but I didn't think I'd see you so soon. I would've dressed up a bit more."

"You look great," I told him, looking over his white shirt and dark jeans.

He turned to face me, leaning his arm on the bar. The bartender came with a fresh glass for me, and Aaron slid it my way.

"To something new," he said and lifted his glass toward me. I lifted mine to his and drank.

"What's your major?" I asked.

He shook his head and sat his drink on the bar, leaning against it again and eyeing the low cut of my dress. It made my entire body warm.

"I'm more interested in you. I could never play an instrument," he said.

"Have you tried?"

"Once," he said and inched closer to me when a guy slipped behind him to talk to the bartender. "My mom made me take piano lessons as a kid. I was shit though."

"Maybe you just didn't practice enough." I shrugged. "It's all about practice."

"Well, if you were my teacher, I probably would've sat at the bench more." He gave me a wink. "So, cello. Is that all you play?"

It took me a moment to recover before I could reply. "Um, yes. Cello. I can play most of the strings, but the cello is my thing."

"Is that the big one?" he asked and drew his arms across his body.

"That's the bass," I told him. "The cello sits between your legs."

He smirked and looked down at me again before raising his eyes to my face.

"Between those legs?" he asked.

Just like that, I wasn't so sure I liked this anymore. I felt like I might explode if he looked at my body that way again. I looked away from the bar, trying to spot Anne. It took me a moment before I found her on the far side of the room talking with a girl with locs.

"I think my friend needs me," I said and pointed her way. I took two steps from the bar and when I looked up again, Anne was practically sucking the girl's face off.

"She looks okay to me," Aaron said.

My panic must've been obvious, because the sly look faded from his face and concern replaced it. He ran a hand through his blond curls.

"I'm sorry. I didn't mean... Maybe I came on a little heavy," he said, holding his hands up. "I didn't mean to be creepy or anything. I just thought you were..."

"It's all right. I'm not the best at this. I'm horrible actually," I said and reached for my drink. I took a sip, ready to leave the scene when he took a step toward me.

"I'm sorry. Let's try this again. Please? I think you're really cute and there's something about you when you talk and the way you look up at me with those eyes like a freaking Barbie doll. Let's just start over?" Aaron asked, gesturing back toward the bar. "How about we take a shot? I could use something to settle my nerves. I'm sorry."

"That's okay," I said. "Let's just start over, like you said."

"Good. That's good." He took a breath and turned toward the bartender, flagging her down with the wave of an arm and asking for four shots before I could stop him.

"Don't drink that," a deep voice said in my ear, startling me. I whirled around to face him, stunned by the seriousness in his face but the sincerity in his chocolate-brown eyes. He wore dark jeans and a black pullover. His dark hair was tied in a topknot.

"W-what? Excuse you." I said and scooted closer to Aaron. The guy reached out and knocked the last of my margarita over on the bar with the flick of a finger. "Hey! I was drinking that," I cried out.

"Were you?" the stranger asked, more concerned now. It was weird. Why fuss over a drink when he'd just made a sticky mess of the bar?

The bartender returned with the four shot glasses, plopping down a rag to clean up the mess before she handed us our shots. I turned to explain the mess to Aaron, but he hadn't noticed and pressed a shot glass into my hand instead.

"To starting over," he said and raised his glass to mine. I downed it, my throat burning. Vodka. Not my ideal shot.

"Ready for another marg?" he asked me, nodding toward the empty glass next to the rag.

"Walk away," I heard that deep voice, somehow low enough that only I could hear.

"Yes," I told Aaron, more out of spite for what man-bun was saying than because I wanted another. "I'd love that."

Aaron turned to get the bartender's attention again and I heard a groan behind me, glancing at the man for a moment. He twisted his glass, an amber liquid with a hunk of ice in the center, before downing the last of it. "Keep your eye on the drink," he said, keeping his eyes on his own glass.

I ignored him and turned to Aaron. I lifted the shot glass, sliding his toward him. He stopped waving for the bartender and turned to look at me, a smile spreading on his face.

"This one is for being adventurous," I said with a giggle. He laughed and pressed his glass to mine, and we drained them. I barely winced this time at the taste, sitting the empty shot glass next to the new margarita that had appeared on the bar at some point when we were talking. I noticed the dark-haired guy next to me as I lifted the glass, half-expecting him to swat it away.

"What if we go somewhere a little quieter and just talk?" Aaron asked. "There are some booths on the far side of the room. We could sit there and finish our drinks in private, maybe head out after."

The idea of going anywhere else sent shivers up my spine.

"Let's just finish our drinks here first."

"What? I can't hear you," Aaron shouted and leaned toward me.

"She said she wasn't going," the guy said, leaning across me.

"Do you know this guy?" Aaron asked me.

I shrugged away from man-bun and into Aaron, feeling his arm slide around my waist.

"No. I have no idea who he is," I said.

"Leave us alone, man," Aaron said and pivoted so he was between me and the dark-haired man. "She's with me."

"She shouldn't have to be with anyone for you to treat her with respect," he said, raising his eyebrows as though implying Aaron was up to something. It made me uncomfortable, all of it. Maybe I should've just stayed with Anne. A glance toward the other side of the room told me she was on to the next thing. I didn't see her anywhere.

Aaron pulled me closer to his hip as he yelled a final string of curses at the man and led me away from the bar. We skirted the dance floor until we found a section of booths behind dark see-through veils. He led me down a hall between two of the booths where the bathrooms were along one wall and an exit on the other. He turned to face me, looking over me as though I might be injured.

"Are you okay? I'm sorry about that asshole. He should've minded his own business," Aaron said.

"It's fine. Thanks," I said, adjusting my grip on my glass. Half of the margarita had sloshed over my hand and onto the floor. I took a long sip. It tasted watered down from the ice.

"I can get us a booth, but it might be a while. It looks like they're all full." Aaron peered around the corner at the red leather booths. I pulled him back, my heart fluttering in my chest at the feel of his bicep.

"It's okay. Let's just go somewhere else."

He eyed me curiously, questioning if I was sure.

"Please," I added and downed the last of my drink and sat the glass on the top of one of the booths.

"All right," he said and took my hand. "We'll go."

He pushed the exit door open. It led to the back alley, and we were greeted with the sound of a car horn from the street at the end. I tripped over the uneven concrete on my way out, falling into him. He caught me and I looked up at his blue eyes.

"I got you," he said sweetly, holding me close.

I giggled.

"Now what?" I asked as I regained my balance. My vision blurred and I felt something hard against my back. As I drew in a breath, a hand pressed to my lips, and I felt something cool against the space between my breasts.

"Now, you're going to come with me like a good girl and do what I say," Aaron said, his voice sounding so different now. It wasn't the sweet, boyish tone as before. "I'm going to uncover your mouth and you're going to tell me what you're going to do."

He did. As soon as his hand was gone, I knew I should've screamed. I should've kicked him. I should've bitten the hand when it was pressed to my lips. I did none of those things. I could barely get enough air in my lungs to speak at all.

"What are you going to do?"

"I-I'm going to do what you say," I whispered.

He placed his hand over my lips again and I realized when he moved it to brush my cheek that the cold object was a knife.

"Whatever you say, baby girl," he said with a dark laugh.

My vision blurred again. I felt myself slumping against him despite wanting to push away. He held me against the wall with one hand, saying something I couldn't hear. Then, he was gone. I blinked when I heard a groan of pain, clearing my vision just in time to see a large figure looming over Aaron on the ground.

"No. Please. Come on, man," Aaron begged.

The figure was human... but not. It looked like he was holding an umbrella over his shoulder. Two umbrellas? Wings! At least, I think they were wings. None of this made sense and my vision blurred again and when I was able to see clearly, I was on all fours in the alleyway.

"I got you," the dark-haired man said. "I told you not to drink anything."

"Did he spike it?" I asked, feeling stupid as soon as the words came out. Of course, he had. I should've trusted my gut. I knew something was off, but I thought it was the other guy, not Aaron.

"Where do you live?" he asked, pulling me to my feet. I stumbled into his chest, only staying upright thanks to his arms.

"Not telling some stranger," I said.

"Better than lying in the alley," he retorted. "You tell me where you live, and you can sleep in your own bed, or we can sleep here. Your choice."

We? Who was *we*?

"The apartment down the street," I said and attempted to unzip my purse. His hands replaced mine after the first try, pulling out my keycard and keychain.

"Who the hell would just leave you like this? Whatever friends you came with, drop them," he said firmly. Before I knew it, I was cradled against his chest, my head lying against his shoulder as he walked down the street.

I closed my eyes, barely registering the movement until I heard the door open and the sound of the TV.

"You're back..." Anne started. I looked up, her face blurry next to the girl from the bar on the couch. "Whoa."

"Hello to you, too," the man said, tone heavy with sarcasm. "Some friend you are. Where's her room?"

Anne didn't respond to the insult. I saw her point toward my room. It was getting harder and harder to keep my eyes open, especially once my head came down on my thick pillow. I heard the door shut and the sound of his feet walking around the room. I felt myself drifting away when he draped my fluffy blanket over me.

# CHAPTER 2

I only dream when I'm in a deep sleep and the heavy night of drinking plus whatever Aaron put in my drink was the perfect combination for vivid nightmares. It was the same as usual, only more intense and I couldn't break free from the dream like normal. Even when my brain registered that it was just a dream, I was stuck staring down at the red marks on my essay. The red blurred on the page until it was running over the black ink in twisted rivers. When I held the paper away from me, blood dripped from the bottom edge and onto the floor.

I dropped it and when I looked up, I was standing in a cellar and blood was splattered across the brick wall, some of the blood was old. Mixed in with the gore were red letters that I didn't get a chance to read before I jolted awake.

I was lying on my stomach, one leg twisted in the gray blanket and my other bent beside me like I was running. I pushed my chest from the mattress, head pounding and eyes burning from the dim light of the window. A large figure caught my attention in the corner by the door. I craned my neck to look at him and felt like everything in my body turned to ice.

I vaguely remembered him, but he looked different. He wasn't huge muscular yes but somehow, he was a presence that screamed power and control. He had dark hair that was pulled into a bun on top of his head. Every inch of him was sculpted so precisely that he had to be the kind of guy that ate protein all day and lived at the gym. He wore dark jeans and a black pullover, sleeves pushed up to his elbows. He turned his gaze from the pictures tacked to the corkboard above my desk, his chocolate eyes melting my insides and reminding me that I was still wearing my strappy black dress from last night and the hem was hiked halfway up my ass.

"There's Aspirin on the nightstand. Drink the whole glass of water, if you can," he said as I flipped the blanket over my lower half.

I sat up on the bed, pulling the blanket closer and tucking my legs underneath me just in case. He stood up, over six feet at full height, and opened the bedroom door. He shut it behind him without another word and I let out a breath that stuck in my throat. Tears spilled over as I fought to control my hyperventilating. I scrambled from the bed and grabbed a pair of navy sweats I had tossed on the desk, pulling them over my legs before quickly stripping off the dress and letting it fall to the floor in a heap.

I pulled the NYU sweatshirt on and forced myself to take deep breaths. I thought of my stomach as a balloon, and I pictured myself inflating it as much as I could. Once I felt a little more put together, I pulled my hair into a bun and went to my bathroom to wash my face, the small space comforting until I got a look at myself in the mirror.

I looked horrible. I looked so bad that I started panicking again about what might have happened last night. I barely remembered. I knew Aaron spiked my drink and then I was in the alley outside the club and that's where things started to mesh with my dream. I remember giant wings, the bloody essay, the bricks with the blood splattered and the writing...

I stripped off my clothes and decided to get in the shower. I scrubbed my skin until it was painful. There were pieces of blonde hair stuck to the side of the shower before I felt a strange calmness overcome me. Suddenly, I didn't feel anything at all. It was like time stood still. I let the water wash over me until it went cold, and I got out and back into my sweats. I dried my hair with a towel until it stopped dripping and opened the bathroom door.

My heart leaped in my chest.

"You haven't taken the Aspirin yet," he said. He was looking out my window. He let the curtain go so it covered the view and he turned to look at me.

A plate of food sat on my bed, which he must have made while I was in the shower. He'd cooked scrambled eggs with beef and bell peppers. An orange lay on the fuzzy blanket beside the plate. I looked at the glass of water on the nightstand, but immediately thought about last night.

"I'm not hungry," I whispered.

He looked a little annoyed at my response.

"After last night, you need to eat," he said, his tone not matching the seriousness in his face.

I shrugged, pulling on the hem of my sweatshirt. "I don't really eat breakfast."

"I have a thing about food. Please, just eat," he said, trying to keep his voice sweet.

"So do I. I don't really like to eat. I don't eat when…" I stopped before the tears could spill over again. God, this was bad. Who was I? I wasn't the kind of girl to go out and come back with some man that I didn't remember the morning after. I didn't even know his name and here he was, making me breakfast and looking back at me with more concern than I think anyone has in my whole life.

"You don't eat when you're anxious," he said, the words a statement of fact. He let out a deep breath and moved from the window, keeping his eyes on me the entire way.

I stepped back until I felt the doorframe behind me. He lowered his eyes to the bed, picking up the fork. He scooped up a large helping of the egg dish and took a bite. As he chewed, he moved to the nightstand and picked up the glass. He downed the entire thing and turned back to the plate on the bed, spearing an egg with the fork. He turned to face me, his expression softer than before.

"Eat," he said and raised the fork to my lips. "Please."

I hesitated for just a moment before I opened my mouth and let him place the fork on my tongue. The eggs weren't as warm as I wanted, but they were some of the best I've had. They were creamy and had a little kick of pepper. He let me take the fork and then handed me the empty glass.

"You should fill that yourself," he said. "Never take your eyes off your drink. Hopefully, last night taught you that."

I scoffed, feeling my cheeks heat with embarrassment. I took the glass and turned for the kitchen, blinking back the tears. I turned on the tap and stuck the glass under the stream, hearing him follow me into the room. He sat the plate on the counter and let out a sigh.

"I didn't mean it to come off that way," he said. "I'm sorry."

Water spilled over the glass and ran down my hand. I turned off the tap and dumped out some of the water before I turned to face him. He pushed the plate across the island toward me. Mostly because I didn't want his judgment again, I started to eat. I relaxed a little with each bite, looking around the kitchen for the dirty dishes. He must've washed them because a skillet was lying on the drying rack by the sink.

I ran through the night again, feeling the tightness slowly return in my chest. I remembered the girl with dreadlocks sitting in the living room when I came back last night, but they must have gone somewhere else because Anne's bedroom door was open, and her bed was made. Her lanyard wasn't hanging on the back of the front door like it would've been if she were here.

"Did... We didn't...?" The words stuck in my throat, and I had to sit the fork aside. I was worried I might be sick.

"I brought you here and put you in bed. Nothing more," he said. "I wanted to make sure you were okay after everything. I sat in your room in case whatever drug he gave you was too much."

"You didn't sleep?"

He sucked in a deep breath as though thinking about his answer.

"I'm on a kind of unique sleep schedule," he said and looked back at me. "A work thing."

I took a drink of the water and found myself finishing most of the glass.

"You didn't have to do that. You could've just left. You know, you should've." My voice shaking.

He scoffed, expression tight again.

"You got drugged and nearly taken in an alley. Your friend left you at a bar alone."

"She knew I liked that guy, and it wasn't like he was some stranger," I said, surprised how easily the lie slid from my lips. I was sure the heat in my cheeks gave away the truth, however.

"And you didn't walk me out this morning."

"Why would I walk you out? I don't even know you," I said, dumping the last of the eggs in the trash and setting the plate in the sink.

"To be sure that I left," he said, the words making me shiver. "And your friend should never have left me alone with you. I shouldn't be here now."

"Why are you?" I asked and turned to face him, fear tightening in my chest now that I was looking at him. "Why are you here?" The words were a whisper the second time and his expression softened. His shoulders relaxed, looking smaller somehow. He leaned his arms on the counter and shook his head before looking up at me.

"I don't know," he said, the same softness back as when he'd told me to take the Aspirin. Part of me wished I had at least done that much now that I was nursing the worst headache possible.

"Okay," I said after a beat.

"Okay?" he asked with a snort of disbelief. "You live in New York City. Did your parents never warn you about what could happen? Has no one ever taught you how to handle yourself?"

Now that was offensive. My eyes burned and instead of yelling at him like I wanted to, the words came out more like a whine.

"I can handle myself," I said. "And I think it's rude that you're telling me I have to watch the way I dress in public and that I can't go to a bar and pick up guys."

"It doesn't matter what you wear. Black dress or sweatpants," he said and pointed at me before continuing, "a predator will see right through your mask and peg you for the naive good girl you are."

I blinked back the angry tears.

"A predator," I murmured. "Well, thank you for helping me. I really appreciate it and last night... That's how I know you're not the kind of person you're talking about because you're wrong about me."

He stepped away from the counter and held his hands out by his side, glancing around the room before looking back at me.

"From where I'm standing there are two possibilities," he said and pushed his sleeves down to his wrists. "You either proudly wear the crown and have never bothered to step outside the castle walls, or daddy has his little princess locked away in this tower and last night was a poorly planned escape."

I stood stunned, only brought back to the moment when a tear ran hot down my face. I saw his expression fall as he lowered his arms to his side. He looked at the floor and gripped his fist with one hand before looking up at me with regret in his eyes.

"Just go," I said and yanked open the front door. After a beat he passed me and turned to look at me from the hallway. "Are you happy? I made damn sure you left this time."

I slammed the door and turned the lock.

# CHAPTER 3

I tried forgetting about the dark-haired man, whose name I still didn't know, by diving into YouTube. My channel had picked up a lot since October when I released my second original song. I loved the softness of string music. I always had, but exploring other genres when I got to college was exhilarating and I found myself imagining how the softness of the violin or the deep swell of the cello would mix with the strong chords of a rock song.

The channel started with me mixing popular songs with melodies I wrote and played on my cello. Then, my mind needed something more and I found myself creating my own songs. I found my guitarist online and he played all the music I sent his way. I did the drums myself whenever I needed them, mixing sounds using a program on my computer. The cello and vocals were all me.

I posted the songs to YouTube with stock videos of forests I found online and displayed the lyrics on the screen. The first song did well, and I saw a steady growth in views and subscribers. The second video doubled that overnight and it was still climbing. It was exciting, but also made me nervous about what would come next.

The front door opened, and Anne came in, dressed in a pair of leggings and an oversized sweater. She hung her keys on the door handle and dropped her wallet on the counter, smiling excitedly back at me.

"How was your night?" I asked her. "I saw that you brought a girl home."

"Her name is Jazz and she's awesome and I'm going to see her again tonight, but that's not what I wanted to talk about." She said and plopped onto the couch next to me, closed the lid of my laptop, and moved it from my lap to the coffee table. "Who was that Thor-looking guy that brought you home?"

"Nobody," I said, hoping she heard the finality in my voice. "He's gone now."

"I'm gay as hell, but that guy was a piece, Lily."

"He was just making sure I got home okay," I told her, feeling the headache ramp up again now that she was here. "I might go take a nap. I'm still recovering from last night."

"Wait. I want to know what happened with that other guy," she said and followed me to my room, leaning in the doorway.

I threw back the covers and climbed into the bed. The sun was high enough in the sky now that it didn't shine through the curtains like before, meaning that most of the light came from the magenta lights hanging around the walls.

"He spiked my drink," I said in an exhale. "I'm fine. Nothing happened."

"Is that when Thor found you?"

"He's not..." I ignored the comment. The last thing I needed was the image of that guy's muscles in my head before I went to sleep. I didn't want to risk dreaming of him. "He saw it happen before I did. He stepped in and got me here. Now, I'm going to take a nap because my head hurts and I have a final paper I need to finish for Monday."

"All right," Anne said. She lingered in the doorway even after I'd laid down and pulled the blanket to my chin. "I'll be working on physics in my room."

I closed my eyes and immediately saw the dark-haired guy sitting in the corner of my room, looking back at me with interest.

Great. Just great.

I didn't leave the apartment the entire weekend. I barely left my room. Anne didn't question me, thankfully. She was gone most of the weekend with her new fling from the bar. Jazzlyn. She was a pre-med student and Anne was already hopeful that the similarity to her parents would make them more accepting of her when they got introduced in the future.

I was on edge on my walk to Bartlett's class Monday night. I jogged through the courtyard even though I was twenty minutes early. When our class released and I hurried from the lecture hall, I froze just outside the main doors of the building when I didn't see Aaron leaning against the opposite building like the day we'd met.

The images of the alley ran through my head. I was slumped against the wall while Aaron begged the dark guy with the man-bun. Something happened. That guy who took me home and fed me the world's best scrambled eggs had done something to him and that should've made me feel a lot more concerned than I did. What had me fighting for breath and my heart racing was knowing that Aaron had been so charming, wrapped an arm around my waist, drugged me, pinned me against that dirty alley wall and

"Sorry," a girl said when she bumped into me on her way out of the building.

It was just enough to pull me from my stupor, but as soon as I adjusted my backpack on my shoulders and faced the courtyard again, everything went over the edge. I didn't realize I'd walked in the wrong direction until the student union building was directly in front of me. There were too many people around. That fact only worsened the stinging in my eyes and suddenly I was dizzy.

I hurried inside and instead of going into the first bathroom, where I knew I'd fall apart, I started up the stairs in hopes that the exercise would regulate my heartbeat. I made it to the third-floor food court, which was busy on one side with students gathering for dinner. My eyes landed on the bathroom, and I barely made it inside the doors and snapped the stall door shut before the tears fell.

I opened my phone and started scrolling through my social media accounts in turn, trying to find a distraction. Once the panic dimmed and the exhaustion set in, I left the stall to splash cold water on my face and hoped my red-rimmed eyes weren't too noticeable. It was finals week. Maybe people would just think I was stressed about tests.

I left the bathroom and decided to go to the coffee shop on the opposite side of the busy third floor. It was nearly empty, with just a few people sitting in the small lounge area with laptops open and headphones on. The workers behind the counter were cleaning equipment, a woman handing over a large coffee and a bottle of water to a man.

A man with long hair tied in a bun at the top of his head.

I froze before the lounge area as the man from the bar turned from the counter with his coffee in one hand and the water in the other. His eyes met mine and something about those dark eyes quieted my racing heart the same way they had in my bedroom even as he told me off for not eating breakfast regularly.

He looked away from me and down at the table just to my left. He pulled out the chair closest to me and sat the bottled water on the table before going around to the opposite side. He relaxed in his chair, pulling the lid off the to-go cup and blew at the plume of steam that came from the top. He wafted the steam away for a moment before finally taking a sip. I could feel those dark eyes studying me as he glanced at me, reading the anxiety on my face. Why did it not terrify me? This guy did something to Aaron in that alley. He warned me the entire night about safety and acted like an ass before I kicked him out of my apartment. He was here now, somehow, and wanted me to sit and drink the water he'd bought me. How did he know I was here?

"Are you following me?" I asked, gripping the straps of my backpack.

He lowered his coffee a fraction from his lips, eyebrows cocked curiously.

"I always stop here for a cup of coffee before work," he said. "I saw you scurry across the way to the bathroom, and it looked like you could use a drink."

I scoffed.

"A drink," I echoed.

"Water," he said. "Cold water can help."

He slid the bottled water farther across the table and scooted the chair toward me with his foot. I knew what he meant. It was the first trick my therapist back home had taught me. Cold water for panic attacks. Part of me was relieved that he seemed to know. The other part of me wanted to scream at him again.

I scoffed again and shifted, nearly tripping over the chair and falling into it instead. I let my backpack slip to the ground and I turned to face him, tears threatening to fall as I righted myself in the chair.

"You're some creep. I don't care if you are here every day. You noticed me and you did this," I blurted and shoved the water across the table to him. "And you're an ass for talking about it like the way I feel is... saying I scurried across the way like I'm some stupid, little mouse or..."

"Drink," he said and slid the bottle back toward me. "Please?"

Again, with the eyes. I hated it. I twisted the cap off the bottle, anyway, feeling more relaxed just feeling the seal crack beneath my fingers. I took a single sip. Then, I took a longer one until I found myself drinking half of the bottle while stewing about if he was really an ass or not. Maybe he was just a concerned person. Still, he didn't have to say all the rude things.

Definitely an ass.

"You're feisty for a little mouse," he said with a smirk.

Definitely an ass.

"Too soon," he said and raised his hands in apology before wrapping them around his coffee cup. "I didn't mean anything by my comment, by the way. You were obviously upset and after what happened, you have every right to be. I was worried."

"Why?" I asked as he took a sip of his coffee.

"A girl gets drugged and assaulted, nearly much more, in an alley... From the looks of it, a girl with a whole lot going on that most people don't know about. You haven't been taught how to fend for yourself in this city, Mouse, that much was clear. Knowing you've just been walking around after that..." He looked away from our table, jaw tight. He let out a deep breath, almost a growl, before he looked back at me with that soft expression. "It bothers me."

It bothered him? How did he think I felt?

"You said your sleep schedule is different because of work," I said, eager to shift the conversation from my teetering anxiety. "Are you a bouncer or something at that club?"

He smirked and shook his head.

"Not a bouncer," he said and sipped on the coffee. The idea seemed to amuse him because his smile only grew wider. "A bouncer. That's one I've never considered."

"What is it that you do then?" I asked.

"Easy with the third degree," he laughed. "Again, you already made a mistake when we first sat down."

"I know that the water was unopened. I watched the barista hand it to you and I broke the seal," I said.

He shook his head and said, "I took you home after you were drugged at a club, stayed all night, made you breakfast, and you never once asked who I am. You still haven't."

I shifted in my seat. "Yeah. Well..." I twisted the cap off the water only to twist it back on and squirm some more under his reproachful gaze.

"I can continue to call you Mouse, if you'd like," he said with a smirk.

"It's Lily," I said with poorly feigned confidence. "Lily Thompson. What's your name?"

"Angel Ramírez," he said.

I twisted and untwisted the cap on the water bottle until finally deciding to drink. One of the baristas went to the table next to ours and began wiping it down. We waited in silence until he was finished and moved farther away. I downed the last of the water, twisted the cap back on, and sat it purposefully in the middle of the table before standing up.

"Well, um, thank you for the water, Angel," I said and lifted my backpack onto my shoulder.

"Lily." He said the words like a goodbye, but that same dark concern had returned in his eyes. I didn't allow myself another moment to read too much into it though before I walked back toward the stairs.

# CHAPTER 4

The nightmare was relentless. I woke up each morning already on edge after replaying the night of the attack in my mind. It wasn't until I was halfway through my finals that I realized I was looking for Angel at every turn, almost expecting him to swoop in with a bottle of water before each panic attack.

He didn't, and the panic attacks were worse than usual. I told myself it was just a high-stress week. Everyone was anxious.

I felt a little better after my last paper-and-pencil final and I could focus on the recital at the end of the week. The music department hosted a mixer at a large botanical garden not far from campus at the end of each semester. Students from the program performed throughout the entire night and had to be approved or nominated by NYU staff. A few of us from the orchestra developed a quartet in hopes of being approved and we were, which was a huge accomplishment considering we were just sophomores.

"Will there be food there?" Jazz asked from the living room couch, sitting next to Anne.

"Just appetizers, I think. They will have drinks," I said.

"Of course, we'll go," Anne said. "I want to see you play; it's a big moment. What if Jazz and I go watch you play and then we can all meet up afterward and get dinner?"

"Sure. That sounds great," I replied and set aside the last of my sandwich.

"Want to watch the movie with us?" Anne asked, sending me a look that told me that not only did she *not* want me to watch a movie with them, but she was hoping I would leave them alone for a bit.

"What are you guys watching?" I asked, just to be polite.

"Some new superhero movie?" Anne shrugged, getting a groan from Jazz who launched into a detailed explanation about how important this particular movie was to the entire series.

"I'll catch up with you guys later. I'll let you know when I head back," I said and went to gather my things from my room.

I spent a lot of time away from the apartment since the attack. Jazzlyn was over most days and she and Anne tended to get increasingly more handsy as the night went on. I was relieved when the rest of the quartet agreed to schedule night rehearsals the rest of the week leading up to the recital. I was nervous enough that I spent extra time practicing in the apartment. I'd try focusing on the notes and let my mind imagine what the night would be like only to find him in the middle of the crowd, staring back at me with those deep-brown eyes and intense interest that I was sure I'd never garnered from anyone else before.

I never made it through the entire piece when I practiced alone.

---

The gardens were illuminated with bulb lights strung around the topiaries and sending a romantic glow over the flowers. Music stands and chairs were set up under a wooden arch for the performers, a senior quartet already set up to begin the night's event. Anne stood with me as I took it all in while Jazz fetched glasses of wine from the bar.

"You'll be great," Anne said.

"I know it will be fine. We've had nearly perfect rehearsals all week, but that doesn't mean I'm any less nervous." I adjusted my curls over my shoulders. I was wearing a long black dress that I only ever wore for concerts. My heels would have sunk into the grass if I wasn't careful. I could just see myself tripping and spilling wine all over the dress before I got a chance to perform.

"I hope red is good with everyone," Jazz said when she joined us. I took a glass of the cabernet from her and took a sip, wondering if I should be drinking at all before the performance. What if it made me sloppy?

"I think I'm going to walk around a bit, you know, mingle with some people," I told them before taking my first cautious step onto the grass. Anne gave me an encouraging look and promised one last time that I'd be great before she turned back to Jazz and I was free to move to a less crowded area.

The first group of the night started to play, so I didn't notice that anyone was speaking to me until I felt a tap on my shoulder. I turned to face an old woman no taller than me. She held a glass of wine in one hand, the other held a fancy navy clutch that matched her sparkly dress.

"Are you a student?" she asked with a smile.

"Yes. I'm a music major at NYU," I said and sipped from my glass.

"What do you play?"

"I can play most string instruments well, but the cello is my primary."

"Are you playing tonight?" she asked, waving to a man carrying a tray of finger sandwiches nearby.

"I'm in the third quartet," I said as the man approached. I thanked him when he offered me a sandwich. I wasn't sure I could eat anything until after the performance.

"Well, I'm sure you will be lovely. This event is always done well. I'll be in the audience," the woman said kindly before joining the crowd.

I walked the outskirts of the garden, smiling awkwardly at the guests as I passed, making small talk with other students milling about. The quartet finished their first piece and moved into the next one as the applause died out.

"Sorry," I said as I nearly walked straight into a girl holding a viola. I looked up after scooting past her and my breath caught in my chest.

Angel Ramírez stood down the path, alone, holding a wine glass and staring at a statue at the end of the path. Raised on a pedestal was a crouched figure of stone, wings spread wide from his shoulders. Angel lowered the glass from his lips and turned, his eyes meeting mine. He didn't seem surprised to see me. I took two steps toward him before my ankle nearly gave out and I stumbled into a boy.

"Oh God," I gasped. The wine glass tipped from my fingers, spilling red liquid over the concrete. I nearly caught the stem of the glass before it tumbled, the sound of it shattering grabbing everyone's attention around us.

"I'll go get a waiter," the boy said and handed his own glass to his friend.

"Um, okay. It's not that bad, just a bit of glass," I said even though I knew it was much worse. I bent down to pick up the pieces, realizing how stupid an idea that was as soon as I'd collected several shards in my bare hand.

"Let me," Angel offered, twisting my hand so the glass spilled into his. "You're bleeding. Let's get you somewhere to clean up."

I hadn't felt the cut. I wasn't even sure where it was, but he'd already grasped my arm and helped me to my feet as two waiters joined us with a metal trash bin and a broom. Angel led the way down the path toward that gargoyle statue.

"I'm fine. Not a scratch," I said as he led me toward a stone bench on the left. He sat down, pulling me down with him.

"Look again." He leaned toward my heels.

Before I was prepared, he lifted my right leg and propped it on his knee. He brushed the fabric of my dress away, so it rose to my knee, revealing the cut on my shin that dripped blood toward my shoe.

"Oh," I gasped. "I'm sorry."

I lifted my leg as the blood began to roll toward my calf and his slacks. Angel hesitated a moment before he pulled his tie from his neck. He sucked in a deep breath as he brushed the blood away with a light touch, revealing a shallow cut that made my stomach turn.

"It's not that bad," he said and began wrapping the tie around my leg like a bandage. He tied it off before looking up at me with a smile.

"Thanks," I said, my heart thumping in my chest as his hand rested just above the tie. He smiled back at me for a moment, something in his eyes different, darker... It was the same urgency I saw there the night he helped me in that alley, the night he did whatever he did to chase away Aaron. Whatever I saw in his eyes had me transfixed until he moved his hands. My heart sped up and my breath hitched when he slipped a hand behind my knee, the other grasping my calf.

He lowered my leg to the concrete and as soon as he scooted a few inches away, everything within me slowed down. It felt like that moment of exhaustion after sprinting. Breathless. Heady.

"A-Are you playing tonight?" Angel asked, tugging at the collar of his shirt. He undid the top button revealing the gold chain of a necklace.

"Yes. I am playing," I said and turned on the bench, so my knees were facing the statue in the center. Now that I was closer, I understood why Angel was so interested in it. The gargoyle didn't make any sense among the beautiful flowers and the elegance of the party. It was ugly. It was hunched over on its perch, face and nostrils elongated. It even looked like it had claws where its hands held the side of the pedestal.

"Strange choice for a garden so lavish," Angel said.

The wings stretched before me pulled me back into that moment in the alley. I could see the scene so clearly now. I slumped against the alley wall as Aaron was wrenched backward. He collapsed onto his back, scrambling over the cracked pavement as the large figure suddenly appeared next to him in a blur of darkness. It straightened up, taller than it seemed it should have, wings stretching from his back wider and wider until they hung high over his back the way a raven might display them before dive-bombing a threat.

Aaron begged for him to lay off, that he would go, but the figure stretched his wings high and lurched forward. Aaron screamed. I remember the screaming. It had died out quickly. I assumed that he ran. That's what Angel had hinted at when I asked him in the student union, but that's not the image I remembered now.

Black wings shrouded the figure and Aaron from view. The scream died off in an echo in the alley, but Aaron was still lying there, slumped against the pavement while the winged man lowered himself over him. My vision blurred and I made a sound, at least I must have, because the wings began to recede so I could see the blurred outline of a man. A man with hair pulled into a bun at the top of his head. A man who lifted Aaron from the ground and moved him into a dumpster across the alley before he turned to face me.

"What are you?" I asked. I kept my eyes on the gargoyle. My voice came out so quietly that I wasn't even sure I'd spoken aloud. I wanted to believe I was just stretching the truth, not that I was accepting that the man next to me really had wings and had done something beastly to save me from Aaron at the club.

"Cursed, Mouse," Angel said, voice low.

I studied the gargoyle a little longer, noticing the notches near the pedestal where part of the stone had chipped away.

"Why do you keep appearing everywhere?" I turned my head to look at him, wrapping my arms around my stomach. It was strange that I could still feel the gentleness of his hands on my leg after remembering the horror that I feared he'd unleashed in that alley. Even now, the darkness in his eyes rooted me to the spot when I wondered if it should've sent me running.

"I don't know," he said, his tone pained. "Why do you keep attracting people who would hurt you?"

"I don't know."

He scoffed. "Even a mouse doesn't accidentally wander into a lion's den. They're too clever for that."

"Why would a lion bother a little mouse? It wouldn't even make a good snack. Maybe for a house cat..."

Angel snorted and looked up at the gargoyle again. His smile faded as he let out a sigh.

"Maybe that's what makes the mouse so clever, she knows which predator is the threat."

"I'm not a mouse," I said meekly. My stomach twisted at the lie. I didn't appreciate the way he talked about me skittering across the student union, but I knew he was right I was a mouse. I was a homebody. I left every morning to go to school, but stayed as under the radar as much as I could, then came back to the apartment where I lived my true self on my quickly growing YouTube channel, where I never showed my face or gave my real name. I was a mouse skirting along the baseboards of life. I hated it.

Angel turned on the bench, looking at me with those dark eyes, the same ones that always seemed to precede the lecture about my safety.

"What's wrong with being a mouse?" he asked.

I shrugged. "If I'm a mouse what does that make you, the lion?"

Wrong thing to say. He turned back toward the gargoyle again, pain in his expression. My stomach twisted in knots and I felt my chest tighten. I didn't mean to insult him. I wasn't sure why, but I didn't want to push him away. I didn't know why our paths kept crossing or why he seemed to be in the right place every time I messed up, but he was and somehow it made me want him closer, not farther away.

"I'm sorry," I offered.

"Don't apologize. I should be apologizing to you," he said, fists tightening before he released them and ran his palms over his knees. "I shouldn't even be here."

"You are following me, aren't you?" I asked, scooting to the far side of the bench and turning to face him. He didn't react at first, just glared up at the gargoyle before looking my way.

"You are a mouse, Lily, a mouse that stumbled into my den. And instead of letting the clever little thing that you are become..." He looked back at the gargoyle like it offended him. Applause broke out up the path where the party was that I'd forgotten about until now. Normally, I would've been panicked that I'd miss the warm-up with my quartet, that I might not be prepared enough, but I was more concerned with the dark-haired man next to me who looked like I'd asked him something that shattered his view of the world.

"I'm really not that clever," I said, hoping to steer the discussion away from whatever had upset him. Again, he acted like I'd just said something insulting. He looked at me in awe. I knew what people probably thought. I was smart enough to get into NYU, I was a great musician, but my SAT was average, and I got what I had because of my family name. That was it. I really wasn't that special. Just like he said before, I was a princess whose naivety about the world got her into huge trouble the first time she tried stepping out of the castle on her own.

No wonder my anxiety was so bad.

"It's been days since the club. We've seen each other twice now," he said.

"I was drugged," I defended.

He shook his head. "Still. You aren't intimidated or intoxicated by me."

"Are most people?"

He shrugged. "One or the other." This time his expression was full of curiosity when he looked my way. Somehow, it was more unsettling.

"Like you said, I'm a mouse," I said, trying to sound flirty and failing.

He didn't smile.

"I wish you weren't," he said. "It would be easier."

"Easier to watch me leave your den?" I asked, my heart skipping in my chest. I don't know where I got the guts to say it, but everything felt alive inside me now that I'd said the words. I couldn't deny that he was attractive, even with the overprotective attitude and the fact that he seemed to show up wherever I needed him. I should have been more concerned by that fact.

"Most people would run away at the mere sight of me after what happened that night. You were drugged, but you can't deny that…" Angel sucked in a deep breath and stood up. He looked taller, but maybe it was the way he was standing over me, stepping right in front of the gargoyle with his expression hidden in the shadow cast from the moon.

I knew what he meant. I didn't want to admit what I'd seen because it was insane. It couldn't be possible, but I knew what I saw. I could feel that it made sense even though the rational part of my mind told me it was just whatever drug Aaron had slipped in my drink.

"Why can't you just let me walk away?" I asked, knowing it wasn't the question he wanted me to ask. He wanted me to ask if the wings were his. He wanted me to ask if he was a monster or if he'd killed Aaron. That was a real thought I'd pushed deep into my mind, not wanting to wrestle with the possibility.

Angel shrank before me, the tension fading from his shoulders. He stepped back, turning to look up the path. The music faded into a single note, applause following as Dr. Tennison started speaking over the microphone.

"You should go warm up," he said.

He was right, I should. But I wanted to stay. I wanted him to answer me. He didn't look at me though. He turned his back on me to stare at the statue again, making it abundantly clear that he was finished with our conversation.

I stood up and made my way back to the party.

# CHAPTER 5

I swore I was fine, but the rest of the quartet could tell I wasn't. Thankfully, they left me alone during warm-ups and didn't say anything as we took our places before the crowd. I positioned my cello between my legs, tucking the fabric of my dress around it so it wouldn't get in the way of my bow.

I messed up twice. It wasn't at all like me and it garnered a surprised look from the violinist next to me as he hit every note perfectly. As soon as we finished our final piece, I led the way back toward the main house where I quickly packed up my cello and then abandoned it before the others could ask what was wrong.

I started for the bathroom, but turned at the corner when I saw how crowded it was. I went as far as I could down the hallway before exiting the building at the end. I was on the far side of the garden now. The bulb lights stretched over the tall bushes. I followed the path until it opened to a round courtyard. In the middle was a fountain. The stone paths were broken up by sections of flowers, all a different vibrant color that did not help to lift my mood at all.

I was a second from bursting into tears when someone spoke behind me.

"Dr. Tennison speaks very highly of you," she said.

I whirled around to face the old woman I'd met earlier, the same sincere smile greeting me. It melted me and the tears fell before I could help it. I tried to swipe them away as new ones came, probably smearing mascara under my eyes in the process and forfeiting any chance I had at rejoining the party and pretending I was fine.

"Oh, it'll be all right," the old woman said and pulled me into a hug. She smelled strongly of flowers. "No one is perfect. We all have our days. This was a lot of pressure for someone so young."

"I know," I managed to get past my lips.

"You're a beautiful girl, talented," she said in my ear, brushing my hair from my face before pulling me tighter to her chest.

Something switched in my brain, silencing the panic in my chest and clearing everything from my mind. I was aware of my surroundings, where in the garden I was, and that we were very much alone when the pain shot through my neck. It was so sharp that it cut off my scream and my knees buckled. I didn't fall. The woman held me in place, her grip so tight that it felt like her nails were embedding themselves into the back of my dress.

A sound between a roar and a hiss sent shivers up my skin. A second later the woman was ripped away, and I fell. I barely caught myself against the pavement, managing to keep my face from smashing into the concrete. The pain came white-hot again at my throat, dulling into a new sensation; numbing, almost calming, trancelike...

The roar behind me interrupted my dream-like state and threw me into a panic again. I rolled to my back just in time to see the woman cowering before a tall figure. It had wings that made the courtyard look small. They were like leather, rapier-like claws at every scalloped tip. The monster stretched them out wide as it let out a guttural sound. It had the body of a man dressed in a tattered button-up shirt, only it didn't look like a man. Its face was elongated, its nose flat on its face with just two long slits for nostrils. His lips were pulled back to expose razor-like fangs to the woman who hissed back at him, her own fangs visible under the warm lights.

The man brought his wings down, propelling him with amazing speed at the old woman. He grabbed her arms as they were launched through the air and into the side of the building with a bang that would've drawn the attention of everyone at the party had applause not broken out at that very moment.

The woman hissed and the man let out a roar in response, his teeth inches from her face. My stomach turned and as much as I wanted to run, I was frozen in place when he sank his teeth into her throat, shaking his head back and forth like a shark before pulling away and spitting a mouthful of gore onto the pavement.

The woman opened her mouth, but no sound came out. Somehow, he seemed larger now than before. His wings stretched outward again, nearly to the ends of the building. The woman was unable to utter a sound as he seized her by the front of her dress and lifted her several feet, so they were at eye level. A gust of wind nearly sent me onto my back as the man's wings propelled them backward across the courtyard.

He slammed the old woman onto the ground before he ever landed, hard enough that I was sure it would kill her. Somehow, she was in one piece. She opened her mouth again, her own fangs exposed before the anger in her expression was replaced by fear. The man snapped the wooden pole of the gazebo like it was nothing, pulling it free and raising it with the splintered end pointing down at the woman. I watched in horror as he impaled her through her chest, feeling faint when she began to disintegrate. Her body broke apart around the wooden pole until it was a pile of gray ash and then nothing but a thin layer of dust.

The man let go of the pole and it clattered to the concrete. Instead of looking at me like I assumed he would, he turned the opposite way. He let out a roar, loud enough that I was sure someone would hear. His body relaxed after, his arms open and his head bowed toward the dark sky. His wings drooped so the ends scraped the path beneath. I noticed after a moment that they were receding, growing smaller until they were small enough to retract toward the man's back. He shrank as well, no longer over seven-foot tall but only inches taller than me. The back of his shirt was ripped in two places along his shoulders. The animalistic look of his head rounded out until I recognized the bun at the top of his head.

This time, when he roared, it was more like a groan of relief.

"Angel," I whispered.

He turned to look at me. Where the monster once stood was the man who'd saved me from Aaron days before. There was a ring of darkness around his mouth and chin, liquid stretching from his chin and thinning as it slowly dripped to the ground below.

I pushed myself back mere inches before he was hovering over me. His face was clean of the blood now, smeared across his left bicep instead and he looked over my body before his eyes met mine.

"Lily," he said and brushed my face. His hands went to my neck next, pain burning across my throat as he brushed the wound there. He lifted his hands to his own face, fear in his expression as he stared at his bloody hands. My blood. I hardly felt the pain now as I watched him. After what he did to that woman, I should have been fighting for my life. I should have begged. I should have done whatever he wanted. Instead, he stared at my blood like it was poison. He lifted his right hand to his lips and for a moment I thought he might lick his fingers. I was sure I saw a pair of fangs past his parted lips.

Instead, he lifted me into his arms and when I looked down the garden was far below.

I wrapped my arms around his middle as we flew, my hair whipping around my face and making it difficult to know which way was up. He landed so softly that I didn't know we were on solid ground until he lowered me to my feet.

"Lily," he said as my knees buckled underneath me. "Lily, how do you feel?"

I leaned back, cold stone making me shiver. I looked around us to figure out where we were, but his hands cupped my face and kept me from looking anywhere but into the worry in his dark eyes.

"How do you feel?" he asked again, his voice like velvet.

It felt like my heart had leaped from my chest. I felt light in the best way. It was exhilarating. The pain was there, but it didn't hurt. Not in that way. I felt like I'd had an entire bottle of wine and not the half-glass I actually had. Everything was sensitive, like electricity was pulsing through my veins and even the gentle stroke of his thumb across my cheek made every inch of me sing, ache for more.

"Good," I said, drawing my lower lip between my teeth.

"The venom will do that," Angel said, turning my head slightly to the left to look at the wound on my neck. "Believe me, it's a lot worse than it feels. That feeling is what keeps you from running, like snake venom to a rat."

Venom?

The gardens came back to the front of my mind until I was replaying the attack.

"You have wings," I said.

"Not here." He stood up. "Let me clean you up first."

I could tell now that we were on a rooftop. There was nothing up here except for an old lawn chair and several packs worth of cigarette butts littered over the concrete. Angel offered his hand, and I took it, glad that he scooped me into his arms as soon as I stood up rather than let me walk.

He pushed open the door in the middle of the roof and started down the dimly lit stairs. The halls were tight, old construction by the looks of it. It was an apartment building, the white paint on the walls and doors the newest thing about the place in the last decade from the looks of it. We passed a single-bedroom apartment a few floors down that had the door propped open, a man asleep in an armchair while three small children played on the floor.

I felt the anxiety building in my chest. Whatever venom Angel mentioned earlier must be wearing off because my chest hurt. I had an urge to leap from his arms and run very far away. But also, I wanted to hug him tighter and ask all the questions swirling through my mind. He turned down a hall and stopped outside an apartment before I could decide.

Angel pulled a set of keys from his pocket and unlocked the door in seconds, closing it and locking it before moving toward a couch by the window. He sat me on the cushions and left for the kitchen sink across the room.

The apartment was empty aside from the couch and a round table with a single chair. It didn't look like anyone lived here. The only items I could spot in the kitchen were a bottle of dish soap and a couple of glasses. Angel stood at the sink, giving me a view of his tattered dress shirt. I could see where his wings protruded earlier, long slits from his shoulders to lower back. As he leaned over the sink to ring out a towel, the slashed fabric pulled apart and I could see scars crisscrossing over his skin. It was like someone had cut him a thousand times or maybe something had raked its claws over his back in a fight like the one I witnessed tonight.

"Lily," Angel said cautiously. He turned from the sink and slowly walked toward me, a glass of water in one hand and a couple of clean towels draped over the other. "I swear, I won't hurt you."

"Where are we? I don't think this is... This can't be a safe place..."

He relaxed and closed the space between us. He sat the glass on the floor as he got on his knees.

"After everything you just saw, your concern is that we're in a bad neighborhood?" he asked with a snort of disbelief. When I looked toward the door at the sound of footsteps in the hall, his hand slid across my cheek, pulling my gaze back to him. "Do you feel safe?"

The question seemed ridiculous at first until I realized I did feel safe, behind that locked door with him, with Angel who apparently had wings and could literally rip apart someone like it was nothing. That dark look of concern in his eyes was enough to melt most of my fear away.

"Yes," I told him.

He nodded and lowered his eyes from mine to my throat.

"Can I take care of that?" he asked, pointing at me with one of the rags.

I nodded and he dipped the rag into the glass of water before raising it to my neck. He inhaled deeply as the wet material met my skin. He was gentle, the wound not hurting until he'd barely pressed the spot. He sat back with a worried look as he studied the wound.

"Is it that bad?" I asked, starting to wonder what it actually looked like. I raised my hand, finding the wound. I ignored the burning sensation as I ran my finger over the mark. One, two, three, four holes set together in pairs with a gap between. I remembered the way the woman held me close, the sounds she made in my ear...

"She bit me," I said, my stomach turning as I lowered my hand. Before I could look, Angel wrapped the wet cloth around my fingers and wiped them clean.

"It's a clean bite. I don't think I'll need to seal it." He began dabbing at my neck again with the cloth. "I hope not," he said under his breath.

"What does that mean?" I asked as he worked. "Seal it?"

He hesitated before dabbing at my neck again and dipping the rag into the glass of water. His shoulders tensed the way they had in the garden before I performed.

"We don't always finish," he said slowly. "We can stop the bleeding, help our victims heal by sealing the wound. The marks fade within a day that way. The venom, if we remain attached long enough, can disorient our victims enough that some don't even put together what's happened."

He spoke so quietly that it sent chills over my skin. He sat back on his heels, shrinking before me and looking up with something like guilt in his expression. I knew it was intentional, him placing himself beneath me. He was trying not to scare me.

"Did she...?"

He shook his head. "I had her off in seconds."

"How would you seal it?" I asked, lifting my hand again to touch the spot and then lowering it when I remembered the way my stomach had turned before.

His jaw tightened and he looked at my knees, shaking his head.

"I won't," he said.

"What if it scars?"

I saw the distress cross his face even though he kept his face lowered.

"I won't."

"I may be squeamish about all the blood and stuff," I said with a shudder, "but I have a higher pain tolerance than you think."

"It's not painful," Angel said. He let out a groan and looked up at me. "Are you afraid of me?"

"No."

"Why not?"

"I don't think you're someone to be afraid of."

Angel's mouth parted in surprise. He lifted his head and slowly rose to his knees. Instead of straightening up, he drew closer to me. I sat back until I was lying against the couch cushion. Angel hovered above me, his hands resting near either side of my head, but never touching me. I could smell the strange scent at his neck as he leaned in, a primal sound, almost a growl, rumbling from his throat.

"You should be afraid of me. Did you see what I did back there? Did you see how easy it was?" he whispered.

I didn't answer. It felt like everything in my body had slowed down. I could feel each thunk of my heart in my chest, every deep breath that passed my lips...

"You want to know how I'd seal that bite mark?" he asked and pulled back, so his face was inches from mine. I knew he was trying to intimidate me, but his eyes gave everything away. As dark as they were, I could read every emotion within them easily. He was concerned that I wasn't terrified. Most people would have been. *I* should have been, but I knew he wasn't the monster that he appeared to be in the courtyard.

"To seal a bite, we must lick the wounds. Each stroke of the tongue stops the bleeding and speeds up the healing. To seal that bite of yours, I'd have to taste you. I can't do that. Here's the thing you need to know about me," he said and lifted my chin with his fingers, so I stared straight into his eyes. "I always finish, Mouse."

My breath caught in my chest. I felt dizzy for a moment and once I'd gathered myself again, he was kneeling before me with a package of gauze pads and a roll of cloth tape between his hands. I watched him work, glad to see that the tension in his shoulders and jaw slowly faded as he finished taping the gauze over the wound. Before I could rise from the couch, he lifted the hem of my dress to my knee and began removing his tie from my calf.

"Does it bother you?" I asked. "All the blood?"

He glanced up at me before assessing the shallow cut.

"Bother isn't the right word for it," he said and dipped a clean towel into the water and began cleaning the dried blood from my skin. "If you walked into a five-star restaurant, could you resist ordering an entrée?"

I shrugged. "Yeah. Sure."

"It's a little like that."

"What if you haven't eaten in a while?" I asked.

He finished taping the gauze to my calf and leaned back on his hands. I was glad to see that he wasn't offended this time. He actually looked a little amused.

"Are you asking if I get hangry?"

"Well, kind of. I guess what I wondered is how often you... What exactly do you... How does it all work?"

He did look a tad disappointed at this question. He thought for a long moment before standing up from the floor and taking the supplies back to the kitchen. My stomach twisted when he dumped the red water down the drain, making sure to rinse the basin clean before he turned to me again.

"You are remarkably calm for someone who just saw two..." He let the words hang in the air, clearly waiting for me to say the words we'd been dancing around the entire time. Saying it aloud, speaking it into existence, would only confirm my fear that I was even more different than everyone else. It was one more secret, one more thing that separated me from the rest of the world.

"Vampires," I said.

He nodded, slowly walking toward me and stopping halfway across the room.

"We're closer to Bram Stoker's version than Stephanie Meyer's," he said.

"In what ways?"

Again, the calm way I'd asked seemed to surprise him. A small smile pulled at his lips before the serious expression returned.

"There is no substitute for our diet," he said carefully.

"You said you didn't have to kill to, um, feed," I said.

He nodded, biting his lower lip until it looked painful.

"I also said that I always finish." He looked straight at me. It was the same serious way he'd stared at me when we were inches apart, feigned intimidation.

"I'm not afraid of you," I said, impressed by the confident way the words spilled from my lips.

"Why not? You know what I am. You saw only a fraction of what I'm capable of. You know that I need human blood to survive and that I never leave a victim alive. I kill, Lily. Why aren't you afraid of me?"

I had to admit that the words were terrifying, but they didn't match the man standing in front of me. I knew that good murderers were charismatic and charming in a way that made them the perfect villains, but that wasn't Angel. I don't know how I knew that, but I did. It was the same conversation from the gardens: the lion and the mouse. He could feed from me if he wanted to. I wouldn't be able to fight him. Just like Aaron knew I was a stupid, inexperienced girl, Angel could make quick work of me. I wasn't the target, though.

"I don't think you feed on just anyone. If you did, then you wouldn't have a problem sealing my bite. I think you kill other kinds of people, people like Aaron," I said.

He knew exactly who I was talking about, and I could tell that I was right from the curious way he looked at me now. It was like I'd stumped him.

"I only feed on the worst of humanity, people who have committed truly horrific crimes of a grand scale," he said, his face scrunching in disgust.

"You only kill people who deserve it."

"Who am I to decide?" Angel snapped, relaxing when he looked at me. "I'm sorry. I didn't mean to..." He let out a sigh and turned his back on me. He pulled the elastic from his hair and took a long moment to pull his dark locks back into the bun at the crown of his head. He went to the far side of the room next. There was a closet, which he opened to reveal his scant wardrobe.

He didn't bother to unbutton his shirt. He ripped the front open with a single tug and slipped his arms out. Even from across the room I could see that his torso was covered in scars. He pulled a long-sleeved shirt from the rack and smoothed it down his chest. He took a jacket from a hanger next and started back across the room.

"I have one more question," I said once he was close enough.

"Okay," He held the jacket to me.

I slipped it on, snuggling in the thick fabric and inhaling the subtle floral scent of him that hung on the fabric.

"You said that when she bit me she released venom. What does that mean?"

"You won't turn," he said and led me toward the door. "Let's get you home."

I almost asked him what would have to happen for me to turn, but I was sure the subject was a sore spot. Instead, I let him lead the way back into the hallway.

# CHAPTER 6

Anne must've been out with Jazz still, because our apartment was empty when Angel and I got there. I checked my phone to make sure I hadn't missed a call from her, but there wasn't as much as a text. I bet they got distracted by each other and found a quiet corner or romantic restaurant.

"Do you sleep?" I asked as I went to the kitchen to fill a glass with water.

Angel locked the door behind us before joining me, not as eager to answer all my questions as I was to ask them.

"No," he said. "Are you aware that you talk in your sleep?"

Really? No one had ever told me that before.

"No. I didn't know that," I said, now a little worried about what I'd said. "Does that mean you just watched me sleep that night after the club?"

"Not intentionally." He lifted himself onto a bar stool. "Do you have nightmares like that often?"

"Like what?"

I wasn't sure he bought my feigned innocence. I remembered the nightmare well because I'd been having a version of the same one since that night.

"You tossed a lot. You said some things that…" He eyed me cautiously. I felt my cheeks heat. What did I say?

"Oh my… What did I say?"

"You don't remember?" he asked, surprised.

"Oh no," I gasped and lifted my glass to my lips more to hide my embarrassment than drink.

"You sure you don't remember saying…"

"I said something sexual, didn't I? Oh my God," I groaned, wishing I hadn't said the words at all as I saw the smile spread across his face.

"No, you did not say anything sexual," he laughed. "You *were* having a nightmare, right?"

"Yes, it was a nightmare," I blurted.

"You never know." He shrugged, eyebrows raised. "Some people are into—"

Oh God.

I inhaled a gulp of water, leading to a coughing fit that only worsened my embarrassment. Once I stopped coughing, I took my time sipping the rest of the water to avoid continuing the conversation.

"So, um," I started once I felt brave enough to face him again. "Can you step into the sun?"

Angel reached under his shirt and withdrew the gold chain I spotted before. A glass vial hung from the chain that contained what looked like dirt.

"I may be cursed to the shadows, but I'm not bound to them," he said before tucking the vial back under his shirt. "It's soil from my homeland, where my human life ended. As long as I carry it on my person I can come and go as I please, day or night."

"Where are you from?" I asked.

"Spain," he said as he adjusted his shirt.

"How have you gone this long undetected? If I flew to Spain right now, went to the capital, and looked through the archives or whatever…"

Angel smirked. "I've gone by many names. I haven't gone by my given name since I became a vampire. Not until you."

Angel got a curious look on his face as he raised his gaze to me. My heart fluttered in my chest. I felt the heat rush to my cheeks and I lowered my eyes to the counter before I burst into flames.

"Do you all turn into bats like you did back there?" I asked. I looked up again as the room fell silent.

He didn't reply right away. He leaned his elbows on the counter and stared down at his hands.

"All vampires can change shape. We don't become bats. We're different. Not all vampires are able to change shape after they turn though, at least not for a while. It takes time to grow that strong. It's a primal thing, something that develops the longer we exist. It's a little like losing your humanity. When we hunt, when we fight like I did back there, certain instincts take over that are easier to summon the longer you've been a vampire."

He looked up at me, eyebrows raised as though challenging me to ask the follow-up question. I couldn't resist.

"How long?" I asked.

"From my experience and those I've encountered like me," he started, sucking in a deep breath as though tallying the years, "over a century. The wings come first. I've never met a vampire with wings who hadn't existed for at least that long."

I hadn't expected that.

The silence stretched on as I stood at the counter. I don't know what I expected from a vampire who'd lived several centuries. It wasn't like he would speak in Old English or something.

The front door opened, and Anne and Jazz stumbled inside, lips pressed together until Jazz noticed me and pulled away. Anne didn't seem surprised to see me at all, but her mouth parted when she saw Angel sitting at the bar.

"Oh. Hello," she said awkwardly, stepping away from Jazz. She looked at me again, her gaze lingering on Angel's jacket still zipped over my dress.

"I'll see you in the morning," Angel said and stood up, not bothering to acknowledge Anne as he passed her for the door.

"The morning," I started slowly, straightening up from the counter with my glass between my hands.

"Brunch," Angel said with a smirk as he opened the door. "I'll be here at nine."

He shut the door, leaving Jazz and Anne to stare at me curiously.

"What happened?" Anne asked and took Angel's spot at the bar. "Are you actually seeing Thor?"

"He's not a Thor," I said, barely containing my smile at the joke. "Maybe a Batman, though."

<hr>

I put on my favorite brunch dress, a navy A-line tennis dress that was comfortable enough to wear on the country club golf course back home and fancy enough to wear to brunch afterward with my mom and her girlfriends. Angel wore a pair of dark jeans and a blue button-up. I darted out the apartment door when he got there before Anne could send me any suggestive looks.

"Do you have a preference for brunch?" Angel asked as we left the building for the sidewalk.

"No seafood. I'm allergic," I said. "Are you going to actually eat?"

He smiled as he led the way to the crosswalk.

"I can. It won't sustain me. Most don't see the point after they've turned."

We waited until traffic slowed to hurry across the street. The sidewalk was full of people, forcing us to walk closer. Angel knew how to navigate a crowd, positioning himself so no one moved between us.

"It's going to be busy," I pointed out once I realized where we were headed. Silver and Gold was an elegant restaurant that Anne and I liked to go to for lunch on Saturdays, mostly because it was too expensive for people on a college budget, and we never ran into anyone we knew there.

"The city never sleeps," Angel said and pulled the door open.

"It will be kind of hard to keep talking here," I said. The corner of his lips twitched with a smile and that's when I realized what this was. He didn't want to talk about it anymore. He was distracting me.

"Table for two," Angel told the host at the podium.

"It'll be a wait. There's room at the bar if you'd like," said the host, gathering a couple of menus. Angel turned to me, the question in his expression.

"The bar is fine," I said. I followed the host through the main floor and to the room at the back. This one was much quieter despite being just as full of people. The bar smelled strongly of coffee. Most of the people sitting along the granite-top bar were nursing steaming mugs of coffee. We sat next to a couple of middle-aged women enjoying mimosas and gossiping about their kids.

"Can I start you with a couple of coffees?" the barista asked as the host sat our menus on the bar.

"I'll have a black coffee," Angel said and lifted himself into his seat. It took me a moment to climb onto the barstool without flashing everyone around us.

"Um, can I get a latte with a splash of vanilla?" I asked her.

She turned toward the impressive coffee machine and I looked at Angel who was already looking over the menu.

"So, what is your plan?" I asked.

Angel lowered the menu, brow creased with surprise.

"What do you mean?" he asked.

"Is this a distraction to keep me from discovering all your, you know, secrets?" I asked and waved my hands in front of my face like a pair of wings. I wished I hadn't as soon as I finished the gesture, my face burning with embarrassment.

"You haven't been on a date in a while, have you?" he laughed.

Was that what this was?

"I haven't been asked," I said, sure my cheeks were bright red by now.

Angel smiled and turned in his seat to face me, leaning one forearm on the bar top.

"I hope you'll forgive me for making assumptions," he said. "Lily Thompson, would you like to go out with me?"

The formality of the words along with the expectant way he looked at me had my insides squirming.

"Yes," I said, gathering my hair and twisting it over my left shoulder. Angel's eyes went to my neck. I'd forgotten about the bandage there. I pushed my hair from my shoulder and let it fan around me again. Still, he seemed transfixed, his jaw tense as he continued to stare at the spot despite my efforts to cover it again.

"Is it difficult for you?" I asked.

My question pulled him from the trance, but before he could

answer the barista returned with our coffee. My latte was such a light color next to his cream-free cup that it was almost funny. He pulled the mug closer to him, waiting until the barista had moved to the opposite side of the bar to speak.

"You smell different than anyone I've encountered," he said, voice low.

"Different how?" I asked, letting a strand of my blonde hair fall across my cheek so I could sniff. Thankfully, I washed my hair that morning. It smelled like honey.

"Like magic," he answered and stared at me with the same curious expression he had last night when I told him I wasn't afraid of him.

"Magic?" I asked, nearly knocking my mug over.

"I've met people with... special abilities in the past," he said carefully as he lifted his mug to his lips. "They smell similar, but you... I've never met anyone like you."

"What do you mean? Are you saying there's more? What else is there?" My heart was picking up pace.

It was annoying the way he smiled back at me. It was like I'd just said something funny.

"I'm the first you've met," he said.

"There's more than just... people like you?"

He nodded and took a sip from his mug. The barista reappeared to take our order. I told her that the coffee was enough for now and Angel ordered a traditional breakfast: eggs, toast, bacon, and fresh fruit.

"I think that was the first time I actually saw you freaked out," Angel said with a snort.

"I'm not afraid," I said.

He saw right through the lie. The idea that vampires were real was enough, but knowing there were more supernatural creatures out there turned my entire understanding of the world upside down. My phone vibrated in my pocket. I pulled it out to glance at the text from Anne asking where I was. I felt just a little annoyed at her since Angel said she was a bad friend for leaving me alone at the club. She never checked on where I was unless we were planning to meet up. I turned my phone over on the bar top, so I didn't have to look at the screen.

"You are studying music. What are your plans after NYU?" Angel asked.

I hated this question. My initial response was to give the usual excuse about hoping to join the New York Phil or some other big orchestra, but the way Angel looked at me had me frozen. I could tell that he didn't have any assumptions about me. He didn't expect anything from me and it was refreshing, calming. So, I told him the truth.

"I have this YouTube channel that's been doing really well," I started slowly, gauging his reaction. He seemed interested, not surprised or disapproving the way I'd always expected people to react. "I do the vocals and most of the music myself. My channel recently got monetized and it's grown a lot since. I think I gained... I don't even want to think about how many subscribers and views I get a day now."

"Why not? That's a huge accomplishment, people enjoying what you create."

I pushed my hair behind my ear before I remembered the gauze at my neck. I gathered my blonde locks at the nape of my neck and draped it over the wound.

"I know. I'm really happy. The kind of music I create on that channel is what I really love. It's a combination of mainstream with classic phrases you'd find in most any string piece. At the rate it's going, I could afford to focus on the channel and then maybe creating albums and even perform, eventually. That's kind of a big dream though. I think just having the channel take off like it has been might be good enough." I shrugged.

"No, it's not," Angel snorted and took a sip of coffee.

"W-What?" I asked.

Angel shook his head. "It's not really good enough for you, is it?"

"Why, because I'm some rich, white heiress?" I asked, lowering my voice when one of the ladies behind Angel glanced our way curiously with her mimosa raised to her lips.

"That's not the reason I meant, not the real reason you don't think it's good enough anyway," he said and moved his empty coffee mug toward the opposite side of the bar. "Are you really an heiress?"

"What did you mean, Angel?" I challenged, heart racing in my chest. I was already preparing to storm out of the restaurant. I worried about bursting into anxious tears instead of standing my ground against whatever insult he'd hurl my way.

"I meant that you want this," he said and leaned against the counter. "Tell me deep in your heart, you don't want this YouTube channel to lead toward albums and performances in sold-out venues."

"I, um..." Any anger I'd felt before melted away. "I do want that."

Angel looked at me for a moment, a smile pulling at the corner of his lips.

"I take back what I said before," he said, his warm eyes locking with mine. "You're not daddy's little princess at all."

My breath caught in my chest, and I fumbled my words, the truth I didn't even know pouring out before the embarrassment could seal it away.

"But, I really am though. I have no idea what I'm doing. I just create these songs with my computer in my bedroom and toss in the stock videos and post them. I don't have any strategy. I don't even know how to do taxes or what running a business like that looks like. I can barely go out like a normal person because I'm not a normal person. I don't know what real life is like because mine isn't normal and I know that."

I looked back at him as soon as I realized the pathetic whining was from my own mouth. I was horrified. How fucking spoiled I was complaining about my privileged life. I had more money for no reason than most people and I wasn't happy. I had panic attacks about things like sitting through a lecture or the fact that I missed a couple of notes at the garden recital. There were far worse things to worry about in the world that I couldn't even fathom from my stupid expensive apartment.

"It's not your fault, Mouse," Angel said like it was the most obvious fact.

"I shouldn't complain."

He snorted.

"You have every right to feel the way you do. Don't apologize for that," he said with a laugh. "Everyone has problems, but not everyone deals with them the same way. So, there are people out there managing with a shit hand. They've worked with those cards before. They've learned how to play the game with what they have. You've never had to learn those skills. It's not your fault."

"Okay, so what do I do with that? Am I just supposed to look like an idiot as I figure it all out?" I asked as our waitress returned with Angel's breakfast. She looked at me and I was sure she was going to ask if

I needed anything. Instead, she awkwardly turned and went back to the other side of the bar.

"Be honest that you're learning. No one can fault you for that. You are learning. You're just finding success on your own, doing something you love, and you're afraid. That's normal. If anyone calls you an idiot for trying to find your way in the world, then let me know. Not everyone who bares their teeth has the balls to actually bite," Angel said and cracked a smile. He unrolled his silverware and sat the knife on the plate before sliding it before me.

I shook my head. "I'm really not that hungry."

"That's the anxiety. Take a couple bites, just a few," Angel said as he pulled his phone from his pocket. He unlocked it and when he sat it on the table between us it was open to YouTube with the curser blinking in the search bar. "Tell me more about your YouTube channel."

He slid the phone away from me with a flirty smile, nodding toward the plate. Once I took a bite the eggs were almost as good as the ones he'd made days before he let me search for my channel and show him the dashboard. After telling him about the most recent video, I found myself talking more about how the channel started and what I wanted to post next. He helped me plan for the next video, promising to help me record it.

"I don't usually film anything," I said, lowering my fork with the last bite of eggs.

"You won't have to. Let me take care of that."

"I'm not against filming the video, I just don't..."

"You don't want to be in it," he finished. "Why?"

How did I explain it without divulging everything about my family? I didn't like talking about them. I was an only child, a prized possession as my father liked to say. I felt more like a pawn though. They weren't bad parents by any means. They were attentive and doting and gave me whatever I wanted, but they were very judgmental people. They cared a lot about bragging about my accomplishments and that often turned into gossiping about the failures of others at the country club and talking behind the backs of people they called friends.

"I don't want anyone to know that this is me," I said and motioned to his phone.

Understanding crossed his face as embarrassment burned like fire across mine.

"Your parents wouldn't approve," he said.

I shrugged. "Probably not. At least, not yet."

He snorted in disbelief. His smile faded to a tight frown for a moment, disapproving.

"Not everyone gets to see this side," I said. "Not everyone sees it the way I do, not even Anne."

Angel relaxed and looked up at me from the counter.

"I do," he said and reached out to brush the hair away from my face, pushing it past my shoulder to reveal the bandage over my neck. "I see you."

I relaxed under his brief touch, surprised how much more I wanted. It felt like our fifth date, not our first, like this was a normal Saturday morning tradition and not some kind of exploration into what more was between us.

My phone buzzed against the counter, drawing attention from the people sitting next to us. I snatched it from the counter as it buzzed again, two new messages from Anne on the screen.

Isn't this that boy from the club?

I had to unlock my phone to play the video she sent. A reporter stood on the sidewalk. Behind her, bags of trash were piled outside a store and a couple wearing mismatched clothes too big for either of them were lingering at the mouth of an alley to watch. I pressed play on the video and turned the volume up just loud enough as Angel watched across from me.

The reporter said, "The body of a man found mutilated behind a bookstore was identified this morning as that of Aaron Hunter, a student at NYU. More was released about Hunter's background, uncovering details that linked him to drug activity and several unsolved crimes in the area. Police matched Hunter's DNA to three rape kits from the last few years, one of which makes Aaron Hunter the prime suspect in the rape and murder of a young woman who was discovered back in September while she was visiting New York with her sorority sisters. Drugs were found on Hunter's body when he was discovered behind the bookstore. It's believed that his murder was drug related due to the state his body was found in. For more information on this case and those currently suspected to be linked to Aaron Hunter, visit our website."

Chills ran over my skin.

"Lily," Angel said, voice low.

"I need..." I didn't finish before sliding off the barstool and starting toward the front of the restaurant. My stomach twisted so tight it hurt. I tasted the bile in the back of my throat, sour. I pushed past a couple waiting to be seated and shoved the front door open, heading straight for a trashcan near the corner of the street.

"Lily," Angel called out to me as I was forced to stop only feet from the trash can, vomiting on my shoes.

# CHAPTER 7

Angel held my hair away from my face while I threw up all of my breakfast. Once I recovered, he walked me back toward the apartment to clean up. He scooped me into his arms once we got into the building, not saying a word when the mess over my feet transferred to his pant leg.

"I'm so sorry," I said and hid my face in the nape of his neck.

"Not the worst thing I've been covered in," he said, apologizing a moment later when I gagged into his shirt. My only saving grace was that my entire stomach contents laid outside Silver and Gold.

Angel took my keys and unlocked the apartment door. He carried me past the living room where Anne sat on the couch with her computer propped on her knees. She looked up at me in surprise.

"Do you let her walk anywhere?" she asked him, moving the computer to the coffee table.

"Do something useful for once and get her some water," Angel shot back as he carried me into my bedroom. He walked into my bathroom, sitting me down on the lid of the toilet and draping my feet into the bathtub.

"I'm sorry," I said again as he turned on the water, testing the temperature with his fingers.

"You don't have to apologize for getting sick," he said as he waited for the water to warm. Anne appeared in the doorway with a glass of water.

"You okay?" she asked me as he held out the glass.

I nodded and took it, sipping cautiously. My stomach had mostly settled now. I was more concerned with Angel. I knew he'd done something. I knew he hadn't just chased Aaron away.

"Give us a moment alone, please," I asked her. She looked over me for a moment, glancing at Angel before nodding and leaving.

"*Now* she's concerned," Angel said under his breath. He pulled the shower wand from the tub and pressed a button near the tap, warm water spraying from the wand over my shoes. He washed them off and then pulled them from my feet, rinsing the last of the vomit from my legs.

"Did you... Was that you?" I asked.

He replaced the wand and turned off the water. He stood up to take a towel from the wall.

"Yes," he said, looking back at me with disgust in his expression. He held the towel so tightly that his knuckles were white.

"Is all of that true about him? Was he a bad guy?" I asked.

Angel snorted like what I asked was funny, some kind of dark joke. He nodded and then shrugged.

"Yeah. He did some bad things. I was tracking him that night when he showed up at the club and found you. He wasn't my usual type."

"What do you mean not your usual type?" I asked.

"Warlock," he answered, turning the towel between his hands. "Aaron was a warlock. I don't usually attack warlocks. It's a little like taking a swing at a beehive. It was just luck that I was tracking a serial rapist and the trail led to him, to that club, to you... I don't hurt people who haven't done anything wrong. I don't normally hurt other supernatural beings at all, but when I sat down next to you and you smelled so different..." He relaxed his grip on the towel, lowering it so it hung in one hand. He looked so disappointed, like it physically hurt. "Are you afraid of me?"

"No," The words flowed easily from my lips.

"You should be," he said. When I didn't say anything, he knelt before me and began drying off my legs. He sat the towel on the counter and went into my bedroom. I looked at myself in the mirror. My mascara was smudged under my eyes. I splashed water on my face and did my best to wipe it away. Then, I brushed my teeth and went back into the bedroom.

Angel wasn't there. I went back into the main room. Anne's door was closed, and I could hear loud rock music behind it. I noticed the doors to the balcony were open and then I saw Angel leaning against the railing. He didn't look up when I joined him.

"Does it bother you that I'm not afraid of you?" I finally asked.

He let out a sigh and said, "Yes."

"Why?"

"Why?" he asked, turning from the rail to stare back at me in frustration. "You found out I'm a vampire and I have to drink blood to survive, human blood. There is no substitute. That fact alone should have kept you well away from me. I silenced that vampire woman with my own teeth. I ripped apart that warlock and dumped him behind a random business. How can you see me as anything but bad news?"

"I don't believe in good and evil," I said, watching the confusion set into his eyes. He froze for a moment before he glanced into the apartment to make sure we were still alone.

"This isn't some kind of moral gymnastics," he said under his breath.

"I don't think it's gymnastics at all." I closed the doors, so we were alone on the small balcony. "The whole world is just a ton of gray. There is no black and white. I think that we are all just doing the best we can to do the right things. Some people have no choice but to do bad things to survive. Maybe, some people do bad things to prevent worse tragedies from happening."

I spoke carefully, but he could see right through my message. I thought my rationalizing murder might tip him over, finally make him truly mad at me, but he wasn't. He looked sad. The disgust on his face wasn't for me or what I said, but something he was grappling with as a result.

"Gray or not, I'm a monster," he said. "I kill people so I can survive. It doesn't matter if they are bad, sick people. I'm still a murderer."

"So, are you hanging around me because you feel…"

"No," he said, stepping toward me and cupping the side of my face. His touch was there for just a moment before he lowered his hands, and we were separated by just inches. He looked anxiously back at me.

"Thank you for saving me at the club," I said and placed my hands against his chest, my heart skipping at the muscles I felt under the material of his shirt. "You may think you're a monster, but what you do saves lives. You saved mine."

"I shouldn't be allowed to decide who lives and dies," Angel hissed. "One day, someone will destroy me for what I am and if I'm still a vampire then, I'll welcome the moment."

His words made my chest ache. I couldn't imagine anyone who does the things he does and still has this level of sanctity for life. It was more than self-deprecating. It was self-sacrificing. In his mind, he was worthy of hell for what he was doing, but he still did it to save others.

I took a deep breath and prepared myself for the panic that would surely take hold in my chest after what I had to say.

"You could've left that morning and never seen me again. You could've left me alone when you saw me, but you didn't. You've been there for every moment of assault, panic, and even sickness in the past week of my life and you could've walked away from each one."

"You should've told me to fuck off when you woke up and I was still in your apartment. You should never have spoken to me again."

"Obviously, you're watching from the wings, swooping in when I need you," I said and slapped my palms against his chest. "You want me to send you away, but you won't stay away."

"If you want me gone, you will never see me again."

"And if I don't?" I challenged, standing as straight as I could and still only reaching his chin. He stared over the balcony, watching the traffic below us for a moment as he reigned in his frustration.

"You should tell me to go away," he said.

"I won't," I told him, gathering the fabric of his shirt in my hands and studying the buttons as I fought against the mix of fear and excitement twisting in my stomach. "I want you right here, with me, because I feel better when you're around. I feel grounded, like I can be my full self without worrying about anything else around us, even the stupid thoughts in my head telling me I should be afraid."

"You really shouldn't fall for a vampire, Mouse," Angel said, stepping closer. He didn't touch me until I felt the railing of the balcony at my lower back. He placed his hands on either side. "I'm stronger than even the strongest human. I could crush you. I'm older than most vampires. I have wings. I could fly you to the clouds and release you. There are so many ways I could kill you, Mouse, but oh how easy it would be to lose myself in you. How easy it would be to be overtaken by how crazy good you smell, how soft you feel under my fingers, the taste of your skin on my lips…"

I wasn't sure when I tipped my head back, but he was at my throat now. His floral scent was all around me, soothing the way a spa was, a trip to the salon, the feel of gentle hands combing through your hair. He brushed my hair away from my face and I arched my back against the railing when I felt his breath against my skin. A hand slid up the nape of my neck and into my hair, gently adjusting my posture so his lips were at my ear now.

"All it would take is kissing your neck, feeling your pulse beneath my lips…"

Angel pressed his lips just beneath my ear, a groan rumbling in his throat.

"You won't hurt me," I said and pulled on the front of his shirt.

"No. I'll never be rough with you, because you're smart enough to know what's good for you. *I'm* not good for you, Mouse. I'm not the man for you, Lily."

"I'm not a fragile princess either," I said and leaned forward. "Maybe I want a little roughness."

My lips brushed the side of his jaw. I thought it was his jaw, I couldn't be sure. Before I could catch my breath, he'd leaped from the balcony with barely a sound. When I didn't see him below, I looked up just in time to see the scalloped edge of a wing disappear on the roof of the building.

"Lily, are you okay?" Anne asked from the living room just a few minutes after I'd run from the balcony, barely making it into my room before I burst into tears. "What's wrong? Was it that guy? I'll fucking kill him. Say the word."

I leaned against the door, holding my breath against the sobs as I slid to the floor. After a few seconds, they broke through anyway, pathetic squeaks piercing the air. I couldn't help it. I wasn't sure why he'd left, and it sent me spiraling. Maybe I came on too strong. Maybe my comment about wanting a little roughness had scared him off. Even worse, maybe he'd gotten the guts to leave me alone and I'd never see him again. I'd never know if I was a freak or not.

"Lily, let me in," Anne said and knocked on the door. "Please?"

I scooted from the door to the end of my bed, intending on inviting her in but not able to find the words. I pulled my legs to my chest and forced myself to suck in deep breaths. I fought against the urge to hold my breath against the sobs, letting them happen and feeling the tightness in my chest ease as I focused on my body. My thoughts went from the feeling of my own breathing to how Angel's breath felt against my throat. He'd barely touched me and yet, I'd felt so relaxed that it was like he'd been touching me the entire time.

"What are you doing here? Whatever. Go away!" Anne yelled, snapping me out of my trance. I scrambled to my feet and by the time I'd opened the door, she was shutting and locking the front door. She turned with anger in her eyes that melted the moment she saw me.

"Oh. Um, hey," she said and sat something on the counter before hurrying across the room toward me. "Are you okay? Did he try anything sleazy?"

"No. It was just me, a panic attack, nothing about him. Who was at the door?" I asked, moving past her before realizing whoever it was had probably already made it to the elevator. I turned to look at Anne and her concern melted into an apology. She groaned.

"It was Batman," she said and passed me for the kitchen. She lifted a piece of paper from the counter to show me before saying, "He said he'd pick you up at six tonight for dinner. I told him to go away."

I'd never seen her look so embarrassed, not even when she accidentally called a girl at school hot and was a little too into the way she said it.

"He'll be back," I said. I knew he would. He wouldn't leave me for good unless I made it clear it was what I wanted. He'd show up at six to take me on a real date. I felt a little like I was made of air.

"I don't mean to hate on him, but this guy seems really into you, like more than someone you just met a week ago," Anne said as she moved to the couch.

I stopped at the armchair, running my finger back and forth along the seam of the cushion.

"I could say the same thing about you and Jazz."

She opened her mouth to argue but stopped short.

"Fair," she said with a nod. "So, how did you get that cut on your neck?"

"It sounds crazy, but I broke a wine glass at the garden recital. That's why I didn't text you. I ran into Angel and he helped me and then things kind of just went from there."

"Not crazy," Anne said with a snort. "Sounds exactly like the kind of thing that would happen to you."

I was glad for that fact. I sprained my ankle at school once slipping on a banana peel in the cafeteria like I was in a cartoon. I got a concussion senior year after I slipped on a pencil on the floor of a classroom. It turns out that head injuries bleed a lot.

"We were supposed to meet up for dinner that night. I should have texted at least. I went back to Jazz's place. I guess we both found distractions in sexy packages." She stopped before she could give any more details, glancing up at me in shame. "I've been a shitty friend."

"It's okay," I said.

"It's not. You can tell me it's not, you know? You should tell me. Sometimes, you're too nice."

I wasn't sure what to say. I felt like I should apologize, but after getting told off for doing that, I caught myself before the words could slip out. I sat down in the armchair instead and waited for her to speak.

"I didn't mean to forget about you," she said. "I think I really like her."

I could tell from the surprise on her face that she meant it. Anne had dated around a lot since high school. She wasn't shy about anything and to see her squirm on the couch was funny.

"I think I really like him, too. I know I don't have a lot of experience with this and it's only been a little over a week..."

The understanding was there in her eyes. She was in the same place I was. How was it possible that you could feel something like this so deeply? It wasn't the same girlish feeling I was used to when I found someone attractive; it was easy the way meeting up with an old friend was after several years. It was strangely familiar.

"Weird, right?" Anne asked.

"Very."

# CHAPTER 8

I had lots of date-worthy outfits, but that didn't make picking one any easier. Jazzlyn and Anne helped me pick a lavender dress that would look appropriate at pretty much any restaurant we went to. Just like he said, Angel knocked on our apartment door ten minutes before six o'clock. Jazz and Anne made jokes at me from the couch as I went to answer the knock, Anne's crass comment making my face heat so much that I paused before I pulled the door open.

I froze in the doorway.

He stood in the hall dressed in a pair of black slacks and a black button-up. The way he smiled, and the way his eyes roved over me, made my heart speed up and reminded me of our earlier conversation on the balcony. He held out a small vase to me that held two white lilies surrounded by a few red roses. After a beat, I took the vase and stepped aside so he could enter.

"Lilies for Lily?" I asked slowly.

He smiled and nodded.

"Maybe it's a little on the nose," he said.

"Does that make you the rose?" I asked and felt the velvet-like petal of one of the roses.

"A classic," he answered. "A date-night staple."

"Timeless, sort of like..." I said and looked up at him. When I saw the humor in his face, I turned toward the kitchen before the embarrassment could overtake me. I sat the vase on the counter and Anne chose that moment to speak up.

"Good seeing you again, Batman," she said with a wave. "No hard feelings about earlier."

"I'll text you before we come back," I told her and grabbed Angel's hand. I tugged him into the hall as Anne called back that they were staying at Jazz's apartment. I pulled the door shut and had made it just a few steps down the hall before he asked if I had my keys.

Anne and Jazz laughed as soon as I walked back inside.

"I'm staying at Jazz's tonight. He's already been in your bedroom twice without seeing any action, so I thought..."

"I'll see you tomorrow," I said, my cheeks burning as I grabbed my purse from the kitchen counter and hurried back into the hallway. Angel noticed my embarrassment, but thankfully didn't comment on it as we walked to the elevator. We waited in silence as the elevator rose to our floor, the sound of pop music from an apartment around the corner the only sound. When the doors slid apart, everything in me froze.

I stared back at my shocked expression in the mirrored wall of the elevator. I glanced to my right to make sure Angel was still standing beside me. He smiled weakly and stuck his hand between the door and the frame before it could slide shut. The metal doors opened again with a ding, and he slipped inside.

"Coming?" he asked.

I forced my feet forward and into the elevator, the doors sliding shut behind and the silence enveloping us. I looked in the mirror on the other side of him, seeing only my left side and curious expression.

"I don't have a reflection," Angel answered the unspoken question. "I won't appear in photographs either."

I immediately thought about how difficult avoiding family photos would be, catching myself as I imagined Angel standing next to my parents before the tree at Christmas. Before I could ask any more vampire questions, the elevator slowed to a stop. The doors opened and we slipped out. I smiled awkwardly at the couple that was waiting to take our place, hoping neither of them noticed the reflectionless man next to me.

"Can I pay for the cab?" I asked as we left the front doors of the building. It was dark enough that the streetlights were on, casting a warm glow over the busy sidewalk.

"I thought we could use the walk to talk. The restaurant is just around the corner," Angel said and moved to one side of the busy sidewalk. "That's if it's okay with you?"

"Sure," I said. "Where to?"

"Have you ever been to La Fée?"

I knew the restaurant he was talking about. It was the closest French place, and my mom loved it. I'd only been once, the last time my parents visited. That had also been the *only* time they visited and the day I moved into the apartment before freshman year. I was for sure the spoiled only child, but NYC wasn't the easiest place to just come for an afternoon when you lived in the countryside estate, especially when you were their age.

"Once, but I don't really remember it," I said. The truth was that I couldn't remember if the escargot and amazing soup I ate was from La Fée or from our trip to France when I was in high school. "I remember what it looks like though. Their sign is adorable."

The restaurant had a fancy neon sign above their door that displayed La Fée in cursive, complete with a set of fairy wings on top of the final E that were a light lavender color, a subtle contrast from the bright white of the cursive. La Fée was a restaurant I heard about around campus sometimes, but one that no college student could afford to go to.

"It's not a far walk," Angel said, slipping his hand into mine.

I laced my fingers with his as warmth bloomed in my core, relaxing me as we started down the street. It was too busy to have a conversation, so I was glad the restaurant was just a few blocks away. There was a group of people outside dressed in beautiful cocktail dresses and suits. Angel held the door open for me and I walked into the restaurant and was greeted by the inviting smell of bread as a waiter dressed in black walked by with a cutting board holding a long baguette.

"Reservation for six-thirty under Angel Ramírez," Angel told the host at the podium. He checked the iPad in his hands before motioning for us to follow. I let Angel lead the way, following the man through the restaurant. The main room had a large chandelier above the diners. Golden fairy wings sprouted from the center; each wing complete with strings of crystals that glittered under the light.

"We reserved a booth in the back, if that's all right," the host said as we moved from the main room into a second area that was much darker. Smaller versions of the fairy chandelier hung over the booths we passed. In the center of the small room was a crystal sculpture that stretched from the floor to the ceiling. It was a series of angelic wings that rose in a spiral to the ceiling, lit below by lights that faded to different colors. The host led us to the third booth and motioned to the seats.

"Thank you," Angel said and slid into the far side. I sat down on the dark leather bench as the host sat our menus on the table. We weren't separated from the rest of the room, but our booth felt very private thanks to the dim lighting.

Our waiter appeared in record time to take our drink orders. We both ordered wine, reds, and the waiter left us alone in silence again. I was starting to feel nervous as the silence stretched on before he spoke.

"Do your parents know all about your YouTube channel?" Angel asked.

"Um, no," I said, still processing the sudden question. "They don't know about it at all. They think I want to join the New York Phil or play the cello in some big orchestra."

"Why haven't you told them?"

"I want to," I said. I wasn't sure how else to explain it. They'd never rejected any of my ideas before. There really was no reason for me to believe that they wouldn't approve of my alternative idea to mix string music with pop and rock. There really wasn't. Still, I'd heard enough of their disapproval of other people's decisions that I could work myself into a panic thinking about all the ways they might react to my new take on classical music.

"Cabernet," our waiter said as he returned with two wine glasses and a bottle. He opened it tableside and poured a mouthful into each glass, waiting for us to approve. Once we both thanked him, he left the bottle at the table and disappeared again, leaving me to confront the anxiety of my family that I tried to shove below the surface.

"I looked further into your channel," Angel said and lifted his glass to his lips. "You're very talented. I don't understand why anyone, especially your parents, wouldn't support you."

"It's not that they wouldn't. They would. At least, I think they would. But they wouldn't see it the way I do. They wouldn't see what I do as the same as what I'm in college for, not really anyway. I'm not making any sense, am I?" I asked, the room heating around me. There was no middle ground. I either shut down and didn't say anything because I was nervous or everything sped up and I said too much because I was nervous.

"They either don't understand your goals for yourself or they don't understand that there's more to be desired than a spot in a prestigious orchestra," Angel said and sipped his wine.

"Yes." I sighed, feeling the embarrassment creep into my face. When he smiled, I relaxed a little. Each time he'd made an assumption about me, it was spot on. I had no reason to believe that he didn't understand. I felt like he could see right through me. There was no point in hiding. It didn't matter, anyway. I didn't want to hide from him.

"How about we talk more about you?" I asked, watching the way he glanced toward the rest of the room before looking back at me. "Not *that*," I added and watched the tension in his jaw melt.

"What would you like to know?" he asked just as our waiter returned. Neither of us had taken time to peruse the menu. I ordered the first traditional dish I saw, a bouillabaisse, and Angel ordered the beef bourguignon without even looking down at the menu. The waiter took our menus and hurried toward the kitchen.

Angel turned his gaze to me, dark eyes that made me forget the list of questions I was ready to ask before the waiter interrupted.

"Are you actually going to eat that?" I asked, remembering what he'd said before about his diet.

He smiled. "No, but I thought you might like it."

"I already ordered my own," I said, ready to defend myself against whatever weird notion he had about my appetite.

"You're allergic to seafood," he said with a laugh.

I paused, trying to remember what I'd ordered. I'd butchered the pronunciation, I was sure, so there was no telling. Angel smiled back at me, making me squirm.

"Okay, so you pay attention to the little things," I said and reached across to playfully slap his hands on the table. "I told you a bit about my family. You told me you're originally from Spain. Tell me about your home."

His smile dimmed a little as he sat back from the table.

"I lost both of my parents to the Spanish Inquisition," he said.

Stunned was the closest to what I felt. First, I had to sort through all the history that I knew to put the timing into perspective. Second, the horrors that flashed through my mind at the mention of that time period were enough to send a chill over my skin.

"I-I'm sorry," I said, the words barely audible.

"I've had a long time to reconcile the fact."

A long time was an understatement.

"I'm sorry," I said again, feeling that pang in my chest that usually came before the anxiety built up, before the tension settled in and made things too awkward to salvage. Angel continued the conversation like we were talking about the weather. It was strange, considering the magnitude of what we were discussing, but it set me at ease.

"My grandfather raised me," he said. "Our family was of nobility, though my parents were cast out. I was fortunate that my grandfather took me in after I was orphaned. I think the fact that I was so young worked in my favor. I was young enough that whatever it was about my parents that had angered the family couldn't have rubbed off on me, I suppose. That was such a long time ago that sometimes I forget."

Angel stared into the room, but I could tell his thoughts were far away. If he was a little boy during the inquisition, then how long had he been a grown man? He said a few days ago that it took hundreds of years for a vampire to grow strong enough to produce wings, longer even for their body to change shape and become the giant bat-like creature that he had when he saved me in the garden.

"I know that my grandfather loved me, and I loved him. He was a good man. I don't remember why my parents were disgraced. I'm sure it was for something ridiculous, but I know that he was a kind man all things considered. He wasn't kind by today's standards, but he loved me and cared for me and treated others well compared to many nobles of the time," Angel said and took another sip of his wine. "I was raised with his wealth and inherited it when he died."

"So, how old are you?" I asked slowly, twisting my wine glass by the stem.

"I can't be sure when I was born, not anymore." He shrugged. "I know that I was turned at twenty-two years."

I saw the subtle way his grip tightened on his glass as he lifted it to his lips, though his expression remained calm as ever. He'd hated being a vampire from the beginning. I could tell that the day he turned was the day everything changed for the worse in his mind; it led him to rationalizing that even making the best of the situation still made him a monster.

We must've been talking for a long time, because the waiter came with our dishes. Just as Angel said, mine was full of seafood. Once the waiter refilled our wine glasses and left, we swapped entrees. Angel didn't even bother pretending to eat while I indulged. The beef bourguignon was amazing and my worries about his past faded with each bite.

"What is your favorite movie?" Angel asked after I was nearly finished with my meal and the second glass of wine. I was a little taken aback by the sudden shift from medieval Spain to my guilty pleasure of cheesy romcoms.

"Don't laugh," I said and pushed the last of my bowl aside. "If I'm sad or just need something on while I'm hanging around the apartment, I put on *Pretty Woman*."

Angel stifled a laugh by taking a drink.

"I said don't laugh," I groaned, though I couldn't help but giggle.

"You're a fan of romantic comedies?" he asked.

"If Julia Roberts is in it, then yes."

"I love a good comedy," he said as the waiter sat the bill on the edge of the table. He pulled his wallet from his pocket and slipped out some cash. "Is there anything you don't like to watch?"

"Horror movies," I said, remembering the time I threw up at Anne's house in high school after we watched *The Texas Chainsaw Massacre*. I still had nightmares sometimes.

"You hate horror movies, and you agree to go out with one of the biggest tropes of the genre," Angel said with a laugh. "I find it a little hard to believe that you could hate being scared after everything we've been through. Everything you saw and you can't stomach a little jump scare in a film."

"Don't make fun of me!" I laughed as he stood up from the booth.

"Surely, there's one scary movie you've seen and liked," he said as he led the way toward the front of the restaurant. It was getting busy. I was glad we came before the bulk of the dinner rush. It was too loud in the main room to answer him, so I waited until we were back on the sidewalk to speak, slipping my hand into his and was greeted with a gentle squeeze.

"I can think of one, but it's not a movie I've seen," I said. Before he could ask for the title, I pulled him down the street.

<hr>

I was on my third glass of wine when I accidentally spilled it over my dress thanks to the jump scare on the TV. Gary Oldman dropped from the ceiling of Winona Ryder's room with a hiss, upside down. It surprised me enough that I screamed. Angel plucked the glass from my hands and sat it on the coffee table, but half the glass was already soaking into the lavender fabric of my dress.

"I'll get you a towel," he said and stood up.

"I'll just change. Pause the movie, please," I said and hurried into my bedroom, shutting the door behind me. The sound of screaming stopped as I looked around my room. It seemed stupid to put on another dress since we were just spending the night on the couch. I picked out a pair of comfortable shorts and a black tank top.

After running my dress under the water in the bathroom sink, I wrung it out and left the bedroom. Just off the kitchen was a small washer/dryer combination. I tossed the dress in the washing machine and started the load. When I turned around, my eyes went to the TV screen. Dracula was standing tall in Mina's bedroom, more bat than man, with slits where his nose once was and long pointed ears. It was chilling how similar Angel looked to the vampire on the screen. If Dracula was a foot or so taller and had giant bat wings stretching from his back, they would look almost the same.

"You're scared." Angel had moved from the kitchen back to the living room, blocking the TV from view.

"I'm not," I said, glad that I sounded confident. "I was just surprised. Besides, there is more wine left." I said as I walked around him, noticing the glass of water on the coffee table when I lifted the bottle to refill my wine glass.

"All right then," Angel said and picked up the remote. He started the movie again and sat down on the couch. Dracula backed into the shadows and when the light was cast over him, he was nothing but a bunch of rats.

"You can change shape..." I started, holding the wine glass closer and shifting a little so our shoulders brushed.

"Not like that," he answered, draping an arm over the back of the couch. "We can't become anything more than what you saw in the garden and only after we've grown stronger after a long time."

"The mirror thing is accurate though," I said, glancing his way and watching the smile spread on his face.

"Yes," he answered. "We have no reflection."

"What about the mind reading, control thing?" I asked. I said it jokingly, but now I was a little worried. I blushed and readjusted in my seat, trying not to think about all the images he'd have seen if that piece of lore was fact.

"No, Mouse," he said with a laugh. "I can't read your mind, but from the way you're squirming now I do wonder."

I forced myself to sit still, focusing instead of the TV even though I'd already lost interest in the ending. I stared down at my half-empty wine glass. He had no reflection. He could change shape, appearing more bat-like, and had incredible strength. He was centuries old. He was forced to drink human blood to survive and chose to feed only from the worst of humanity. He could not read my mind. Thank God for that.

"How do you make a vampire?" I asked and took a drink. The glass stayed suspended near my lips as his expression fell. He looked at the TV, sadness in his eyes.

"That is one trauma I'm not ready to revisit," he said and looked at me, his smile forced.

I sat the last of my wine on the coffee table and drank from the glass of water instead. Of course, losing your entire human life would be traumatic. It was probably a painful experience if any of the vampire movies ever made were correct. I couldn't imagine what Angel went through.

My internal chastisement was interrupted when he slipped an arm around my waist. I looked up at him, my heart skipping in my chest. He pulled me closer, and I relaxed against his side and let my head rest on his chest. That floral scent at his neck was relaxing even with the eerie horror music in the background. The arm around me fell into place, his hand sliding onto my bare thigh and began tracing gentle patterns on my skin.

"I think I've scared you enough for the night," he said as the credits rolled on the dark screen. He exited from the film to the main menu and turned on an episode of some cooking show.

"Not scared," I reminded him. Butterflies filled my stomach when his lips pressed to the top of my head. I inhaled his heady scent and closed my eyes, so comfortable I fell asleep.

# CHAPTER 9

I was so unbelievably snuggled. I never slept this well, especially with the light this bright which was what pulled me immediately from dreamlessness. I struggled to prop myself up, stopping when I realized I wasn't wound in the sheets but pressed against a body. I looked at Angel who was reclining against one side of the couch with a pillow propped under his head. He smiled at me and shifted so I could move from between him and the back of the couch into a sitting position.

"Good morning," he said.

"Have you been here the entire time?" I asked, remembering that he didn't sleep.

"Lying next to you was probably the closest I can ever get to sleep," he said with a snort. "And I didn't want to wake you. You seemed like you needed it."

I thought about the way I must have looked. I hadn't taken my makeup off from last night and I could tell. The mascara flaked off and into my eye as I sat there, prompting me to get up and go back to my bedroom.

"I'm going to, er, get ready for the day. Just make yourself comfortable," I said, not that he hadn't been perfectly cozy on the couch this entire time.

I closed the bedroom door and went straight to the bathroom, groaning at the dark smears under my eyes. This man had seen me with eyes red-rimmed and puffy from crying, in a full-on panic attack, drugged, and had cleaned vomit off my shoes. If I hadn't scared him away after all of that, surely smeared makeup wouldn't do the trick.

I waited for the water from the shower to warm up before getting in. Angel was right about needing the rest. I was so used to tossing in the night, waking up before my alarm, and struggling to fall asleep at all. I knew it came with the anxiety, but I had no idea just how bad my sleep was until I stood under the warm water. I felt like a new person.

When I finished dressing in a pair of jeans and a T-shirt and left my bedroom, Angel stood at the stove tending to a skillet. I lifted myself onto a barstool and watched as he tossed what looked like a mixture of potatoes and bell peppers. The skillet to his right held the same scrambled eggs I liked so much. My stomach growled in response.

Angel glanced back at me and smirked.

"Did you hear that?" I asked.

He turned off the heat and scraped the potatoes onto a plate and then did the same with the eggs. He turned to face me, sliding the plate across the counter to me.

"My hearing is much better than yours," he said and held out a fork. I took it and immediately speared an egg.

"How much better?"

He thought for a moment, dragging a rag over the countertop around the stove.

"There's really no comparison," he said and sat the rag aside as the coffee maker beeped twice. "I can hear you breathe across the room if I focus. Most of the time, we aren't paying enough attention to notice the subtle sounds. Being human doesn't really go away when you turn, not at first anyway."

I wondered how often he slowed down enough to pay attention to my breathing.

"Latte with a splash of vanilla?" he asked as he pulled a mug from the cabinet above the coffee maker.

"Um, yes, please," I said, taken aback that he remembered my order from brunch. I watched as he moved a bottle of vanilla from the cabinet.

"Do you have a frother?" he asked.

"Yeah, in that drawer." I pointed to the drawer in front of the coffee maker.

Angel pulled out the frother and sat it on the counter. He took the half-gallon of milk from the fridge. He poured a little bit of the coffee and the vanilla into the first mug. Then, he pulled a tiny saucepan, the one I laughed at Anne for owning when we moved in, and he poured some milk into it. He placed it on the stove and turned the burner on.

"You like lattes?" I asked as he watched the milk, placing the frother in the liquid as it began to heat up.

"No. They aren't for me," he answered as he focused on mixing the milk. I could see that it was thickening. "I like my coffee black. There are only a few foods that don't make me sick these days. Liquids are easier. Anything with added sugars or syrups tends to turn my stomach. I can have a few bites of solid foods, but much more than that and I feel sick. Meats that are cooked rare seem to be easier." He moved the pan from the stove. He poured the warm milk into the mug with the coffee before setting the pan back on the burner and continuing to froth the milk.

"I didn't realize that living hundreds of years made you a coffee connoisseur," I said and took another bite of the eggs.

Angel smiled and continued to froth the milk until what was left in the pan had grown so thick that he was able to scoop it out with a spoon and plop it on top of the coffee in the mug. Once finished, he sat the mug in front of me with a smile.

"I've worked as a barista," he explained and began gathering the dirty pans from the stove and setting them in the sink. "After I figured things out as a vampire, I decided that I liked the daily life of humans more. I tried to live as normally as I could and that started with getting a job. I worked for a butcher and when I expressed interest in how he prepped and cooked the meat, he passed me on to a chef as an apprentice."

I took a sip from the mug. Heavenly. It was every bit as good as any cup of coffee I'd ordered in a shop.

"It would be better with espresso," Angel said and turned on the tap.

"It's great." I took another sip. "Almost as good as your eggs."

"Talk about good, you're a pretty good cellist. I'd like to hear you play again sometime," Angel said and finished rinsing off the last of the pans. He opened the dishwasher and began loading them into the bottom rack.

"I have a cello here. Want a lesson?" I asked. I was surprised. I could feel the blush creep onto my face, and I fought hard against the uncomfortable giggle threatening to break free as Angel looked up at me from the dishwasher, a smile spreading.

"I definitely want that lesson, Mouse," Angel said with a laugh. "After you finish breakfast."

"What is your deal with food?" I asked, not that I was complaining. The eggs and potatoes were too good to let go to waste. I planned on eating the entire meal.

"Food like this is a luxury I can't indulge in anymore," Angel said. "Besides, I take care of the people I care about. I've lived through the pain of hunger. No one should have to do the same if I can help it."

His words made my stomach twist into a knot, and it took me a moment to realize it was guilt. I lived in this spacious New York City apartment without a job, and I still worried like crazy. I worried about everything. I had a panic attack a few months ago because I dropped my pencil while studying.

"Lily," Angel said.

When I looked up, he was gone. He stood to my left, a couple of feet away, and looked at me with concern. He took a few slow steps toward me until he was within reach.

"When you feel uncomfortable like this, what triggers it? What makes you anxious about the world?" he asked, stopping inches away.

"Safety," I said in an exhale. I wanted to explain, but I couldn't bear to say more. I was safe at home, kept away from it all thanks to my family's money, thanks to the expensive apartment only tenants could enter. That was one thing money could buy, or usually could. I've always struggled with anxiety, but things are different now.

I haven't always been safe. I haven't felt completely safe since.

"You're safe with me, Mouse," he said, his voice low. "That's the only good thing about being around a monster like me. No one would dare lay a hand on you."

My heart skipped in my chest.

"I know," I whispered. I could see in his expression, in that brief fade of his confident eyes, that he wanted to follow up by telling me how dangerous he was for me. It passed quickly, a darker look replacing it that made my stomach knot in a new way.

I reached out and touched his face, feeling the strength in his jawline. I traced down to his neck, lacing my fingers behind his head and pulling him closer. Only, I didn't have to pull at all. His lips were on mine, voracious at first and then softening to the point of frustration. I shifted in my seat, so my knees moved apart, making space for him, but he didn't step any closer. Just as I thought about attempting to pull him to my chest, his lips were gone.

"I don't want you to teach me," he said, his nose brushing mine. "I want to be that cello. I want to rest between your legs the way it does. Play whatever melody you want, I'm yours."

Everything inside of me sped up. I moved my hands from the back of his head to the front of his shirt. I tugged, but he didn't move. He stood inches away, almost close enough for me to wrap my legs around his hips.

"I want you," I breathed.

He stroked the side of my face and groaned.

"I can't. It's not safe."

Everything came to a stop. My heartbeat was fast, but it felt like my ribcage was slowly capturing it, vicelike. My breath hitched in my chest and started to catch before I could fill my lungs.

"No. Not that, Mouse. I want you. I'm yours, if you'll have me," he said cupping my face, lifting my eyes to his. "I can't give you more. I shouldn't have said those things when I can't follow through."

"What if I want you to follow through?" I asked, fighting the tears. "If it's about me..."

"Sex with me would be too much. It's too primal, too honest. It would strip me down to my true form," Angel said and brushed away a tear that slipped down my cheek. "You wouldn't like me in my true form."

"You don't know that. I was there in that garden and I'm still here now."

He smiled and stepped closer, bringing his forehead to mine and weaving his hands into my hair. He breathed in deeply and when he exhaled there was a deep rumble in his throat.

"What I mean is that I can't give you more right now," he said and pulled back so I could see the sincerity in his expression. "My natural instincts, the vampire in me... There's truth in what many know of us. It's natural for us to lure our prey into bed first. It's easy to let go of humanity during those moments and I don't want to risk that. Even after hundreds of years, I struggle to maintain my manners in those moments. I don't want to be rough with you, Mouse."

The darkness in his eyes told me that was exactly what he wanted, and I was a little surprised that I wanted the same. My core tightened at the thought of those gentle hands rough on my skin.

I heard laughter in the hallway and then the sound of keys in our door. Angel had vanished from under my fingers before the lock clicked in the door. I looked around the room, but he was gone, probably flown from the balcony like he had yesterday.

"Hey, Lily," Anne greeted and tossed her purse onto the counter.

"Hi," Jazz said as she came in behind her. "How was your date?"

"It was really good," I said, still trying to shake the feeling deep in my core.

"Are you and Batman together yet?" Anne asked, making flirty eyes at me.

My embarrassment betrayed me immediately and they both burst into laughter.

"Are *you two* together yet?" I countered and pointed at them both in turn.

The laughing stopped and Anne and Jazz exchanged glances. It was a little funny. They'd spent almost every day together since meeting at the club and they'd never talked about their status.

"I'd say so," Jazz said with a shrug to Anne.

Anne looked at me like she was getting ready to drop the best come-back of all time.

"Yes," she said, clearly trying to contain her smile. "Jazzlyn is my girlfriend."

I couldn't pretend to be mad anymore for their intrusion. We stood there for an awkward moment. Then, Anne started walking toward her room and Jazz trailed after her.

"We are just here for a little while," Anne said as she went. "We might leave in an hour or so. There's a thing. I'll let you know."

Anne pulled her door shut behind them and I heard two sets of giggles far too girlish to be anything wholesome. I glanced at the balcony. He really was good. Angel didn't leave a single sign whenever he came or went. The perfect predator.

I went to my bedroom and shut the door. The curtain was still pulled close, plunging the room into darkness aside from the purple glow from the Christmas lights around my room. It reminded me of the club. I thought through every moment I'd had with Angel so far, starting in the club.

I opened my phone and scrolled through Spotify until I found a club mix with songs in deep reverb. It was sexy. It pulled me back into the moment in the kitchen. I replayed every word he said. I could still hear his deep voice in my ear. I swayed to the music, dragging my hands up my neck and through my hair to try to replicate the feel of his. Once I bumped into the bed, I sat down. I moved my knees apart and imagined what it would feel like if instead of resisting he'd stepped between them. Maybe his hands would slide up my thighs like mine were now. Maybe his touch would grow firmer the closer he got. I wanted him to grab me, pair the softer touches with a firm grip on my thighs or that deep growl. I'd gotten lost in that sound before.

I gasped. I would've screamed had all the air not shot from my lungs.

Angel was leaning against the closed door, smiling at me.

"Please, don't stop on my account," he said with a laugh.

"I thought you left," I said, trying to calm my heart.

"I like when you blush like that." He straightened up and moved closer, stopping just out of reach. "Is that what you like?"

"What? What do you mean?" I asked. My face was so hot that I knew all hope was lost of pretending what I was doing was anything other than what it was. The sexy club music was still playing on my phone. I reached for it, but it was gone as soon as I moved. It took me a moment to spot it sitting on my desk behind Angel, the deep music still playing.

He had that darkness in his eyes again, almost like hunger. It made my stomach clench.

"Is that the way you like to be touched?" he asked.

"I-I don't know. I don't really. I've only been with one guy."

"Do you want me to touch you like that?"

My mouth went dry. I didn't realize I was leaning away from him until he was standing at the end of the bed. I pushed myself back on the mattress with my feet, propping myself up on my elbows as I reached the pillows. Angel didn't stop. He kept a foot away from my face, climbing gracefully onto the bed and then hovering over me.

"When we were back in the kitchen," he started, looking down at me beneath him before lifting his eyes to mine. "What were you hoping I'd do?"

"I don't know what you mean," I breathed. My heart was like a caged hummingbird in my chest. He was so close that the heady floral scent of him was everywhere. I felt hot, like I was wearing more layers than I was.

Angel let out a hum of a laugh. Still, he didn't touch me. The suspense was almost too much.

"Oh, I think you do, Mouse." He leaned toward me. I sank farther back in response, flattening myself onto the pillows under me. "You said you wanted me. How?"

"How?"

"How do you want me, Mouse?"

A little gasp burst from my lips before I could contain it. I hated how close we were without touching. The way he hovered over me effortlessly. I arched my back, but still didn't even brush his chest. He was doing it on purpose, keeping us apart just to make me squirm. It was working.

He smiled and asked, "What do you want me to do?"

"Touch me."

"How?"

A little squeak of protest I didn't know I could make escaped my lips. Could he not just put his hands on me? Why did I have to say anything? I wasn't sure I could.

"Touch me like a vampire," I said, the words sounding more like a whimper than a real request.

"No. Not like that," Angel said, the humor in his expression dimming a little. "But I can do this."

He remained perfectly balanced above me as he moved his right hand away from my shoulder. I felt chills prick my skin when his fingers met my thigh. He slid his hand slowly up my leg. He paused at the top of my jeans.

"Too soft," I whispered.

He gripped the top of my jeans, gathering the fabric in his hand so that it tightened around my hips. My heart leaped in my chest and as soon as he'd tugged on the fabric, he was back to his gentle touch. He slid his hands under my shirt, inching upward. I heard that throaty growl build in his chest and I bowed my back in response. Just as his fingers approached the band of my bra, the pressure went from soft to firm and then that same squeak slipped from my lips when I felt the brief sharpness of his nails threatening to take hold.

His hand vanished and my eyes flicked to his face. He took a deep breath as though steadying himself. I reached out to touch the side of his face with one hand gingerly before I cupped his cheeks and raised his gaze to my eyes. He closed his eyes and breathed deeply again, this breath much calmer than the others. When he opened his eyes, he captured my left hand in his. He kissed the back of it before lowering it to the pillow beneath me. He did the same with my right hand, both now resting next to my ears.

"I don't want to risk letting go with you," he said and brushed the side of my face with his thumb. "I can't, Lily. I want it just as much as you, but I can't. Maybe with time, but not now."

I squirmed beneath him again. He the adjusted his stance over me so that his hands laced with mine, pressing them against the pillow. Once I stopped moving, he shifted again, freeing my hands. I knew what he wanted. No touching. His body inches from mine. I hated it, but I loved the proximity all the same. The smell of him was intoxicating and I didn't want to risk him backing away again.

"I take care of the people who are important to me," Angel said. His right hand moved from my cheek to my neck, gently tracing its way down my chest and stopping at the top of my jeans. "Especially you, Mouse."

With a single hand, he pulled the button of my jeans free and pulled the zipper down. Before my gasp could escape, his hand slid beneath the fabric. His movements were slow and light, drawing out each stroke just to the height of pleasure before moving to a new gentle touch that started the build-up all over again.

"I don't want you to know the real me. I'll never let myself be that way with you. I want to be gentle. I want to take care of you, Mouse. Isn't it enough to feel this way, to have me like this?"

I pressed against his touch, but he pulled away, relentless about torturing me with his soft touches. It was everything I dreamed of, but also not nearly enough. It was so good, so damn good. Still, I wanted to feel him, really feel him pressed against me and let go the same time he would. I didn't care if it stripped him to the vampire underneath. Maybe I wanted that. Maybe I wanted to feel his hands, rough to match that dark voice that came to the surface whenever I needed him.

It was so good. It was too good, but I wanted more of him. Tears burned my eyes and finally spilled over when it was all too much, the gentle stroke of his fingers lulling me to safety before the last of my control spilled over. I felt shattered like everything inside of me had let go all at once. He stifled my cry with his hand, continuing that tortuous rhythm of his fingers until it all spilled over again, and I whimpered into his palm. It was like waking up from the best sleep of your life and then, very quickly, being pulled under again with exhaustion. I was still recovering when I realized that Angel had pulled me against his chest. He was under me now, his arms draped around my waist while I panted against the crook of his neck.

He brushed my hair away from my face as I came back down. He shifted to one side so he could kiss my forehead.

"Happy tears?" he asked and brushed away the last of the moisture from my face.

I bit my lip as the heat rushed to my cheeks. I'd never... My first time was far from that.

Angel smiled. "I like making you blush and other things."

My cheeks hurt from the smile tugging at my mouth as I spun around to climb out of bed. As soon as my feet were on the floor, muscles like Jell-O under me, I wished I'd stayed in bed where I could lie against him. When I turned to face him, his gaze left me frozen in place. My jeans hung low on my hips, low enough to reveal the band of my underwear. How was it possible that not a single item of clothing was shed, and I felt more naked than I ever had before? That deep look in his eyes made me want to cover myself and throw myself onto the bed all over again.

When he lifted his gaze to my eyes, his expression changed. He looked conflicted. His hands went to his hair. I thought he was going to pull the elastic free for a moment before he lowered them and sat up.

"I want to try this. I want to be with you. I want every inch of you, mind and body." His eyes flicked to my waist for a moment before his eyes met mine. "Against my better judgment and the serious risks, I want to be yours. I am yours, if you want me. I can't leave you now and spend the rest of my days worrying about you. I want to try this because I don't think I can stay away now."

"I want you, too."

His arms were around me before I knew it. As fast as he'd moved, his lips came down on mine softly and we were back where we started.

# CHAPTER 10

Angel pressed me against the wall of my bedroom, hands on my face, in my hair. He kissed his way down my neck, the hollow of my throat, and over my chest. When he straightened up again, his hands were on the hem of my T-shirt. He dragged it up my body and over my head, tossing it aside before returning his lips to mine.

I fumbled with the button of his jeans, my heart skipping when I finally freed him. My hands froze on the fabric of his jeans.

"I'll be gentle, Mouse," Angel said. He was smiling when I looked up at him.

His hands were on the button of my jeans, pulling it free easily and pushing the fabric down until they pooled at my feet. I stepped out of them and kicked them aside, watching as he did the same with his own. He stood back and removed his shirt, the sight stopping my heart.

First, he was gorgeous. Every muscle was defined, and every curve was perfect.

Second, his torso was covered in scars. They were all long, some deeper than others. It looked like someone had dragged a knife over his body. I had just glimpsed a grouping near his left shoulder that told me the truth. Claw marks.

Angel was inches away again, the comforting smell of him thick around us. He slid his hands into my hair as he moved closer. Instead of kissing me, his fingers wound into the hair near the nape of my neck and gently pulled, guiding my head to one side to expose my neck to him. He placed feather-like kisses there, working his way down my neck and over my collarbone. His hands followed. They glided over my skin, unclasping my bra as they went. He didn't stop kissing me until his lips were on my navel.

I gasped as his hands slid to my hips and grabbed the last piece of clothing on my body, tugging them down my thighs where they fell to the floor. I let out a squeal as I rose into the air. My legs wrapped around Angel as he held me up, hands cupping my ass. He turned and lowered me onto the bed, hovering above me like before.

I reached for his chest, my fingers immediately finding a scar. I couldn't help but run my index finger down the raised mark. My hand was immediately captured in one of his. He raised it to his lips and kissed my knuckles, smirking down at me when he then laid it on the bed above my head. He took hold of the opposite hand and laid it with my other, holding onto both my wrists in his left hand.

"If you want me to stop, will you tell me?" he asked, brushing his nose against mine. I could feel him against me now. It made me squirm, attempting to press tighter to him. "Lily, please?"

"Yes. I'll tell you," I said, realizing why he'd stopped moving.

It was what he was waiting for.

He released me so he could sit back, both hands going to my hips and pulling me closer so my thighs spread farther around him. He leaned over me, my heart skipping in my chest when those dark eyes found mine. My mouth fell open as he found my center and moved deeper and deeper until I ached around him. I inhaled a small gasp when he tilted his hips even more, enough to know I'd still feel him much later. He lowered his forehead to mine with a groan, a hand cupping my cheek. He kept his eyes on mine as he slipped away only to draw closer again with a roll of his hips. This time he didn't stop, moving with slow thrusts as I adjusted to the feel of him.

He kept that same pace, brushing my hair away from my face, tracing his way down the valley between my breasts and toward my navel. I reached around his shoulders as his hand went lower and found that sensitive spot, making my legs press tighter around him. My hands tightened on his shoulders, and I had just pressed my nails to his skin when he thrust into me hard.

A whimper escaped my lips, and my hands were pinned against the pillow above me again. I saw the worry flash through his expression for just a moment before he let out a deep exhale and moved his right hand to my face again. I bit down on my lower lip only for him to pull it free with the pad of his thumb.

"When you touch me..." he breathed. A deep sound like a groan came from his throat and I knew he was taking a moment to slow his thoughts. I could see it in his expression.

"Then I won't," I whispered and tilted my hips upward to meet his.

A smirk replaced the awe on his face. He tightened his grip on my wrists and picked up where he'd left off with a swift thrust, already moving with a quicker pace that made my heart race. I fell apart beneath him in moments. He was gentle, so much so for someone who could rip people apart effortlessly. He got rougher near the end, gripping my hands tighter. Just when I thought he might release a part of his true self, he let out a loud groan and was lying next to me a moment after.

I snuggled closer to him, pulling my fluffy blanket from the foot of the bed over us as the air conditioning kicked in. He draped his arms around me and traced patterns on my shoulder and kissed my temple.

"Angel," I started tentatively. I knew he wouldn't like the question, but I had to ask. "Where did you get all the scars on your body?"

His finger stilled at my shoulder. He didn't move, his chest not even rising or falling with breaths I knew he didn't need to take. Finally, he sucked in a deep breath and shifted me to the side so he could sit up. The worst marks were on his back. There were two that stretched parallel from his right shoulder to his lower back. He turned on the bed to look at me, obscuring the view of the marks.

"Vampires don't play well together most of the time," he said.

"Are those from the same fight?" I asked, reaching for his chest again. I saw his hand twitch, but he didn't stop me. I lightly touched the worst mark near his shoulder.

"Different fights," he said. "None of the vampires that left these walked away in one piece."

I pulled my hand back, laying it in my lap and rubbing the back of it with my other hand.

"I don't mean to scare you," he said in a sigh and brushed the side of my cheek.

"It doesn't scare me," I told him, pulling his hand away from my cheek. "It makes me sad."

"Why?"

"Because I can see that it makes you sad," I said. Angel relaxed, looking down at the marks on his stomach. "I know you hate what you are, but there must be something good that came from this. I wouldn't know you."

"It may seem like a superpower to cheat death, be strong, and be more beautiful than you were in life," he said and looked up from the marks. "It's all a curse."

I didn't reply. What else was there to say? It wouldn't change the way he saw himself.

"I'm yours, Lily. I swear it. I will never hurt you and anyone who tries will find themselves in pieces." Angel twisted the end of a piece of my blonde hair around his finger. "Being with me comes with some risks and not just because I am what I am. It's everything that surrounds me, the world that I'm a part of. There's something I need you to do to make sure that you stay safe."

"What is that?" I asked.

"Stay away from Washington Square Park, Minetta Street, and Washington Street," he said with a sigh. "Please, just keep away from those areas."

"So, steer clear of tourist traps?" I asked with a forced laugh. It didn't work to break his serious mood. "Okay. I'll stay away."

He smiled and leaned in to kiss me.

"Lily, your mom's calling," Anne called from the other room.

That was enough to send my heart racing. I nearly fell out of the bed when I rolled away from Angel. I pulled on my jeans and T-shirt, not bothering with the underwear, and ran from the room. Anne held my phone out as she crossed the living room, glancing toward my room as I took it.

"Um, hi, Mom," I said as I pressed the phone to my ear. Anne gave me a shocked look before I shut my bedroom door on her. I was a little stunned at the sight of Angel, naked from the hips up, lying under my favorite blanket, and lounging so casually against the headboard.

"Lily? Are you listening?" my mom asked.

"Oh. Sorry. I'm in the middle of folding laundry," I said, looking away when Angel let out a laugh.

"I was asking if you were still able to come home a few days early. Your dad is playing in the charity golf tournament again this year and I'd rather not ride in the cart all alone," she said. Before I could respond, I heard her talking to someone. I recognized his voice as it grew closer.

"Hand me the phone, Donna, baby," he said before there was a shuffling sound as my mom handed the phone to my dad. "How's my little water lily?"

"Hi, Dad."

"Are you going to be here for the tournament? I've been playing a round of golf every Saturday with the guys to prepare. I think I'm going to place a lot higher this year," he said. I could hear my mom chide him in the background. "Your mom would love for you to be here."

"I know. I was planning to be there, but things have been a little complicated for the last couple of weeks." I glanced back at the bed only, Angel wasn't there anymore. He stood right next to me with a look on his face that made my stomach twist with guilt.

"Lily? Did I lose you?" my dad asked, pulling my attention away from Angel who shook his head and mouthed the word "go" to me.

"Um, I'll be there. I just have to sort a few details out," I said.

"I got you on speaker with Mom, Lilypad," he said. *Water lily* was a nickname I had let go, but hearing another childhood pet name made me cringe. "What kind of things do you have going on suddenly? The semester just ended and the last time we talked you said you'd passed all your finals."

"Um, well, I made a friend," I said. It almost sounded like a question. Angel smirked next to me, so I turned my back on him to try to hide my embarrassment.

"That's great," Dad said.

"Oh, is this a male friend?" Mom asked in the background. "You haven't told me about any boys since you got to NYU. Tell me you at least go on an occasional date between all those cello lessons."

"He's not a guy," I blurted, lowering the phone from my ear as soon as I realized my slip.

"Tell us what to call him or her and we'll have a nice time," said Dad. "The club may not be so welcoming, though. Tell him or her to just wear pants that night."

"I mean... Dad, it's not like that. It's—"

My mom gasped and I heard shuffling through the phone again. My parents exchanged words I couldn't make out and then it was my mom in my ear again.

"It is a boy, isn't it?" she asked. There was more shuffling in the background, and she muttered, "Thank the lord."

I heard my dad arguing in the background and my mom was quick to defend herself, saying something about Anne and that her parents were never at the club now.

My heart thumped heavily in my chest. Movement on my left caught my attention and I turned to see Angel, fully dressed, next to me. He held out a hand for the phone.

"May I?" he asked, keeping his voice low.

After a few more seconds of listening to my mom's questioning, I handed the phone over and walked straight into the bathroom. I fully intended on shutting myself inside so I couldn't hear, but my nerves got the best of me. As soon as I walked across the tile floor, I turned around and walked right back out.

"I don't want to impose," Angel said to my parents.

I waited in silence for far too long, probably my mom's doing. I knew she was just excited about the idea of me bringing a boy home.

"Lily and I will be there, Mrs. Thompson," he said, pausing a moment before continuing. "I'm sure she'll tell you all about me. Know that I'm not as great as she makes me out to be. Yes, your daughter is one of the kindest women I've ever met, too good for me. I can't wait to meet you both. Yes. I'll hand the phone off to Lily," he said with a laugh.

I took the phone from him and hurried into the living room, shutting the bedroom door before I burst into tears of nerves.

"Lily?" Mom asked.

"I'm here."

"He sounds nice. He reminds me of your dad," she said.

At least Angel only had one pet name for me, one that came from something of an insult, but still.

"He's pretty great, Mom."

"Well, I can't wait to meet him. I didn't know you had a boyfriend all this time."

"It's relatively new," I said. I was mentally kicking myself for revealing the fact. My Catholic parents would have lots of questions about me bringing home a serious boyfriend I'd met just a few weeks ago. "We met at a school thing a while back. We've known each other a while, just never tried out the whole dating thing until, like, recently. I think it's been like a month or two."

"Anyway, he seems nice. Do you still want us to come and pick up the two of you?"

"No," I said a little too quickly. I held my breath for a moment before continuing. "We have a way to get there. I'll let you know when we leave. Mom, I have to go. We have plans. It's why he came here."

"Okay. Have fun," she said, my dad yelling something in the background as I hung up. I noticed a text message waiting for me and opened it out of habit, blushing as soon as I read it.

Did you just fuck Batman?

I looked up, expecting to see Anne sitting on the couch in front of me just waiting for the gossip. Instead, her bedroom door was closed, and I could hear faint rock music playing behind it.

---

I should've known I'd never get away from Anne.

"I want to know everything," she said across the kitchen aisle from me.

"I just told you that we had sex," I cried out, turning away from my Chef Boyardee in the microwave.

"Yes, but I want to know if he was good to you in bed," she said, raising her eyebrows in a way that made me uncomfortable. It made me think about the moment he hovered over me.

"Oh, my God," Anne said, lowering her spoon back to her rice bowl.

"Anne," I groaned, turning back to the microwave again to hide my burning face. It let out a ding as soon as I turned and finished cooking my meal. I used it as an opportunity, pulling the hot container out and sitting it on the counter.

"At least tell me he got you off. He did, didn't he?"

"Anne," I groaned again, mixing the ravioli inside the plastic bowl.

"I knew it!" she yelled.

I turned around, shushing her. She burst into a laughing fit.

"You are so..." I couldn't think of the right word, so I took an ice cube from my glass of water on the counter and tossed it at her. It didn't stop her from laughing. If anything, it only made her laugh more.

"I was starting to worry that our Catholic girls' school had rubbed off on you in the wrong way," she said with a giggle.

"I'm surprised you're even here tonight," I told her as I mixed my ravioli, hoping it helped cool them off.

"Jazz went home for the weekend. She's going to talk about me to her family before I come next week to meet them." She was unable to hide her smile.

"You two really are serious," I said, noticing the way Anne fidgeted with her spoon. It was a big deal, more than I knew she'd admit. Anne's parents basically disowned her when she finally came out last year. They wanted her to come to visit them, but they couldn't help but spew their usual speeches. That just wasn't who Anne was and they didn't make any effort to understand. So, she didn't bother anymore and as much as she acted like it was an easy split, I knew it wasn't. She wanted a family life. Maybe Jazz could give her that.

"Wow. That's a big move. It's exciting," I said, unable to think about what Angel would look like next to my parents' country club friends.

"They are super inclusive. Jazz has two gay relatives and they're the normal ones," Anne said, taking a bite from her bowl.

"I'm bringing Angel home for the country club's Summer Social," I said, the words pouring from my lips before I could think about it. I knew I would hesitate if I thought about it too hard and even now, I turned to the fridge to fill my half-empty glass of water.

"Donna and Kenneth are meeting Batman?" Anne asked.

"His name is Angel," I said, forcing myself to face her again once my glass was full. "And yes, I'm bringing him home to meet my parents."

"And you say *I* must be serious," she joked, tossing the melting ice cube right back at me. It bounced off my shoulder and fell to the floor.

"My parents are more progressive than yours," I said. "Bringing a boy home isn't that big of a deal." That wasn't entirely true, but not for Catholic reasons. My parents loved gossip, even my dad who pretended to be all macho and not care. As soon as it came out over the phone, I knew that it would be all they could talk about until we got home, which meant that all their friends would also know about it.

"How much did you tell them?" Anne asked.

I opened my mouth to answer before realizing that I hadn't really told them anything. I don't even think I'd told them his name. I know Angel hadn't introduced himself when he took my phone to tell them we'd be coming.

"All they know is that I have a boyfriend and he's coming home with me."

Anne let out a dramatic gasp and said, "Scandalous."

"That doesn't say much considering showing your knees was scandalous at our school," I said and took a bite of ravioli. I remembered Anne being told off many different times for wearing her skirt too short.

She rolled her eyes.

"So, I'll be visiting Jazz's family next week and you'll be back home with Batman and yours."

"You can call him Angel."

"Batman suits him better."

Oh, if she only knew how well it suited him.

"Fine, but you should know you didn't make the best first impression on him, so maybe don't call him that when you see him next," I said, blowing on the ravioli I'd speared before I popped it into my mouth.

Anne made an annoyed face and asked, "What did I do?"

"Well, in his defense," I said as I chewed, pausing to swallow, "the first time we met, you left me at a bar."

"I didn't! You were having a great time when I saw you. I swear, I wouldn't have left you if I didn't think you were. Nothing seemed wrong," Anne said, her cheeks turning pink.

My stomach twisted the way it always did when I felt guilty. I never should've said anything. I should've just left it and never mentioned why things were tense between them. But Angel was right. She shouldn't have left me. She should have checked with me herself, not from across the room. She should've stayed with me. I couldn't bring myself to tell her that now. I knew she meant well.

"I know," I said. "I've known you since grade school. He doesn't know that though. All he knows is that I went to the club with you, and he found me alone."

Anne groaned.

"I was a bad friend that night. Shit. I know I was."

"I forgive you," I said.

She groaned again and sent me a pointed look. I knew it well. Her eyes stared daggers, one eyebrow slightly raised. She gave me that look whenever I wasn't being wholly honest, and it worked every time. I'd spill my guts, just like now.

"You should've checked with me. I did get drugged and pulled into an alley."

"God, Lily!" Anne gasped, nearly knocking over her rice. "I didn't know that. I thought you just left that other guy and ended up getting a little too drunk with Angel. I didn't know he brought you home because of that."

"I know. I'm not proud of what happened."

"He really is Batman," Anne said under her breath. "And you shouldn't be embarrassed. I'm glad you left before everything happened with that guy. You could've been caught up in it all. The news said he was connected to gang members and that's who they think got him."

My stomach was in knots as I remembered what really happened to Aaron.

"I need to get a new outfit for next week. I don't have anything that's not club-worthy or sitting-in-a-lecture-like-a-hobo-worthy. Want to come?" Anne asked, sliding her half-empty bowl of rice across the counter to me. I stopped it and tossed the last of her rice into the trash next to the counter before setting the bowl in the sink.

"I need to work on some music stuff for YouTube."

"Oh! When is the next song coming out?" she asked as she pulled her purse over her shoulder and lifted her lanyard from the front doorknob.

"Not sure." I said. This wasn't normal for me. Not having a scheduled plan for the week, or at least knowing what to expect next, usually made me so nervous. I didn't feel anything this time. It was weird. Anne noticed, hesitating before she turned to the door.

"All right. Well, I hope it goes well. I'll let you know when I come back so we can do something together," she said and left the apartment.

# CHAPTER 11

Angel spent just as much time at the apartment as Jazz did. I barely saw Anne; we were both locked in our bedrooms with our significant others most of the time. I didn't ask Angel about the scars on his torso again, not even tracing them, as much as my fingers wanted to reach out and try rubbing the memory of the attacks away.

"Promise me that you'll be free tonight?" Anne asked me as she followed Jazz toward the front door. Jazz looked back at her fondly from the open door. Whatever was so important, she knew about it.

"I have no plans. Why?" I asked, looking up from my phone. I was expecting Angel to appear at any moment. I was hoping he'd walk through the front door like a normal person and not just swoop in from the balcony, mostly because he always commented about the sliding door being unlocked.

"There's a band at this cool bar I want to see. It's a place we've never been to. I want to go, just you and me," Anne said.

"Okay. What do I need to wear?"

"What you have on is fine," Anne said. "I'll text you later. We can leave from here." She ignored Jazz's encouragement to follow her into the hallway.

After the door shut and locked behind them, I went back to my laptop on the couch to focus on the music I was editing. The song was almost done, a rock ballad that I'd been tinkering with for months. Just when I thought I was ready to post it, my chest would tighten, and my brain would tell me it wasn't ready. The rational part of me knew it was fine. It was more than fine. It was a really great song, one of my best, but I was afraid to release it because I loved it so much and it felt raw. It was the song I was hoping would take my YouTube channel further. I dreamed of being in the video but couldn't bring myself to film anything. I'd tried. I'd tried even just filming myself, not my face, playing the intro on the cello. Every video I recorded that featured myself, I deleted.

"You should really lock this," Angel said.

I looked up from my computer as he slid the glass door shut behind him, locking it in place. He joined me on the couch, pressing a kiss to my temple and pulling me close to him.

"Can I listen?" he asked, pointing to the computer screen.

My chest tightened and I forced myself to take a deep breath.

"Yes," I said and sat the laptop on the coffee table. "I'm just about done. I should be done. It's good. I just need to finish a few things."

He snorted and moved the MacBook onto his lap.

"I'm sure it's perfect," he said and pressed play.

The cello sang a deep crescendo that grew slowly into the melody. The vocals came in at a distance, singing over the strings as the tempo finally took hold and the rhythmic drumbeat stole the spotlight.

"Is that you?" Angel asked, looking away from the screen.

"Y-Yeah," I said softly.

A small gasp of disbelief escaped from his lips as more strings joined the drums. I held my breath against the embarrassment as the vocals faded in again.

"It's beautiful," he said.

"It's not professional quality."

"Stop," he said. His tone startled me. It wasn't sharp. It wasn't even firm, but it was enough to make my heart skip. He looked at me with admiration, a smile on his face that eased the tension in my shoulders. "You are a great musician and it's about time you acknowledge that."

"Okay, but I'm an average singer."

Angel cupped one side of my face, his expression serious.

"You have thousands of followers on YouTube who think you are amazing. Own it."

I didn't respond, not sure how to accept the compliment anyway. Angel leaned in and his lips met mine, soft at first. I sucked his lower lip between mine and he groaned. He moved his hand from my face to the back of my neck, holding me in place. The other slid from my knee to my thigh, gripping it as he lowered me onto the cushion.

I pulled his lower lip between mine again, lightly biting. The groan that reverberated from his throat made my core tighten and a jolt shot through my body when he squeezed my ass. His eyes were dark, the same ones that I remembered from the alleyway and the garden. Another growl emanated from his chest. My back arched as his grip on the back of my jeans tightened, the hand at the base of my neck sliding into my hair. It was a tight fist at the roots, tighter than the last time, and the feeling of his hands so firm on my body elicited a small gasp from me.

Angel took control of the kiss. He held my lips to his, rolling his hips slowly against the most sensitive spot between my thighs. Just as I had, he sucked on my lower lip. I grabbed the front of his shirt and attempted to pull him closer, making him moan and roll his hips again. Everything sped up, his hand squeezing my ass and the other hand tugging my hair all while he continued to press against the apex of my thighs. He drew my lower lip between his again, this time softly dragging his teeth over it before sucking again.

I gasped as he bit my lip. It wasn't hard, but the initial sting made me ache with need. I arched against the couch, realizing that his hands were gone. My eyes flew open when he let out a sound between a yell and an animalistic growl. He stood at the front door with his back to me, his shirt ripped to his lower back, and his large bat-like wings dragging across the ceiling.

"Angel?" I asked, sitting up on the couch.

He whirled halfway around, his wings curling around him so that all I could see were his dark eyes over one wing.

"Stop," he snapped, his tone cold.

My entire body tensed. I realized what was wrong a second later when I tasted metal.

"I'm sorry," I said.

"Don't apologize. It's not your fault," Angel turned his back on me again. "Just stay there."

I did. I watched as he fidgeted, back muscles tensing beneath his ripped shirt and relaxing several times until the wings had started to recede. He let out a sigh that quickly turned to a frustrated groan as the last scalloped edge of his wings vanished. He turned halfway around again, freezing when he lifted his left hand to his lips.

"I'm sorry," I said again, tears burning my eyes. I knew it wasn't my fault. We were having such a good time. His touch was everything I wanted, more himself than he'd been in bed so far. I wasn't sure if I was crying now because I was frustrated or if I just felt guilty that it had ended with him struggling.

"I won't do that again. I won't let it get out of hand," Angel said and lowered his hand, looking at me. His expression fell and I tried to swipe the moisture from my cheeks, pivoting on the couch to hide my face from him.

"Lily?"

He'd moved with that silent speed I was still getting used to, a gentle hand turning my face to look at him again. The concern in his eyes made my heart speed up and each breath I took caught abruptly in my throat.

"Did I hurt you?" he asked.

I shook my head, chewing on my lower lip to keep it from trembling. I could feel the cut on the inside of my lip with my tongue, most of the bleeding stopped now.

"Lily, if I ever hurt you, if I take things too far again, there's always a knife at my lower back. You take it and shove it right here," Angel said, pressing my right hand to the fleshy spot between his ribcage.

"No," I blurted.

He cupped my face with both hands and said, "It won't kill me. I'll heal quickly, but it will force me off you."

"No, you won't hurt me," I said, the words coming out more clearly through the tears than I anticipated. "You didn't hurt me, and you won't."

Angel's hands were soft on my face, but I could see the tension in his face and shoulders. I even noticed now how dark his eyes were, almost completely void of their usual chocolate color.

"You're safe with me, Mouse. I won't let anyone hurt you," he said, his voice cracking. "But I let things go too far. I'm sorry. I promise it won't happen again. I'm going to take better care of myself. I'm going to feed more often. I don't want to take any risks with you."

He brushed a tear away with the pad of his thumb only for two more to spill over. I groaned as he worked to swipe them away.

"I-I like it when you're rough," I said in a whisper. My cheeks heated beneath his fingers, and I wanted to turn away. I would have if my eyes weren't locked on his. I pressed my thighs together as he stared back at me, mouth parted. The moment was brief. He lowered his hands to mine, looking at them.

"I know." He snorted and I was glad to see he was smirking when he looked up at me again. "And I want to give you that if it's what you want. I want to give you everything you want, but when you grabbed me like that and when you bit me..."

"I didn't mean"

"No. It's not your fault, Mouse. You didn't do anything wrong," Angel said and swiped my face again. "Can I ask what I did to make you cry?"

I scoffed. Oh, this was embarrassing.

"I'm sorry," I said, catching myself as soon as the apology left my lips.

"Do you feel like I rejected you?" Angel asked gently.

I wasn't entirely sure what I felt. I forced myself to take a deep breath, fighting against the vice-like grip around my chest.

"Maybe." I shrugged. "I don't know. I'm not very good at these kinds of things. I haven't..."

He sat back, concern crossing his face as he slid his hands from his temples to the crown of his head where his hair was gathered.

"H-Have you been able to have sex with women in the past?" I asked as he recovered.

"God, Lily," he said under his breath, lowering his hands and looking back at me with enough concern that it made my heart skip. "Have you been with anyone before me?"

"Yes," I said a little too defensively. My cheeks warmed at the memory. "Well, not like, since I learned more. I've had sex before. It wasn't good sex, but it wasn't... I was inexperienced."

Mortified. I was mortified and before I could turn away, Angel brushed my hair behind my ear and his warm gaze melted me. Stupid tears. I cried about everything. Happy. Sad. Confused. I cried. No wonder he worried about me.

"Most of our first encounters leave a lot to be desired," he said, reaching across the coffee table for my water bottle. I took it from him and drank deeply before lowering it to my lap and fidgeting with the cap.

"You didn't answer my question," I said, relaxing against the pillows the best I could.

Angel nodded and let out a long sigh.

"I couldn't tell you how many women I've slept with, but none of them were you," he said. "I didn't have sex at all until I'd been a vampire for nearly a lifetime and never with a human. It's always just been sex since and never... I've never been aggressive in bed before. Everything with you just feels deeper. Being with you feels more intense to me than I've ever experienced, and I just wasn't prepared for that. I swear that I will never hurt you. Bloodlust is not something I've ever faced and I'm much too old to succumb to it."

"That's a long time. Did you have like, a type?" I asked, lifting the water to my lips and drinking. Angel smiled. He lifted a piece of my hair and twisted it around his index finger.

"Blondes," he said with a laugh and let the strand fall back into place. "I think I like blonde girls who act innocent in public but have the confidence of a mountain lion behind closed doors the best."

He leaned in to nuzzle my neck, making me giggle. He pressed a soft kiss to my cheek before standing up, using the darkness of the TV screen as a mirror to assess the damage to the back of his shirt.

"Still," he said and looked back at me. "I want to be the most in control when I'm with you. We're visiting your parents in a few days, and I want to make a good impression. I'm going to hunt tonight. That's why I don't want you anywhere near those places I told you about."

"Anne and I are going to a local bar for a concert tonight for some girl time anyway," I said and stood up from the couch. "We won't be anywhere near the tourists on Washington."

He smiled and pulled me into a hug that didn't last long enough before leaving, thankfully through the front door this time.

# CHAPTER 12

I couldn't stop replaying the moment in my head after Angel left.

*"I think I like blonde girls who act innocent in public but have the confidence of a mountain lion behind closed doors the best."*

I was a mountain lion? The words made me feel more at ease with myself than ever.

I was a mountain lion behind closed doors? That comment made me feel strong as hell.

I didn't have any footage I could use for my YouTube video, but that was for the best. I had more ideas now. My heart beat like crazy as I looked over my closet. No outfit seemed right. This song was raw, emotional, and a little sensual. I thought everything about string music was a little sexy, but this song had the right lyrics. The melody from the cello pulled on my heartstrings every time I played it. The edge of the electric guitar underneath the verses made the song more than just a beautiful love song. That's what inspired my outfit.

Anne was a couple of sizes larger than me, so I went to her closet. I found a white T-shirt and took it to the bedroom. I stripped all my clothes off and slipped it over my head. I didn't own any lingerie, but I did have a pair of seamless black underwear in a cheeky cut that made my head spin as I thought about what I'd do next.

I pushed the anxious thoughts to the back of my head, channeling the mountain lion behind closed doors, and I took my cello from my bedroom and brought it into the living room. I kept the curtains over the balcony windows open, letting the sun stream in. I started rolling the camera as I got set up, keeping my back to it. I got less than a minute of that footage, enough to use in the YouTube video to display the name of the song and my branding. Then, I started the camera again and sat down on the chaise of the couch. I played through the entire song, looking over when I got a chance to make sure my head was out of the shot.

I moved the camera to a new angle and played the song again, focusing on the long notes of the song and the way the music would swell as the electric guitar melted with the chorus from the cello. I thought about the lyrics when I hit the chorus for the final time. I thought about Angel and how he looked hovering above me on the bed. I thought about how I felt pulled into another world when he lowered between my legs for the first time. My thighs tightened on the cello, and I missed a few notes, pulling me from my thoughts. I ended the song a verse early. It was fine that's what editing was for.

I put the cello back in the bedroom and came out with my laptop. I played the finished version of the song and danced in front of the balcony. It had been so long since I danced, but I remembered so many steps I'd been taught throughout my childhood lessons. Just like the song integrated the classic sounds of the cello and the gritty edge of the electric guitar, I switched from graceful ballet turns to more modern hip-hop. I danced several times, moving from the floor to the chaise. I felt so free. I wanted to be more of whatever this was, whatever that lion was that Angel said only existed behind my bedroom door.

I forgot what I was doing for a moment and found myself sitting on the chaise, swaying side to side with the music. I raised my hands high above my head as I swayed, slowly bringing them down, through my hair, over my chest, and down my torso. I laid back on the chaise and let my hands drift farther, arching my back and throwing my head back. I was pulled from my thoughts by my own voice. The final verse echoed around the room and my heart sped up as I remembered the camera recording just a few feet away. I let my butt slip off the end of the chaise and to the floor, pulling my knees to my chest and looking toward the balcony as my voice held the final note and the cello returned to play the last measure.

Oh my God. What was I thinking?

I thought about how many subscribers I had on my YouTube channel. Our apartment was pretty inconspicuous, right? I'd been an internet enigma for a year now, but this video would narrow the pool of possible suspects. Blonde. Short. You could clearly see my underwear. Holy shit, more of my ass was out than I'd ever shown in public.

I heard the key in the front door, but I didn't have a chance to do more than shift to my knees. Anne froze in the doorway, her eyes going from me to the tripod set up in front of the coffee table. Her eyes went back to me, mouth forming a shocked O before she looked at what I was wearing.

"Is that my shirt?" she asked, finally shutting the door behind her. Thank God.

"Um, yes."

She dropped her keys and the plastic bag she was holding on the kitchen table and hurried over, plopping down on the armchair at the opposite end of the coffee table from me.

"Are you filming porn in my shirt?" she asked with a coy smile.

"Anne! Oh my..." I stood up and only felt more embarrassed when I remembered I didn't have any pants on. I hurried to my bedroom and snatched my sweatpants from the bed, practically jumping into them as she laughed wildly in the living room.

"It's not like that," I shot back at her when I went back to the living room. "My face isn't going to be in it."

She gasped and started laughing again as I stuttered through the truth, giving up as she leaned back in the chair with her face behind her hands.

"Okay, the truth," she finally said as she recovered. She sat up, face red. "What are you doing?"

"I just filmed the video for..."

Anne waited for me to finish. This song needed a different name. I'd been calling it "Dark Meets Light" since I wrote it because of the classic sounds of the cello and the rock moments of the electric guitar. It just didn't suit it, especially after my performance.

"I revamped that song I've been working on forever," I started and moved to my laptop. I typed in my password and began editing the title on the audio file. "It's called 'Lion Inside.' It's going to be the first video on my channel to feature me."

"Everything except for your face," Anne said and pointed toward my butt.

I felt my face heat. Was this a good idea?

"Yes," I said with more confidence than I felt.

Anne looked back at me, impressed. I let her take my laptop and she hit play on the song. She'd heard it before, but it had been months. I had only made small changes, but she acted like it was a whole new song.

"I think Batman is good for you," she said a few moments after the song ended. She sat my laptop on the couch next to her.

"Good how?" I asked.

She shrugged. "He brings this side of you. Do you remember Noah from grade school, and how we used to laugh at his pranks on Father Rick?"

"Everyone laughed at Father Rick," I scoffed. It was true. He was a little weird. He was nice, so nice that I felt a little bad when I thought about how we made fun of him. We were stupid kids. I laughed at dumb stuff then. Nothing was too serious, and my favorite part of school was the few times a week we went to music class.

"Yes, but then we got to middle school and you told our teacher that Noah was the one who kept putting shaving cream on her desk before class started."

"She pulled the whole Catholic guilt speech."

"So did every other adult when it came to Noah and his stupid pranks. But you had always laughed before," Anne said.

"What's your point?" I asked, taking my laptop from next to her and holding it against my chest.

"That you started to worry about everything when we got into middle school and things like grades and religion and boys suddenly mattered," she snorted. "You loosened up a bit by junior year of high school after I came out, but you were still super paranoid that someone would find out and I'd get kicked out or disowned."

"I just wanted to be a good friend and not mess things up for you."

"Lily, I tried to wear a tux to Catholic prom."

I hugged my laptop tighter. I remembered that moment probably more than any other through high school. I remember crying the Friday before the dance because I thought she was going to get in trouble at prom and end up getting expelled. It didn't happen. I went with my date in my blue dress, Anne coming over to my house to take pictures with us in her tux. I went to prom. Anne met up with her girlfriend at the time to see a movie.

"What I mean is that as we got older and adults told us to take things seriously *or else*, you focused on the or else part and ignored the reality. It's like, just because someone choked to death on a hotdog doesn't mean hotdogs are dangerous."

"That analogy was a choice," I said slowly.

Anne laughed and I couldn't help but join in.

"You know what I mean!" She threw a pillow from the couch at me, and I turned, letting it bounce off my back as I went to set my laptop on the charger at my bedroom desk.

I wore my high-waisted jeans and a long-sleeved black crop top for the concert. Anne, as always, looked more fashion-forward than I did. She wore a pair of black sequin pants and a white bralette under her jacket. Her suede loafers would garner comments on the way to the club just like they always did.

"Ready?" she asked, eyeing my outfit. I knew she was dying to do something to it, but she didn't say a word.

"Yeah. What's this place again?"

"The Nighthawk," she said as she started for the door. "This band is amazing. I've been listening to them on repeat since I heard about them a few weeks ago."

"How did you hear about them?" I asked as we got in the elevator.

Anne smirked in a way that told me the answer.

"Jazz."

"You think Angel is good for me," I started and elbowed her as I leaned against the back wall. "Jazz is good for you. You are a lot more, well, less."

Anne laughed.

"Funny way of saying she grounds me," she said as the doors slid apart.

We waved at the doorman as we went to the street. It didn't take us long to get a cab. Our driver barely acknowledged us as we climbed in the back, adjusting the loud pop music on the radio.

"Can you get us close to the Nighthawk on Minetta?" Anne asked, leaning between the front seats to talk to him. He gave her a curt nod and pulled away from the curb before she'd clicked her seat belt into place. "Tomorrow is your last day before you go home, right?"

I pulled my eyes away from the people walking the sidewalk to look at her.

"Yeah. Angel and I leave Monday."

"I don't go to see Jazz's family until next week. You don't have a problem with her being over all the time while you're gone, right?" Anne asked.

Weird. Jazz and Anne were always together anyway. If they weren't at our apartment, then they were over at Jazz's.

"No, why?" I asked cautiously.

Anne looked a little nervous, keeping her eyes on the road ahead.

"Would you have a problem with me moving in with her at the end of the summer?"

Woah. That was unexpected.

Anne dated around a lot; she didn't stay in relationships for long. She'd been in a couple longer than she'd been with Jazz, but never had she said something so serious as this.

"You're moving in together?" I asked. "It's only been like a month."

"I know. I know it's crazy, but everything is so easy with her. Besides, I may be basically estranged from my parents, but they still pay for my half of our apartment and it's just... too weird," Anne said, making a disgusted face. "I got a job on campus this week. I start Monday. I'm on my way toward a grad assistant position to get me through a master's. Really, our apartment is the last thing my parents can wield over me. Financially, anyway."

She wasn't wrong. Anne was at NYU on a lot of scholarships and her savings account. Sure, her parents still contributed money, but it was *her* account. They didn't track it. They didn't pay the bursar. They did send her half of the rent every month.

"I get it," I told her, still trying to figure out what it would mean.

"I'll still see you all the time," she said as we turned at the light. "You know I will. We've been inseparable since grade school."

"I know." I held on to the door handle as the driver took the next turn fast to make the light. "It's just strange that we're both in relationships like this."

"We?" Anne asked and shifted in her seat to look at me. "You and Angel are serious?"

I opened my mouth to answer, but no sound came out. All I could think about was our conversation earlier about the partners we'd had and what we wanted in the bedroom; how different things felt with me than any girl he'd ever been with. Just like Anne said, everything felt so natural with him. Here I was concerned about Anne and Jazz because it had only been a month and I met Angel the same night they hooked up.

"I know what you mean about things being easy," I finally answered. "I like him... I like him a lot."

Anne smiled only for a moment before we were both tossed into our seats.

"Sorry," the driver said with a wave over his shoulder. A few of the pedestrians in the crosswalk gave him dirty looks as they started to cross.

"So, when are you posting 'Lion Inside' to the Wilted Rose Strings channel?" Anne asked, adjusting her bralette.

My stomach twisted into knots. I'd spent the rest of the day editing the videos I'd taken. It went quicker than I had imagined. None of the shots featured my face. Anne told me before I started editing that no one would know what I looked like anyway, so I could assume everyone would think I was just a hired actor. That put me more at ease and made editing my half-naked videos a little easier. I watched the finished video so many times that I knew every moment, every angle of my dancing body. When Anne told me she was getting ready for the club, I quickly posted the video to YouTube and pushed it to the back of my mind.

I was glad I silenced all notifications on my phone except calls and texts.

"I did before we left," I told her. "I don't want to think about it right now."

"That's a really big deal," Anne gasped, only worsening my embarrassment.

"I know and that's why I want to forget about it."

"We'll get you a drink when we get to the Nighthawk and you'll forget about it, especially once the band starts. I can't wait to see them live," Anne said with a moan

We were only a couple of streets away when Anne told the driver to pull over. She paid and we got out, deciding it would be quicker to just walk from here than fight with the traffic. She practically jogged the last block to the entrance. Thankfully, we were early enough that we didn't have to wait in line very long to get inside.

The Nighthawk didn't look like much from the outside. The brick building was original and crumbling in a few places. But inside, everything was new. The theme was very steampunk; the wall behind the large mahogany bar was covered in mismatched gears. The entire ceiling was a network of steel piping, complete with warm light from exposed bulbs. The entire club felt warm and inviting, not the usual dark room with strobe lights that we typically visited on Saturday nights.

"Drinks?" Anne offered over the loud rock music.

I nodded and led the way toward the bar. The bartender mimed for us to show our IDs. Once she checked that we were old enough, she leaned across the bar top to ask what we wanted. Anne ordered the signature cocktail for the night, named after the band we were here to see. I got my usual rum and Coke. We moved to a mostly quiet corner of the room to enjoy the music.

The band started setting up when we got another round, and I followed Anne's lead to get a good spot near the stage. Every member of the band was dressed in dark robes. They looked a little like faceless dementors, all except the lead singer. She wore the same dark robes but kept her hood off. Her face was streaked with red paint and her dark hair was pulled back into braids. She wore the logo of the band on a chunky chain over her robes.

"You said they're local?" I asked Anne before I took a sip of my drink.

"Yes, but they've been doing a lot of touring. I don't think they actually live in NYC anymore," she said.

We stopped talking as they started to warm up, mostly because Anne was too excited. She held our spot while I went for another round of drinks. We'd nearly finished those when it was announced that the band would start soon. Anne made me chug the last of my drink, and get us fresh ones for the show.

The floor was crowded by the time the show started. Our bodies were pressed together, making me a little claustrophobic as the set opened with fog machines. Moments into the first song, I was a fan. I cheered alongside Anne to every verse. It was a mix of metal and rap, the lead singer effortlessly switching between the two. There was barely any pause between songs, just enough to fill the room with fog again once it started to dissipate. At one point, the fog was so thick that we couldn't see the band on stage anymore. The singer finished the song, her voice echoing through the room before the music stopped and all that was left was the cheering of the crowd. When the fog thinned, the band was gone and the same light rock music played through the club's sound system as when we'd arrived here hours before.

"That was amazing," I said.

"So worth it. Definitely my favorite band!" Anne screamed, garnering the annoyed looks of a couple of guys behind her.

"I think I spilled my drink on the guy behind me," I said, looking at my empty plastic cup.

Anne shrugged. "I can fix that. Next one's on me."

"Okay, but I gotta pee first. I'll meet you at the bar," I said as we inched through the crowd. I left her once the crowd thinned a little and I figured out which direction to go.

The women's room was elaborate, with a set of leather couches just inside the door that a woman was already lying across as her friend stood next to her on the phone. I went into the first stall, glad that I was wearing more sensible shoes than the girl laying on the couch.

When I looked up at the back of the black stall door, I saw red. It was just a flash, but it turned my stomach. For a second, I thought I might throw up. Then, the only thing I could think about was Angel, and I had a strong desire to check on him—not just desire, but worry. I pulled my phone from my pocket as my mind was flooded with images of Angel on an empty city street. I imagined that he'd just finished hunting for the night, walking with a much more relaxed gait. The buildings around him looked familiar and it took me a moment to remember them from our drive here. They were the industrial-looking buildings just a few streets over. The thought of Angel so close made me think about his night hunting, how he told me to stay away from Washington Square Park, Washington Street, and...

Shit.

I flushed the toilet and searched my phone for his number, pressing it to my ear before the toilet finished. Angel picked up just as the room quieted again.

"How's your night, Mouse?" he asked.

"Where are you?" I asked. I knew he could hear the nerves in my voice. I knew because he hesitated before he responded.

"I just finished for the night."

"You told me not to go to Minetta Street, didn't you?" I asked, hearing a girl groan outside the stall, probably the same one draped across the couch.

"Yes. Lily, where are you?"

I didn't answer. Why didn't I remember he said Minetta Street? I could just see him now, walking alone down the street, worried about me getting assaulted or worse. Again.

"I forgot you said that," I admitted. "I'm at Nighthawk on Minetta Street with Anne. We came for this really cool band. Everything is fine, I swear."

"Lily," he started with a sigh. He paused for a moment. "Are you okay? Why did you call me?"

"Are *you* okay?" I asked.

Again, no sound. I looked at the phone to make sure it hadn't disconnected us.

"Why are you asking if *I'm* okay?" he asked. I heard the woman outside the stall groan again and the sound of a metal trash can being dragged across the tile before a stomach-turning gag.

"Um, I don't know. I was just worried about you. I told Anne I needed to go to the bathroom, and I was just in here and suddenly worried that something might be wrong. I know it's stupid with you being, well, you."

"Don't go anywhere. I'll be there in a few minutes," Angel said.

Part of me was kicking myself for saying anything at all. It was all going so well. Anne and I were here together, so it wasn't like she'd leave without me. Still, something about Angel being all alone on what sounded through the phone like a very quiet street only had my mind swirling with terrible possibilities.

"All right, but tell me you're okay and that no one is following you or anything," I said. My heart skipped in my chest when he didn't answer right away.

"Lily, I have to go. I'll be there in a few, just stay there." He hung up.

I imagined that he actually was being followed. Sure, he was an old vampire, one with decades of experience and skill, but did that make any difference if you were ambushed? What if the police were following him? What if he got caught hunting and he ended up arrested for murder?

I had to stop. I shoved my phone in my pocket and left the bathroom, going straight for the exit. If he was just a few minutes away, then I had a good shot at finding him. Wherever he was, it was close by and quiet. I started away from the Nighthawk in the direction that seemed the least crowded, recognizing the buildings immediately. I felt a little better as I went, like I was headed in the right direction as fewer people passed on the street. Finally, after turning left, I heard a loud bang down an alley to my right.

Angel's chest was pressed to the alley wall, his wings spread wide behind him. A woman stood between them. Bat-like wings stretched high from her back as she sank her teeth into his left wing. Angel let out a primal roar and as the woman ripped her teeth away with a piece of black wing in her mouth, her eyes met mine.

# CHAPTER 13

Before I could react, the woman was standing inches away from my face, a hand around my throat. I couldn't breathe as I was lifted into the air, staring down at her. Her face was long the way Angel's was in the gardens, nostrils more like slits and fangs just past her red lips. She let go a moment later with a squeal. Angel locked onto both her wings with his feet pressed between her shoulders.

With a sickening snap, he pulled her wings from her back and tossed them behind him. The woman whirled around to face him with a hiss, launching for his throat. They were locked in a fast-moving whirl of limbs as I fought for air on the pavement.

There was a loud snap and then a ripping sound before the alley went silent.

"Don't look," Angel said, his voice so gruff that it hardly sounded like him. I had barely lifted my eyes, only recognizing his jeans feet from me when he yelled, "DON'T LOOK!"

It scared me enough that I kept my eyes on the ground. I didn't look up when I heard the sound of something heavy being dragged across the pavement. I didn't look up when I heard the sound of snapping wood. I kept my eyes on my knees when I heard a single thwack.

"Lily," he said next to me.

When I raised my gaze, I searched for the woman. I searched the alley behind him for the other vampire and instead only found a wood pallet snapped apart and a single jagged piece lying in the middle of the alley.

"Lily, are you okay?" Angel asked, taking my face between his hands and looking over me.

"I-I'm fine. She didn't even leave a scratch," I said, looking again down the alley. "Are you okay?"

He scoffed, his expression hardening.

"You're worried about *me*? The immortal vampire?"

"Yes," I gasped. "Why shouldn't I be?" I cupped the side of his face. It didn't soften his expression at all. Instead, I found myself draped over his shoulder a second later. There was a whoosh like thunder around us and the ground quickly faded farther and farther away until I realized we were too high for anyone below to see.

I wrapped my arms around his waist as he flew. I kept my eyes shut, remembering how disoriented I was the last time. I wasn't sure where we were until I felt him land. I opened my eyes, adjusting to being upside down as I recognized the Christmas lights above the TV and the purple glow of the lights from my bedroom.

Angel let out a frustrated sigh as he slid the balcony door open and said, "You need to keep this locked."

"There's no way anyone can climb up here except for you," I said, a little impressed with how confident I sounded. Maybe it was everything hitting me after our conversation earlier. Maybe it was the annoyance at being tossed over his shoulder like a rag doll. Maybe Anne was right, and he just brought out a more confident side in me.

"Yes, except for people like me," he said, his tone sharp as he walked into the living room with me still draped over his shoulder.

"Yeah, well..." I said meekly.

"Well?" he asked, shutting the door behind him and making a point to lock it, pivoting so my face was inches away when he did so.

"I don't need a lecture," I shot back and slapped the back of his jeans.

The next slap echoed through the living room before I felt the sharp sting of it. I let out a yelp, my hands flying to the back of my jeans when

Angel stood me on my feet. My eyes burned from the shock of it, the embarrassment, and the fact that my stomach was clenched tight now that I was staring up at his strong jaw and deep eyes. I rubbed the spot on my right ass cheek, wincing at the touch.

He took a step toward me. I took a step back, feeling my face warm. The air between us felt charged, and though part of me wanted to burst into tears at being told off for breaking my promise the other half wanted to invade that space between us. I wanted to stand up to him in the hopes that he would put his hands on me again, pull me tight to his chest, kiss me...

"I still don't need a lecture," I said, barely getting the words past my lips as I dared myself to take a step forward. Instead, he moved closer. He didn't touch me, which only worsened the ache in my core. He stared back at me with those dark eyes for a long moment, looking over my body before raising his gaze to my face again and chewing on his lower lip.

"Oh, I think you need more than a lecture, Mouse," he said. I let out a small squeak when he pulled me to his hips, hands cupping the back of my jeans. "And now that I'm fed, I might just even this out for you."

He gripped the cheek he hadn't slapped tight enough that it made my heart race. I sucked in a gasp and inhaled that intoxicating scent at his throat and I couldn't help myself. I pressed my lips to his collarbone and in one swift move, he lifted me so I could wrap my legs around his hips. He groaned, the sound vibrating under my lips as I kissed my way up his throat and to his lips.

"You're going to be the death of me," Angel said as he pulled back.

"Good thing you're immortal," I breathed.

He carried me to the bedroom without jostling me in the slightest. I wasn't aware we'd even made it to the bed until he lowered me to my feet again and the glow of the purple Christmas lights was around us.

"You ready for that lecture, Mouse?" Angel asked with a devious smirk that made my heart skip. "You've been begging for it since we first kissed."

This time, I mustered the courage to step closer. I grabbed the front of his shirt in one hand and looked straight up at him. My entire body was buzzing.

"More than a lecture?" I challenged, tugging on his shirt again.

He smiled, taking my face between his hands. He leaned his forehead against mine.

"Much more."

He slid his hands down my neck and to the scoop neck of my crop top. In one easy move, he ripped the entire front open. He dragged it down my arms until they were free, and it collected on the floor at my feet.

"Your turn," he said.

My grip on his shirt had gone slack. The front of the fabric brushed against the bare skin of my stomach. With my brain busy replaying the moment in my head again, Angel took control. He pulled his shirt off in a smooth motion and tossed it aside. He took my hands and pressed them to his chest, stepping closer so he could nuzzle my ear. He let out a deep groan, almost a growl, into my ear and I nearly melted right there at his feet. His hands moved to the button of my jeans. I winced as he pushed them down, feeling the spot he'd slapped before.

He dropped to his knees as he pulled my jeans down, helping me step out of them. He grabbed the back of my thighs and pulled me closer, kissing the skin just above the band of my underwear. His hands slid over the back of the same black pair I wore to film my music video, placing a light swat on the sore spot. I squealed, my hand reaching back involuntarily.

I bit down on my bottom lip before I could let the little whimper from the throb escape. Angel looked up at me and my face grew warm. The primal desire in his eyes faded and I felt my stomach knot in disappointment as concern washed over his face. He stood up, keeping his hands cupped gently on my ass.

"Did I hurt you?" he asked, lightly stroking the offending cheek.

My face must have given the answer away. Of course, it did. My face burned so much that I thought I might need a minute to get a grip.

"Yes," I said. I lowered my eyes to his bare chest, focusing on the long scar on his shoulder as I admitted the truth. "You said I wouldn't like you in your true form, but that's the part I like the most, when you let your guard down. When you let me see your reality."

He stopped stroking the sore spot to place a finger under my chin, raising my eyes to his. They were deep with a different kind of need, the kind that made me want to snuggle close to him.

"How could you ever love a monster like me?" he whispered.

"I do," I answered, taking his hand. My heart fluttered as I held it, hesitating for just a moment before I lowered it back to my ass.

Everything sped up as that primal look returned to his face and his grip tightened against me. In a matter of moments, we removed the last of our clothes. He lifted me into his arms again before lowering me onto the bed. He hovered over me for just seconds before he was between my legs, moving with more intensity than the last time.

He kissed me hard, the kind of ferocious kiss that had me breathing heavily and it wasn't until I felt his fingers slip between my thighs that I sucked in a gasp and turned away from his lips. He traced a path from my jaw to my throat with his lips, his fingers tracing a rhythmic pattern of their own that had me nearing the precipice. I pulled my legs tighter around him and he adjusted his position in response. He widened his stance, spreading me farther with his knees and leaning back just enough to hold my gaze with those dark eyes and wry smile.

I moved my hands to his shoulders as my head began to spin. I was pinned beneath him, unable to do anything but hold his shoulders as I surrendered to his touch. He groaned and I realized when I finally let go, my body relaxing against the sheets as I recovered, that I'd dug my nails into his back.

"Sorry," I said, worried I'd pressed my luck too far with the whole "letting his guard down" thing. Instead, he smirked down at me, as he shifted himself to lie down beside me. He reached across me and grabbed my bicep. I squealed in surprise when he flipped me onto my stomach. He nudged my knees apart, making space for himself. He grabbed my hips and lifted them, so my knees slid underneath. The slap pierced the air, the sting coming to the left side this time.

"Told you I'd even it out," Angel said, gathering my hair at the base of my neck and using a fistful to guide me onto all fours. "Now, hold on tight, Mouse," he said as he started to move my hands to the headboard.

My lower back ached when I woke up. I was still naked, lying on my stomach with one arm outstretched to the other side of the bed where Angel was. At least, he had been there the last I remembered. I stood up and pulled on my favorite leggings and NYU T-shirt, a comfortable outfit for the drive later that day.

Oh boy. I hadn't thought about the trip ahead since I talked on the phone with my parents. I cringed as my brain swirled about all the different scenarios that could unfold the second we got out of the car. I knew they would like Angel once they met him; I couldn't imagine a world where anyone would dislike him.

I followed the smell of bacon and found Angel standing in front of the stove. He laid the final pieces of bacon from the package onto the skillet with a loud sizzle. The plate next to him had my favorite, the scrambled eggs he made that first morning, and a side of fruit and toast. He didn't turn around as I entered, but I knew he could hear my bare feet pad across the hardwood floor.

I stepped onto the barstool and let out a gasp of surprise as I sat down. I adjusted immediately so I was mostly leaning against the countertop. Angel spun around, ready to come to my aid until he noticed me half out of my seat. A smile spread across his face, and he turned to remove the bacon from the skillet and place it on my plate.

"I think I marked you up a bit," he said as he sat the plate in front of me.

I winced as I slowly settled onto the wooden chair. At least the seats in the car would be cushioned.

"I think I got you, too," I said, remembering the way I dug my fingers into his back.

His smile widened. "Already healed."

"Ugh. Stupid vampire powers."

"Where are you sore?" he asked. When I hesitated, mouth parting in shock when I remembered the last time he used his mouth to heal my wounds, he laughed. "I mean are you sore anywhere else besides below the waist? I don't think either of us could stand it if we tested my vampire powers out that way."

Oh. My.

I couldn't speak. I shifted in my seat, ignoring the ache.

"Nowhere else," I finally said. It was a lie, one he saw straight through. Just as I scratched his back, he left a few scratches of his own on mine before we were done for the night.

"Did you pack any sleeveless dresses for our trip?" Angel asked, eyebrows raised.

Oops.

He came around the counter. He pulled the neck of my shirt back so he could peek inside.

"You'll have to slip it off for a moment," he said.

I lowered my fork to my plate and pulled my shirt off. Angel brushed my hair over my left shoulder. The nail marks weren't deep at all, more like cat scratches. He moved to my right. I looked away from him as it dawned on me what he was about to do.

He kissed the first one before tracing the spot with his tongue. He did the same with the remaining two. I didn't look until he passed me again to take his place at the sink where a stack of dirty dishes sat. I pulled my shirt back on as I watched him clean the mess.

"I'm a little surprised you own a car, and not just because we're in New York City," I said. I relaxed a little more at the first bite of the scrambled eggs. How they were so good with just what we had in our kitchen was beyond me.

"A car is the only thing I've kept consistently through the last decade. I could just fly everywhere, but I like the slow comfort of a long drive," Angel said as he finished scrubbing the last pot. "I have it in a garage not too far out of the way. We'll have to take a cab to get it, but it's on our way upstate."

I nodded, the anxiety hitting me all at once. I'd dated before, though not since high school, but Angel wasn't the first boy I introduced to my parents. He was the first one I felt so deeply about. The idea that things might not go well hung over my head like a boulder.

"Anything I should know?" Angel asked.

I forced the thoughts aside. I could see from the way he looked at me that he'd noticed my nerves.

"Um, my family has money," I started.

He scoffed and said, "I figured that part, Princess." He motioned to the apartment around us with the dishtowel.

I rolled my eyes.

"It's a combination of old money and my parents' business," I said, not even sure where to start. I chose the abbreviated version. "My mom's family owned the house and the land for a long time. They immigrated here before World War I, started a vineyard, and that's how the estate was passed down along with the family business. My mom still manages it, but she wanted something of her own. So, she works as an equine veterinarian. The vineyard mostly runs itself without my parents needing to be so hands-on. My dad runs the business side of things and together, they own a couple of racehorses."

I wasn't about to tell him which horses. That alone was more income than lots of people made. There were also Dad's other business ventures on the side that I could hardly keep track of.

Angel nodded his head slowly, wringing the dishtowel in his hands before he finally sat it down on the counter.

"Do you have any siblings?" he asked.

I shook my head. It was just me. My parents didn't find each other until they were in their thirties. They'd always been honest with me that they never wanted any children. My mom found out she was pregnant on a horse-riding retreat, despite being on birth control. She told me that as she stared down at the results in the hotel suite, she could see a whole life ahead of her. Family trips. Christmas cards. The works, not to mention that it made me the sole heir to the estate and family business. She went home prepared to fight my dad on the issue, but he had the same thoughts. We have been a family of three since.

"It's just me," I said and pushed my plate aside. I ate all the scrambled eggs, but I couldn't bring myself to eat more now that we were talking about the day ahead.

"Are you finished?" he asked. I could see from the way he eyed me that he wanted me to eat more. Always so concerned.

"I'm too nervous to eat," I told him. I was glad that he didn't press me. Instead, he pulled a Zip-loc bag from one of the kitchen drawers and dropped the toast inside.

"Snack for the road," he told me as he sealed it, pulling out another bag and dropping the fruit inside. "Is it bringing a man home that makes you nervous?"

The entire thing made me nervous. How was I supposed to explain why?

"Well, um, my parents are the kind that would go to my orchestra concerts and clap a little too loud between songs and bring an obnoxiously large bouquet of flowers that would block people's view in the crowd."

Angel laughed and moved to the front door where our luggage sat. He tucked the food into the Louis Vuitton I rarely carried. "They sound great."

"They are but sometimes I think that's the problem," I said and stood up from the stool. "I can do no wrong. I'm going to be the best cellist in New York! They're so connected that there's no way I won't do something big with my life, play in grand theaters..."

"But you don't want that."

He didn't say it the way I expected, as though he was finishing my thoughts. His tone was more defensive. It was the tone I always imagined I'd take whenever my parents mentioned the New York Phil or playing in the pit on Broadway. I used to imagine making a scene when my parents bragged about me at brunch at the country club and how good it would feel to be so rebellious and break all the club rules.

"Yeah," I said as he raised the handle on my rolling suitcase to full height. He did the same with the second suitcase, a perfect match to the first one that I'd loaned him for the trip. He owned so few outfits that he packed most of his closet in it.

"They shouldn't put all that pressure on you," Angel said and turned to face me.

I opened my mouth to defend them and couldn't find the words. Angel held out his hand for me and after a moment, I took it and moved closer. He gave my hand a gentle squeeze.

"It sounds like they don't know how much it affects you. Have you told them?"

"No," I said, looking away from him when the guilt settled heavily in my gut.

Angel turned my face back to his before he spoke.

"They clearly adore you. You should talk to them. You need to talk with them."

I knew that. I'd known that for a long time. I told myself I would for years and then, after launching my YouTube channel, I planned to each time I went home for the holidays. I even wrote a script.

"Are you nervous?" I asked. It hadn't dawned on me how he might be feeling. He had spoken so confidently on the phone when they called.

He smiled. "I'm not going anywhere, Mouse."

My entire body relaxed. I wanted to throw myself against him and snuggle against his chest. Instead, I rose onto my toes to kiss him and then we left the apartment.

# CHAPTER 14

Once the cab dropped us off to pick up Angel's car, a black SUV that contained what looked to be the other half of his wardrobe in the trunk, he made me play all my songs from my YouTube channel. Before starting each one, he made me tell him about the piece. I learned after the first one that he wanted to know it all, not just what kind of song it was.

I told him about the recording process, who I hired to record the parts I couldn't play. I told him about writing the lyrics and what I learned to do better after I'd posted the video. If he could only see some of the videos, he'd understand how my most recent video drastically differed. I hadn't looked at any of the thousands of notifications since I posted the video and I'd been avoiding all my social media accounts out of fear.

What if people knew it was me?

What if people thought the song was sappy and stupid?

What if they loved it and it went viral?

God, what if it went viral?

The last bit was enough to send my heart into uncontrollable palpitations and make my stomach turn.

Once we got through all the videos and I was able to relax again, he told me a little more about his past. He told me the last place he lived, a tiny town in Colorado. He worked as a barista for a little money and the goal of living as normally as he could. He told me that a life like his was short-lived in a small town. He told me about the forest there and how being among the trees provided him with a little relief from the mask he wore all day.

"In small towns, you're more exposed. People remember your face," he said as the tall buildings of New York City slowly grew farther apart. The trees soon replaced them as he told me about where he lived before Colorado.

Angel stayed in the cities, mostly. He said that all big cities were crawling with vampires among other things. I didn't ask him what those other things were. It was easier to fly under the radar in a big city. It was easier to find the scum of the world, as he put it. They had their own hellholes and did their best to stay unknown too. When those kinds of people go missing, most don't notice or care to investigate further.

"Anne calls you Batman," I said, noticing the horrified look on his face and adding, "she doesn't know you're a vampire."

"Why Batman?"

"Well, she called you Thor when you brought me home that first night, probably because of the hair," I said and reached over to poke his man bun. I was glad to see him relax a little. Talking about how he lived always made him sit statue straight. "You are a little like Batman though. You hunt bad guys at night."

I stopped when I saw his jaw tense.

"That's where you're wrong. I'm not the hero," he said, flexing his hands on the wheel and exhaling.

"Well, you're not the bad guy either."

"I murder people. I'm not just a murderer, I'm a serial killer, Lily," he said, lowering his voice to a pained whisper.

"I don't believe that it's that simple," I said slowly. I wasn't sure what I believed, but I knew he wasn't a ruthless killer. There was no masking how he really felt. I saw the disgust in his eyes whenever he talked about vampires. It was a physical response he couldn't hide, a secret so abundantly clear now that I knew him.

"I've been alive for centuries," he said in that sad tone. "The most I can go without feeding before I feel the pain of it is a little over a month. That's a lot of people who died just so I can..."

I closed the air-conditioning vent on my side of the car. I understood, but I knew it was stupid of me to act like I knew what life was like for him. If it was my life or someone else's, I couldn't imagine what I'd choose. I thought about his immortality, and how living with the weight of that each month would shape your view of the world. It would've been so easy for him to think less of the act over time, especially after a few hundred years. Maybe it was because of his immortality that death, no matter how much a person deserved it, felt so monumental to him.

"What would happen if you didn't feed?" I asked carefully, watching for his reaction. He stared straight ahead. I wondered for a second if he'd heard me. It was a stupid thought. Of course, he had.

"After I turned, I was so... I couldn't bring myself to do it again. I tried going without hunting. The hunger was intense. It's like going days without sleep. Your entire body starts to hurt. Every breath is like swallowing sand. Trying to drink or eat only makes it worse. It makes you sick."

"H-How long did you go?"

He let out a scoff. He chewed on his bottom lip, tugging on it hard enough that I could see the slight taper of one of his teeth. He let out a deep breath and tightened his grip on the steering wheel.

"Eight months and twelve days," he said, voice wavering.

"Oh," I breathed. I sat back in my seat, crossing and uncrossing my legs. I was surprised when he continued with the story, though in a hushed voice.

"I'd nearly lost myself on a few occasions. I wanted to die. I couldn't face our small community like that. I couldn't bear the thought of killing anyone there. I tried all that I could to end things. I felt my back break, my heart stop, all of it. Nothing worked. I was still too new to understand what needed to be done, not that I could've done it alone. I was so overtaken with hunger that I don't remember much of that time, but I remember the night I threw myself at my maker's feet and begged for death. I'd killed once to complete my transformation and I couldn't bear to do it again. He couldn't bring himself to kill me."

"What did you do?" I whispered.

"He took me to a cemetery; he had a key to a mausoleum. He told me I could complete my penance within those walls. He locked me inside and even when the hunger drove me mad, I couldn't escape. Most vampires don't get wings for another hundred years, but mine came when my humanity died, and the monster consumed me. It was too dark to know what I looked like, but I knew I was nothing but skin and bones. After a few months, my strength faded and I was unable to stand. I was alive, but nothing more than a living corpse. The pain was horrible, but there was no reprieve, no slumber or loss of consciousness to make it easier to bear. I accepted it. I wanted to be punished. I wanted to suffer for the life I took and for defying nature. I would've gladly laid on that floor for several lifetimes."

"Did he come back for you?" I asked.

Angel shook his head, a far-off look crossing his face.

"There was a spare key. I remember feeling like I'd been set on fire when the light streamed in. I was nearly blind from the time in the dark, but I heard a pulse and... God, the smell," he said with a groan, a tear sliding down his cheek and clinging to his tight jaw. "I must've moved out of the sun because it didn't hurt anymore. I felt drunk with ecstasy, more alive than ever. That's when I realized I was latched onto her and had her lifeless body pressed to the wall. I was desecrating from hunger. I drained her and was still attempting to feed when I realized what I'd done."

I sat in silence. I wanted to reach over and wipe the tear from his cheek, but I couldn't move.

"I've never lied to you, and I promise that I never will," Angel said, finally wiping away the tear. "I am a murderer."

After a while, Angel asked me to talk about my childhood. I knew it was meant as a distraction after the heaviness of his introduction to immortality. I felt guilty after hearing about the worst moment of his life, so I told him as much as he wanted to know. Even more, I found myself gladly telling him every embarrassing memory, even the one's my closest friends never knew. He laughed when I hoped he would, but never at me. Once I was out of stories, he held my hand over the cupholders as the sun began to vanish behind the tall trees and the cars grew fewer and fewer along the way.

At first, the familiarity of the road signs and billboard for my family's vineyard made me feel at ease. That quickly changed. It felt like someone had punched me in the chest. I couldn't inhale fully as the trees grew thicker. I held my breath until I couldn't anymore, forcing myself to take a few deep breaths before holding it all inside again until I saw the bridge leading toward the road home.

"Straight! Go straight!"

Angel flipped the blinker off and continued ahead, Siri telling him to take the next left. I kept my eyes on the dash, but I could feel his gaze on me as we drove. I felt myself coming down when we made the next turn onto a dirt road. The SUV bounced over the series of potholes before finding the packed dirt again and coasting slowing ahead.

I focused on what my therapist told me to do. I took deep breaths. A deep breath in as I slid my hands to my knees and then a slow breath out as I slid them up my thighs. I was breathing normally again when Angel took the next left toward the vineyard. Instead of turning right onto the paved road, he remained stopped at the stop sign.

"Lily, are you okay?" he asked, putting the SUV in the park and turning in his seat to face me.

"I'm fine."

"We aren't there yet. If this trip makes you too anxious, I'll turn around right now."

"No. It's not that," I blurted, holding my breath against the truth before it could slip past my lips.

"Will you tell me?" he asked gently, brushing my hair away from my face.

"It's nothing. I'll feel better once we get to the house."

"It's clearly *not* nothing," he said with a snort and continued to stroke my cheek with his thumb.

"It's not them. It's not my parents or this trip. I just" I stopped when I felt the vice-like grip return to my chest. I focused on the road ahead, turning away from Angel. I could see the end of the first row of grapes on the right. I hated that road. I hated this forest. The short drive over that bridge and past these trees knew was unbearable, but seeing the fence line of the vineyard was like finally making it over the finish line in a marathon.

"What is it, Mouse?" he asked.

I shook my head. I opened my mouth to again say that it was nothing, but no words came out. I shook my head again, tightening my arms around my waist and fighting against the grip threatening to cut off the air to my lungs.

"All right," he said and took my hand. Part of me wanted to pull away and hold myself tighter, but he laced his fingers in mine tight enough that I knew he wanted to be included. He had shared the darkest part of his past with me. My entire body hurt so much that I couldn't do the same for him. I wanted to scream. I wanted to crawl over the center console and curl up into his lap and let it all spill out, but I couldn't find the words. Hell, I couldn't even breathe.

I didn't realize how long we'd been sitting at the stoplight until we finally made the right turn. I was mostly relaxed by that point, exhausted but at least I wasn't hyperventilating anymore.

"Wow," Angel said once the main house came into view.

The house was mostly original. It was the same plantation-style white house that was there originally aside from the additions to the right and the left that housed Mom's library and Dad's game room respectively. The main house was three stories with the second having a grand balcony on the back side that stretched the length of the house and overlooked the pool. Behind that was the pool house. It was also three stories, the top two serving as a guest house where my Grandma Thompson would stay during the holidays so she wouldn't drive my parents insane.

"Maybe I should be a little nervous," Angel said as we pulled into the circle drive. "I'm not, but maybe I should be."

I playfully slapped his chest before we got out of the car. Angel opened the door behind the driver's seat and started pulling out our suitcases as the front doors of the house flew open and both of my parents smiled back at me.

"Lilypad!" my dad cried out, beating my mom to the porch stairs. He hurried down the steps, my mom trailing after him. He pulled me into a tight hug that chased away the last bit of anxiety I'd felt from the trip. A second later, Mom brushed him aside for her own hug. We were close in height, which meant that she could easily whisper in my ear.

"Where is he and what is his name?" she asked.

"Angel," I said before I pulled away and looked back at the car. I heard the door shut a moment later and he soon appeared as he made his way around the back of the SUV, carrying both our suitcases like they were full of feathers.

"Hello. Thank you for having me. You have a beautiful home," he said as he lowered the suitcases to the pavement and extended a hand to my mother. She hesitated before she took it and gave it a shake, making my stomach twist into knots.

"Welcome. My name is Kenneth. Most people call me Ken," my dad said as he passed me to offer his hand to Angel. The handshake was stiff and lasted just a second before my dad wrapped an arm around my mom's waist. "This is my wife, Donna."

"It's good to meet you both. I've heard good things," Angel said, looking politely at each of them in turn. "Ken, Lily told me you play a lot of golf. I'm not very good, but I do like spending a Saturday on the course."

"There's no better way to spend a Saturday," my dad said with a nod. "I'm sorry to say my daughter didn't tell me your name."

If it was possible, I would've sunk right through the concrete.

"Angel," Angel said and inclined his head toward my dad. "Angel Ramírez."

"Ramírez. Are you related to the Ramírez family in private planes?" my dad asked.

Angel didn't falter at all. He kept his smile even as he shook his head.

"All of my family is back in Spain," he answered.

"Ah," my mom said, suddenly coming back to life after staring for so long. "Are you an international student?"

"No," Angel replied and bent down to pick up our luggage again.

"Angel works for a company in New York," I jumped in before things could get any more awkward.

"I assume you speak Spanish?" my dad asked, taking one of the suitcases from Angel before he motioned toward the open front door.

"Yes," Angel said and followed him.

Mom tried pulling on my arm, but I ignored her. I knew she wanted to pull me aside to gossip. It was her usual MO. I followed Angel and Dad into the house as they talked about Spain. Dad had only been twice, but he talked like he knew all the local spots. Angel endured it all with grace, nodding his head and agreeing when he was prompted.

"We got your room all made up for you, Lily," my mom said, tapping my shoulder when we reached the main staircase.

"I'll take your things," Angel said, lifting the hand that held my suitcase.

I noticed the way my dad glanced down at the suitcase in his left hand, eyes lingering on my nametag tied around the handle.

"Yes. Sure. I'll show you the way," I said and hurried up the stairs ahead of them. Angel followed and I heard my parents whispering as soon as he reached the top. Angel could probably hear every word of their conversation, only worsening my embarrassment as I went down the hall to my childhood bedroom.

"This is a disaster," I said as I turned into my bedroom.

My room was exactly as I'd left it senior year of high school. There was a cello sitting on a stand in the corner, probably terribly out of tune after all this time. My bed was made with my purple comforter and fluffy throw blanket, the same one I had in white back in my NYC apartment. Angel sat my suitcase down and appeared with lightning speed in front of me, hands on my hips.

"It's fine," he said and kissed my forehead. "Right now, they are negotiating how long they will let us be up here alone. I think they'll settle somewhere between two and five minutes."

"Angel," I groaned and slapped his chest with both of my hands. "I'm twenty years old and they are acting like I'm a kid again."

"You are their daughter," Angel said and slid his arms around my waist. "They are just being protective."

"Fine, but I think it's rude," I said even though the thought of confronting my parents made my heart skip.

Angel looked toward the hall, a smile spreading after a moment.

"What?" I asked.

"Your dad is talking about how far away the guest room is from yours."

"Oh, God."

"Your mom wants me to sleep in the pool house."

"*Mom*," I groaned. When it came to my parents, my mom had never been the one to be conservative about these things.

Angel laughed and pulled me closer.

"Don't be mad at them," he said.

"I want them to like you and they're being judgmental," I moaned. "I'm sorry."

"Again, you are their daughter, and they have some concerns," he said slowly, laughing after a moment as he continued to listen in. "Such as your virginity."

I slapped his chest, though, in hindsight, he wasn't the one who really deserved it. My face burned so hot that I thought my cheeks would fall off.

"If they aren't nice to you..."

I stopped when he lowered his lips to my neck. He pressed a kiss just beneath my ear before whispering in my ear.

"I'll be fine," he said. "I can play whatever part you need me to."

"Then it's worth noting that they don't know I lost my virginity senior year," I said, hating how stupid it sounded. I was standing in my childhood bedroom. There was a freaking stuffed animal on the dresser.

Angel laughed into my shoulder before he pulled back and kissed my temple.

"Then you'll be their good little Catholic girl," he said and squeezed my butt. I gasped and stepped away, more from the worry of being caught than the soreness from last night. Regardless, Angel smiled like it was the funniest thing.

"Now I know what part to play," he said with a wink.

"You—"

I didn't get a chance to respond before he stepped into the hallway, gesturing for me to follow. I ignored the part of me that wanted to pull him closer and instead followed him into the hallway. I caught my mom's gaze as we started down the stairs. They were clearly in the middle of a conversation when we joined them. My mom's smile was forced.

"We're supposed to get hail tonight," my mom said when we joined them. "We had our houseman, Jordan, move some equipment to make a space for the car in the barn for you."

"How about I show you around the area before we move your car? We got about an hour before the rain moves in." My dad said and clapped Angel on the shoulder.

I could see from the strained smile on my mom's face that they'd planned this. Angel didn't act the least bit surprised as he agreed and followed my dad to the front door. He knew. I wondered just what he'd overheard while we were upstairs. My chest clenched. I felt my breath hitch in my chest when I opened my mouth to protest, to ask Angel to stay for a glass of wine, for anything that would keep him here and not push him away from me.

It didn't matter because he followed my dad out the front doors anyway.

# CHAPTER 15

My mom waited until Angel and my dad pulled to the end of the driveway to speak.

"I thought you were bringing home another student."

My stomach sank.

"Angel already finished that part of his life," I said. "He has a full-time job."

"What does he do?"

"Um..." Oh God, no. Could I really not think of anything?

My mom gasped and raised her hand to her temple. "You don't even know what he does?"

"He has a night job! It's hard to explain, one of those business things. You don't know every aspect of Dad's career," I said, thankful I was able to come up with something. She settled down a little at the mention of my dad. She lowered her hand from her head but crossed her arms over her chest a moment later with a huff.

"How old is he?" she asked.

Oh, the irony.

"He's twenty like me."

"Twenty and already finished with school and in a full-time business career?"

"Exactly," I said with a nod. It didn't quell her concerns though because she only pressed her lips into a tighter line.

"Lily, he's not at all the kind of man I thought you were interested in."

"What is that supposed to mean?" I challenged, setting my hands on my hips.

My mom scoffed and just when I thought she was going to respond, she turned and went toward the kitchen, muttering under her breath the whole way.

"What kind of man is he, Mom?" I called out as I followed. She lifted the teakettle from the stove and took it to the sink. She turned the tap on high and filled the kettle before setting it down noisily on the stove. She let out a sigh and shook her head as she turned to look at me.

"Well, he's very rugged," she said uncomfortably. "There's stubble on his face. It's clearly a style to him and not a matter of forgetting to shave this morning. I'm a little surprised he's a businessman unless he's not a businessman." She cast me a questioning look, clearly trying to get me to admit that there was no business career.

My face felt hot.

"He does something with computers for a business company," I said as my mom finished pouring milk into a mug.

"What brought him to the States?" she asked. She had slipped into that sweet tone she used at brunch. It was her backhanded way of feigning interest to learn the good gossip. I was not about to let her use it on me to make me slip up.

"Work," I said simply.

"Don't get short with me. I'm only asking," Mom chided and moved the kettle from the stove, filling her mug. She swirled the teabag around the rim before lifting it and turning to look at me. "If all his family is back in Spain, then it had to be hard to get started. Lots of immigrants struggle to make it here. Who leaves their whole family behind in another country?"

"You're so judgmental," I said as she moved from the kitchen to the dining room. The table was already set with gold runners and an olive-green tablecloth. The wine glasses sparkled, and I could see from across the room that she'd pulled out the China that had been passed through our family for several generations.

"I'm just concerned about you," my mom defended, waving her hand at me like she could shoo away all my anger like a pesky fly at a picnic. "You must admit that it's just not a normal thing to do. Is he estranged from his family? I just think it's a red flag, Lily."

"He doesn't have any family," I blurted.

"He just said himself that he had family back in Spain," Mom said and pointed toward the front of the house. "See? Red flag."

"Fine. He has family back in Spain, but they're all lying in cemeteries, okay? It's just him."

I had expected her shock, but something in me snapped when she shrugged and lifted her tea to her lips.

"I like him, Mom. A lot. I'm not going to let you do your little snobby act with him around."

"Lily!"

"Everything all right in here?" Dad interjected, his voice deeper than normal. He would always drop his tone, keeping his words kind and polite, before he launched into an argument. Even now, with Angel stopping in the doorway behind him, his eyes went from my mom to me in silent reprimand.

I caught Angel's eye across the room. He was studying me, probably for signs of panic. I was at the tipping point. I wanted to storm out of the room like a pouty teenager and hide my embarrassment behind my bedroom door. I also wanted to do what Angel had been encouraging me to do.

"Maybe no one has noticed, but I am twenty years old. I'm an adult. I live on my own. I can take care of myself. I was the first sophomore to be invited to perform at the Spring Garden Recital in a very long time. I am doing fine all by myself," I said, sucking in a deep breath when I finished to keep the nerves from bubbling over.

"We know that and we're both very proud of you, Lilypad," Dad said.

"Ken," my mom said seriously, raising her eyebrows expectantly.

Dad nodded and he looked back at me with an expression that said he'd rather be anywhere else.

"I don't know what was said and I don't think it matters. Lily, we are aware that you are an adult, but you are and will always be our daughter. When you are in this house, you will be respectful to your mother and me."

"I wasn't disrespectful"

Dad held up a finger. We'd gone almost to the top of the chain. Deep voice. Finger pointing. I knew the people-pleaser in me would crumble if we got to the yelling phase.

"Whatever happened, your mother didn't appreciate it. Again, I don't know what was said and I don't care. You may be an adult, but this is our house. Speaking of that matter," he said and then turned to look at Angel, pointing his warning finger at him. "Adults or not, you two aren't married. I noticed, Angel, that you took your and Lily's suitcases into her bedroom. You can have your pick of any of the guest rooms upstairs, but you will not be staying together."

"Of course." Angel nodded. "My apologies. I didn't want to be rude by leaving my things by the door."

"Are you Catholic, Angel?" Mom asked.

If I was standing just a foot closer, I would've stomped on her toes.

"Let's save some conversation for dinner, Donna," my dad said and lifted her mug to his lips and grimaced the way he always did whenever he tried her tea. "Terrible."

"Lily," Angel said from the doorway. "Your father showed me around the front of the house. I'd love to see the grounds."

"Um, okay. Let's take a walk," I said. I avoided my parents' gazes as I passed them for the hall, feeling like I could breathe again as I hurried through the living room for the door to the patio.

Angel appeared at my side as I blazed a trail past the pool and toward the yard behind the pool house. He took my hand and stopped, keeping me from walking any farther. I felt a little better when I saw that he was smiling.

"What did you hear?" I asked.

He let go of my hand, his smile fading a fraction.

"I'm proud of you for speaking up for how you feel," he said, pushing his sleeves to his elbows. "You don't have to stand up for me though."

I groaned.

"My mom always does that."

"I've been through worse than the concerns of my girlfriend's parents," he said with a laugh, pulling me closer by my hands.

It was the first time he'd used that word. *Girlfriend*. It made my heart skip.

"They won't chase me away. As long as you'll have me, I'm right here, Mouse," he said, pivoting so we switched places. He lifted my hands above my head, and I took a step back to keep balanced, my back meeting the wall of the pool house. Angel smiled, keeping just far enough away so as not to touch me.

"I want you," I told him, feeling the heat rush to my face and my stomach tightened when I thought about the position I was in. "I want you to stay."

He adjusted his grip, lacing his fingers in mine. He leaned in closer, just barely brushing the tip of my nose with his and letting out a soft groan.

"What else do you want?" he asked, inching closer.

I arched my back, wanting to feel him against my breasts. He lifted our hands higher so I couldn't brush against him. He moved my right hand so he could hold them both in place above my head with one of his. My heart sped up when he cupped the side of my face. I wondered if he could hear it pounding with desire. I shifted in my spot as he brushed the pad of his thumb across my lower lip. His hand slid down the side of my neck and stopped, spread wide just below the hollow of my throat.

"I know what you want, Mouse. I can see it in your eyes, the way you squirm..." He said and took another step closer. "You may want me to take control, and I get lost in you each time I watch you come undone at my touch, but I'm not the one in charge at all. I want you to be happy. I want to kiss away your tears. I want to hold you when life is too much. I want to be the one who makes you blush like this."

He lifted his hand to my cheeks again with a laugh.

"I blush at everything," I said. I was constantly embarrassed about doing or saying something wrong.

"Not like this," Angel said and lowered my trapped hands. He kissed the back of one before releasing me.

"I want you to take me," I said, reaching for his pants. He brushed my hands away and cupped my face.

"I told your father we would respect his boundaries," Angel teased, kissing my nose. "But that doesn't mean that when I lie down in that guest bedroom, I won't be thinking about you down the hall and how earlier I had you pinned behind the pool house."

My stomach clenched tight as he let go, the frustrating ache remaining as I forced my feet forward for the tour of the grounds.

I showed Angel everything up to the vineyard. My chest tightened as we approached the soft dirt rows and suddenly all I could see were the stars of the sky that night, the cheers from the barn, and the edge of the shadow I couldn't reach no matter how much I willed my feet forward.

"We should go back," I said and turned around, hoping he would follow.

"What's in that barn over there?" Angel asked, falling into step beside me and pointing toward the large building.

"I'll show you later. Dinner's probably ready."

Dinner had never been ready on time my entire life. Angel looked like he wanted to ask me more, but he slipped his hand in mine, and we walked back to the main house.

My parents were talking in the dining room when we entered the back door. I could just barely hear them, but I knew from their tone and the way Angel's grip tightened for just a second that they were talking about us.

"Is dinner ready?" I called out. I let go of Angel's hand and hurried around the corner. I sent my parents stern looks as I entered, relaxing when I saw the table. It was full of my favorites. There was smoked ham and turkey, root vegetables, a Caesar salad, and two more vegetable dishes that my mom always made for special occasions.

"This looks delicious, Mrs. Thompson," Angel said when he joined me. He placed a gentle hand on my lower back, sending me an encouraging smile before he passed me for a seat next to my dad.

Mom shifted the seat next to her and despite taking a step toward the seat next to Angel, I made the unfortunate mistake of making eye contact with her. There was no escaping now. I went around the long table and plopped down on the wooden chair next to her. I gasped at the sudden throb of my butt, my eyes lifting to Angel's when I suddenly remembered the reason for it.

"All right there, Lilypad?" Dad asked as brought a bottle of wine to the table.

I had to look away from Angel's amused expression.

"I went to the gym," I said, hearing Angel snort across the table.

"The gym?" Dad asked as he took his seat.

My mom scoffed. "You barely got your gym credit in high school."

"Yeah, well, I've started working out," I said and adjusted in my seat.

"She's stronger than she looks," Angel said and winked when both of my parents shifted their gaze to me. "She has a lot of stamina."

Oh, God.

"You never answered my question, Angel," my mom said, clasping her hands under her chin. "Are you Catholic?"

"Yes," he answered without missing a beat. "My family's Catholic. More than just that, they're devout."

I was a little stunned. I knew Angel wasn't religious, but of course, he had been at some point. Most people were that long ago. I thought about the time he lived through for most of his childhood, the Spanish Inquisition. Of course, he would have had a very fundamentalist upbringing.

"Lily attended Catholic private schools her entire childhood. One of the best high schools in the state is a Catholic all-girls school," Mom said. She was clearly challenging his alleged piety.

"My schooling was very similar," Angel said and clasped his hands like my mother.

"You went to a Catholic school?" my mom asked.

"Had my knuckles rapped and everything," Angel replied.

Mom let out a moan of disapproval.

"It was a common occurrence. My school was quite strict by most standards," Angel corrected and shot me a knowing look. "I wasn't a troubled kid like it sounds. I'd say I'm pretty eager to please."

I tried kicking him, but I was too far away.

"Let's pray before the ham goes cold," Dad said and rubbed his hands together, launching into the prayer before I could even raise my hands. Angel smiled at me over his hands while both of my parents kept their heads bowed. I tried my best to shoot him a warning look but was sure the burn in my cheeks undermined the gesture.

I made sure to make the sign of the cross when my dad finished, pretending that everything was normal and failing. My mom looked at me suspiciously, not looking away until my dad pulled the cork free from the wine with a loud pop.

"I picked a Sauvignon Blanc," he said and poured it into Angel's glass. We were quiet as he filled out glasses.

"Thank you for having me," Angel said. "I hope I made a good impression."

He looked so sincere that it only made my stomach twist with anger when I noticed the way my mom's lips twitched when she smiled. I took my glass and lifted it to my lips, taking a long sip that didn't go unnoticed.

"Let the grapes breathe, Lilypad," Dad said with a laugh, helping himself to the ham. I accepted the basket of rolls from my mom and passed it across to Angel.

"Tell us about your family, Angel. How is it that you came all the way to the States?" Mom asked as she sliced a piece of the ham in half before putting it on her plate next to the large helping of salad.

Unlike Angel, she wasn't too far away to kick. Angel didn't hesitate despite the glare my mom sent me.

"My parents died when I was young. My grandfather raised me. I moved abroad when he died," he said, raising a forkful of ham to his lips.

"I'm sorry to hear it," Dad said, looking far more contrite than my mom.

"It was a long time ago. I don't have many memories of them," Angel said with a shrug.

If they only knew how long it had been...

"Did you grow your hair out after you left home?" Mom asked.

Angel gave an awkward laugh.

"Mom," I hissed.

"Well, it's only natural for a boy to get a rebellious streak when he leaves home, especially when he crosses a whole ocean."

"Long hair doesn't make you a rebel," I pointed out, my heart racing. Why couldn't we just leave it? Why did she have to pick on him?

"Your mom just means that you don't see a man with long hair very often," my dad said, sending me that scolding look again. Strike one.

"You're more shocked at my boyfriend having long hair than when you found out Anne's gay," I pointed out, avoiding my dad's gaze.

The look my mom gave me was like a punch through the chest. My throat felt thick, and I fought against the tears burning my eyes. This wasn't the time. I wouldn't crumble in a panic right now, not when I'd talked myself up all day to tell them the truth. If I didn't stand up for Angel now, I'd never be able to tell them about my music.

"What's shocking is that you didn't tell us about him before. You two keep making eyes at each other. Don't think I haven't noticed the way you *look* at him," she said with her brows raised. "You're obviously close, but you didn't tell us. I want to know why."

"There's not a reason. I just..." I stopped to reign in the sob that threatened the burst from my lips.

"Why wouldn't you tell us this? You've never lied to us before, Lily."

"It's not a lie."

"Oh, for heaven's sake, Lily!" Mom was shouting now, her disingenuous nice-girl act long gone. "This isn't you, so it has to be something about him."

I'd pushed back from the table and was on my feet before I realized it. My entire body felt charged with electricity, but not from fear. This was new. This was anger.

"Of course, it has to be him. He doesn't fit your country club image. He won't look right mixed in with the other white boys," I said, walking toward the hall before the tears could fall. I heard my mom muttering and the shuffling of feet coming after me. I'd nearly reached the main staircase when she spoke up.

"Are you calling me racist?" my mom yelled.

I whirled around to face her. She'd gotten up so fast that her napkin was still clinging to the hem of her sweater from the static.

"I'm saying that you sound like those snobby bitches you complain about at the club."

My mom raised a hand to slap me, but it stayed suspended beside her. Angel gripped her forearm, staring into her stunned face with those dark eyes and tight jaw. He didn't let go of her until he'd moved between us.

"I know you don't like me. You didn't like me when I got out of the car and I'm sure you really don't like me now," he said.

My mom gasped and looked back at my dad, a silent request for him to step in.

"I think we've all jumped to conclusions. Donna and I just wanted to have a nice dinner and get to know you," he said in his deep baritone before looking at me, pointing a finger at my chest. "And you, young lady, adult or not, will not speak to your mother like that. She's right about you hiding this from us. You've never done that before and I think I'm starting to see why now."

My dad's eyes roved over Angel, sizing him up before he looked at me again. I hated that I couldn't stop the tears. Angel didn't look away from my parents when he reached back for me. His hand found mine and gave it a comforting squeeze, gently guiding me farther behind him as he lowered his voice.

"Your daughter has been unable to stay still the whole time we've been here."

"Because of the way you look at her. You can't keep your eyes off her!" my dad yelled, standing taller.

"Are you aware that Lily has panic attacks?"

Dad snorted. "Yes, we're aware. She told us years ago. We talk about it all the time. We helped get her the best therapist we could find."

"She fidgets when she's anxious. She bites her lip. She tenses her muscles. She won't look at you. When she's had all she can handle, she pulls her legs and arms close. Her voice is even different, higher. That all may seem small. It's the most subtle of reactions and she tries so hard to hide it. Still, she's done each of those since we have been here. I'm not ogling your daughter, Mr. Thompson, I'm paying attention to her," Angel said. He gave my hand another soft squeeze, so unlike the roughness in his voice. Neither of my parents spoke. My mom crossed her arms like the Karen that she was, finally caught in her game. My dad looked a little hurt.

"You don't have to like me, but I will be around if she wants me, as long as she wants me. I am hers. I will make sure that she has whatever she wants and whatever she needs, no matter what you have to say about it. She is so much more. You just have to *see* it." After a second, Angel relaxed and took a step back so he was standing next to me. He reached up and brushed a tear clinging to my face. "Do you want to stay?"

"Yes," I answered.

"Do you want me to stay?"

How was that even in question?

"Yes," I blurted, holding his hand tighter.

"Then we'll stay," Angel told me and then looked back at my parents. "We will stay if you will have us."

"Of course," Dad said, voice soft. "Of course, we want you, both of you." He looked from me to Angel, his cheeks flushed.

"I want Angel to stay with me," I said, the words coming out slowly. I chewed hard on my lower lip, prepared for the argument. My parents exchanged nervous looks.

My mom cleared her throat and just as segmented as I'd stated my terms, she gave her approval.

"The pool house is set up."

Dad let out a sigh and wrapped an arm around my mom's shoulders, giving her a small shake as he nodded to us. "It's yours."

"I, er, need a moment to get my things," I said, my eyes lingering on Angel for just a moment before I hurried upstairs.

# CHAPTER 16

My heart raced as I gathered what little I'd unpacked in my bedroom. I kept my hands moving, knowing that the moment I stopped the anxiety would come crashing down. I still had to walk through the house. I had to get to the pool house. I couldn't let it all spill over yet.

I lifted the handle of my suitcase, and before I could drag it toward the door a familiar set of hands were on mine.

"Go," Angel said gently, eyes full of so much understanding that I didn't hesitate. I couldn't stay another moment without it all becoming too much.

I nearly tripped going downstairs. Thankfully, I didn't run into anyone on my way through the living room and out to the back porch. The fresh air filled my lungs like it was my first breath. The emotions hit like a riptide.

I stumbled toward the pool house as the sobs burst forth, each choked off by the tightness in my chest. I hated it when it got this bad. I hated the pathetic sounds, the weakness in my legs, and the dizziness that lingered as I struggled to fight for air. I could feel my insides screaming, but I was frozen in place. I couldn't remember opening the pool house door and sitting down, but there I was. I was sitting on the stairs to the upstairs apartment, curled over my knees as I tried to make it all stop.

The door opened. Angel didn't look shocked to see me. He didn't seem surprised at all. He set our suitcases aside, shut the door behind him, and was at my side in seconds. He lifted me easily into his arms, starting up the stairs without jostling me.

"I'm sorry," I breathed into his chest.

"It's not your fault," he said and kissed my forehead as we made it to the top of the stairs. With one hand, he opened the door that led into the combination living room and kitchen. The living room and kitchen were slightly larger than my New York apartment, both decorated in navy blue with nautical accents to match the pool vibes. Angel kicked the door shut behind us and took me to the bedroom to the right.

The room was slightly larger than mine in New York, with a king-sized bed. Angel didn't sit me down on the mattress. Instead, he climbed into the bed with me cradled at his chest. He leaned against the headboard. I lay against his chest, trying to control the sobs. He stroked my hair, the motion slow and almost rhythmic. It reminded me of the way I'd draw my bow across the strings of my cello for a whole note.

"I'm proud of you," he said after a long time.

"I didn't want my mom treating you like that. You're so much better."

I heard him inhale as he stifled a laugh. "You didn't have to do that for me."

"It's the same thing you did for me," I pointed out, raising my head from his chest. He kept his hand entwined at the ends of my hair, gently twisting my locks through his fingers. He looked almost sad, drawing in his bottom lip before releasing it and looking down at his fingers in my hair.

"You don't deserve to be treated like that. You know that, right?" I asked.

He looked up at me with those sad eyes and said, "Why is it so easy for you to demand people have respect for others while not demanding the same for yourself?" He moved his hand from my hair to my face, but I stopped him. I could feel the resistance in his hand for just a moment before he relaxed and allowed me to lace my fingers with his.

"You're deflecting," I said.

"And you're altruistic to a fault."

"Don't," I said, my voice cracking. "You deserve to be treated with kindness, especially by people who don't know the first thing about you."

"I don't usually let people know the first thing about me, Lily." His voice was sharp. He sucked in a sudden gasp, looking away from me and closing his eyes. He exhaled slowly before looking back at me again. He cupped the side of my face and said, "I know you don't see it, but I am what I am."

"Stop saying that you're a monster," I groaned, patting his chest.

"You don't see it because it takes all of my humanity to fight it," he said in a low tone. He sucked in a deep breath, relaxing beneath my fingers. "I am a vampire. I only exist because others don't. My instinct is to hunt, and you are the perfect prey. You're my type. You're inexperienced"

"You wouldn't. You won't," I said, more confidently than I'd felt all day.

Angel shook his head before letting his forehead rest against mine.

"I won't. I take every precaution with you. I won't," he said and took my hand. He moved it to his hip and for a moment I thought he wanted me to slip beneath the fabric. Instead, he pressed my palm to something hard. I remembered what he'd told me before about being armed, realizing my hand was wrapped around the hilt of a knife.

"I can't," I squeaked.

"Please," he breathed, gripping my hand tighter around the knife. "It wouldn't kill me."

"It would hurt you."

"I've had worse," he said, letting go of my hand.

I immediately let go of the knife. I cupped his face between my hands.

"You are worth it, Angel Ramírez," I said.

"Then you are worth the world, Lily Thompson." He brushed the hair from my face. "For fuck's sake, start acting like it."

His lips were on mine, moving ferociously. He shifted so I was suddenly beneath him on the bed. Instead of remaining suspended above me, I felt his weight against me. I tugged on the fabric of his shirt, pulling it toward his head inch by inch until he finally sat up and stripped it off himself.

He was pressed against me seconds later, the warmth of his skin greeting my fingers as I spread them across his back. He slid a hand along throat and to the back of my head, letting out a groan as his fingers pulled on my hair. My hands were on his shoulders before I realized it, my back arched and my fingers gripping whatever I could of him.

"Leave your mark on me, Mouse," he said before his grip on my hair was gone. "I'm yours."

His lips moved down my neck, over the hollow of my throat, and down to my breasts. Before the moan could leave my lips, a gasp stole the air from my lungs. He pulled me to the foot of the bed by my thighs, standing tall at the end with a devious smirk on his face as he knelt.

"Angel," I said nervously. I'd been underneath him before; I was no stranger to sex. But I'd never been in this intimate position. He lowered himself, a smile disappearing between my thighs.

---

I saw flashes of red. Someone had painted over the brick with purpose, the cursive looping together almost to the point of understanding.

"Lily," he said with concern.

I rolled over and Angel pulled me closer. I shrugged away from him until I'd risen to a sitting position. Angel was standing inches away a moment later, concern in his expression.

"I'm fine," I said despite barely remembering the dream. There was a brick wall; that was something I dreamt about often. Then, there was writing on the wall. It took a few weeks to realize it was writing and not just brush strokes.

Angel pulled me from my dream as he held my face between his.

"What were you dreaming?" he asked.

"Brick walls with red paint," I said, the words spilling from my lips. "Weird."

"Weird," he agreed with a smile.

The pool house kitchen wasn't stocked at all. I was still full to the brim with embarrassment, but Angel led the way with enough confidence for both of us as we walked back to the house and into that stupid dining room for brunch.

It was clear that my parents had been there. My mom's mug sat near the end of the table with not just one, but two tea bags resting on her saucer. My dad's place at the end was complete with a half-full mug of coffee. Angel insisted on me waiting at the table while he filled mugs of coffee for us. I was surprised that the first person to return was my dad.

"Morning, Lilypad," he said as he sat down at his usual seat at the head of the table. He fidgeted with a spoon in his mug for a moment, despite there being nothing for him to stir into the coffee.

Already, the air felt too tense to bear. I couldn't sit with it any longer.

"I'm sorry for being—"

"It was our fault," Dad interrupted with a wave. "We're more progressive than most in all areas except for you."

I was stunned to silence. My dad stirred his coffee a few times before he looked up at me, sincerity clear in his expression.

"I understand," I said slowly. I was surprised when he smiled back at me, looking away when my mom returned with a platter of fruit.

"Come here," my mom said, pulling on my hand.

I didn't resist, letting her lead me toward the kitchen. I stood in the entryway, my eyes landing on Angel's back before I realized he was standing at the stove in my childhood home. He scooted the eggs to one side of the skillet before lifting the entire thing from the heat and scraping the contents onto a single plate. It was just enough for a single serving, filling a third of the plate between the mixed fruit and the pota-toes. He sent me a smile as he turned from the stove with the plate in hand, not at all surprised to see me.

"When's the last time you played golf?" My dad had joined us in the kitchen and scooted behind us. He took a sip from his mug and watched as Angel sat a fork onto the plate.

"Over a year," Angel said, turning from the stove with the plate in hand. He sat down the plate on the large island, scooting a barstool out for me. I watched the slight upward twitch of my dad's lip when Angel stepped aside so I could take a seat.

"We're going for a final round before the tournament today if you'd like to join," my dad offered. My mom and Angel looked at each other for a moment. Angel must have snuck out of the pool house while I was asleep. They were all in on this little plan. My mom shifted her gaze to me and smiled.

"I'd love it if you came to get your nails done with me, maybe get a haircut. We could get mimosas afterward," my mom told me and pulled a banana from the bunch on the counter. "The boys could golf, and we could have some girl time, just the two of us."

"Um, sure. That sounds like fun," I said, my stomach squirming at the way all three of them smiled. Angel was the only one who looked sincere. After all this time, I was sure he could lie to God himself and get away with it.

"It's a date," Dad said and clapped his hands together. "I'll load the clubs. You're not a lefty, are you? I don't have a left-handed set."

"Ken, let him eat first," Mom chided, slapping his bicep with the back of her hand before peeling her banana.

"That's all right. I'm an early riser. I ate a few hours ago," Angel said and straightened up. "And no, I'm not left-handed."

"Perfect," Dad said, clapping Angel on the shoulder and leading the way. I rolled a grape from one side of my plate to the other as I heard my dad's voice growing farther away. The front door shut and the house went quiet and I still struggled to ask the question. I cleared my throat, finally looking up at my mom who hadn't moved from her spot across the island from me.

"So, erm, did Angel..." I looked down at my plate again.

"He did," my mom said in an exhale. She wrapped up the last third of her banana in the peel and sat it on the counter. "He came in here when your dad and I were just starting breakfast. We were both still in our bathrobes and pajamas; he was dressed for the day and insisted that we needed to have a discussion. Honestly, he was very forward. He was outright rude a few times. Your dad threatened to punch him, but he—"

"Mom," I started, feeling that thickness that rises in my throat before the tears spill over.

"Angel's right. The thing is, you've always been so easy to parent. You never rebelled. You did well in school. You never gave us any trouble and the few times you did, you're so sensitive that you were harder on yourself than we would've been. I guess we never thought that maybe your anxiety was behind it and not that you just chose to go along with it all," she said, sad wrinkles forming around her eyes.

I thought about Wilted Rose Strings. Now was the time to mention it since she was talking about what I wanted for myself. Now was the time to get brave. But I couldn't.

"Since when are you and Dad so religious?" I asked instead.

Mom laughed and shook her head. We were never "by the book" when it came to Catholicism. I had attended Catholic schools because they were the best in the county. My parents never instilled the conservative values of the church in me, not really anyway. They were there, but only when we needed to impress their snooty friends or maintain our reputation for school.

"You've never brought a boy home before."

"I had a boyfriend in high school," I pointed out.

She scoffed. "That boyfriend wasn't really, well, a *boyfriend* the way Angel is. You're an adult. You make your own decisions. You live on your own. You go out to parties. I think your dad and I just heard the word boyfriend and got a little nervous and then when you two showed up... I know you're a grown woman, but somehow, I didn't expect you to walk in with a whole man."

The idea was still a little strange to me, too. It wasn't that it was my first adult relationship. It was how serious it felt and easy it was. When I caught myself thinking about him, it surprised me how much I wanted to be with him and only him. I couldn't fathom my future without him. Even now, the thought filled my stomach with butterflies.

"He's better than any man I've met," I said, spearing an egg. The meal had cooled down, but it was just as good as always. Whatever he did, these eggs were my comfort food.

"I think you might be right," she admitted, letting the annoyance show for just a moment before she moved on to the next subject. "Are you being safe?"

I stuck the prongs of the fork into my chin instead of my mouth, looking straight up at her unbothered expression. I sat my fork down. It wasn't like we hadn't had this conversation before. My parents had both talked with me about sex and all things anatomy, despite how uncomfortable it made me. They were frank and I was sure I was the most educated person at school, next to maybe Anne who knew more than she probably should've at seventeen.

"We, er, yes. It's good. I mean, we're good. I mean, I'm taking birth control and we're doing all the stuff. The safe stuff," I said, sliding my plate aside. After that, not even Angel's five-star cooking could save me.

"Good," she said. "It's never worth the risk, no matter how serious you are."

I understood that part of her comment was from experience. I knew that I was never unwanted, but I was very much unplanned. I was so used to being around adults that kids were never something I thought much about when it came to my own future, and I wasn't eager to start. Between birth control and Angel being frozen in time, it was safe to say that we were protected.

"I bet we can slip in for nails if we go now," Mom said and went to the far side of the kitchen for her purse. "We can get you a haircut, too."

"I like my long hair," I said. I didn't dye it either, so there was really nothing to fuss over.

"We'll just have Josie trim it up a little. Lily, the ends look so dry. If we don't do something about it, it might go all crispy and break off when you style it for the social at the club."

The social. I knew it was part of the reason we came here early rather than waiting for a few more weeks to visit. The social seemed so far away and I knew it was because I kept pushing it to the back of my mind.

"Okay, but I want to keep as much of the length as I can," I said and left the kitchen to get my purse.

# CHAPTER 17

It took a little longer to get our nails done and my hair trimmed, long enough that mid-morning mimosas turned into a late lunch over chardonnay at the country club. We sat on the patio where a few other groups of retired couples and older women gossiped. Just down the stone stairs was a rose garden with a small stage and several areas carved out of the path for a bar and catering to set up. Today, it was empty aside from the roses.

"How is Anne?" Mom asked after we'd caught up on all the basics. I told her about classes, getting to perform at the spring recital, and how Anne got a girlfriend about the same time I met Angel.

"She's good, still in engineering. Don't ask me what kind, I have no idea," I said and took a sip from my glass. "She's visiting Jazz's family. They're going to move in together in the fall."

I felt my stomach twist when I said the words, already anticipating the next question.

"Have you asked Angel to move in with you?" she asked.

I relaxed a little. That wasn't exactly what I thought she'd say. I didn't think she'd be the one to suggest it anyway. No. The answer was no, I hadn't asked him yet because I was so surprised that Anne would move in with Jazz after just a month. Despite my shock at the next step in their relationship, it felt right for Angel and me to do the same. He was already mostly living with me. I felt a lot better about him living in my spacious apartment with security than where he was now.

"Probably soon," I said, the words sounding like a question as they left my lips.

Mom paused with her glass just below her lips, worry lines forming on her brow before she took a drink and smiled up at me again.

"I'm glad Anne is doing well. I'm a little surprised that she's with someone. I assumed she'd never get serious about anyone, not that there's anything wrong with that."

I knew she meant it. She told my dad no the first time he asked her to marry him.

"What's new around here?" I asked, glancing at the group of women gathered around a table behind us. I recognized all of them, though a few of their group were missing. Everyone at the club referred to them simply as "The Ladies Club." There were so few members left in their generation that no one bothered to call them out on their bigotry. All of them were over seventy and met every day in the late afternoon for wine and whispers. Joan in particular, the only woman in the group who still dyed her hair a light blonde, was still making her way around the club to try setting up her rich son who had moved in to take care of her. No one bothered to point out that he was dating one of the tennis pros.

"Oh, nothing," Mom said before letting out a gasp loud enough that Joan and her minions looked up at us. "Olivia Saxon showed back up at the club a few weeks ago. She's been hanging around in the afternoons, but doesn't talk with anyone. You know how she is. She's probably just back to listen in on everyone's conversations and wait for a good moment to spread everyone's business."

My stomach plummeted at the mention of her. Olivia Saxon was a red-haired woman approaching thirty who no one liked. That didn't bother her though, because she didn't seem to like anyone anyway. She sulked around the country club when she came and somehow, always knew everyone's juiciest secrets. She'd outed several affairs and uncovered a group of swingers that resulted in mayhem one summer. No one knew how she did it, but she'd insert herself out of nowhere to state what she knew as if it bored her. After the swingers' scandal, she disappeared for a while.

"More chardonnay?" a waiter asked when he brought a piece of apple pie with two forks.

"Yes. Thank you," I said and finished the last of my glass before letting him take it. I was staring off at the garden, and suddenly it wasn't Olivia making my stomach turn. My mom exchanged her wine glass for the pie and immediately scooped a piece of caramelized apple into her mouth.

"Lily?" my mom asked, pulling my attention away from the garden. "I asked what you're planning to wear for the social Saturday."

"Oh," I said and lifted the extra fork from the plate. "I'm wearing my blue dress."

"The one with the lace or the chiffon?"

"The chiffon," I said. I loved that dress. It was short and with one long sleeve of light chiffon. I packed a pair of nude heels to wear with it.

"The tournament starts at five. They should be done in time to clean up and join us for dinner at seven," Mom said.

I took a bite of the pie and looked over the garden again. You could see part of the golf course in the distance, a cart zipping by to the next hole.

"It will be a fun night," Mom said.

"Yeah," I agreed and took another bite despite my knotted stomach.

***

The tension between Angel, my parents, and me melted over the next few days. My dad warmed to him quickly. Angel played the part of a businessman well, which kept my dad entertained. I got a lot of quality time with my mom, which was nice. She took me to brunch with her friends where she thankfully didn't make her usual backhanded comments. Maybe Angel really had opened their eyes.

"Have you ever been on a horse, Angel?" Dad asked as we sat around the living room after dinner. My mom rested on the arm of his chair, slinking her hand over his shoulder.

"You should take him riding. You could watch the sunset," she said, sending me a look that told me I better say yes. It wasn't necessary. I wasn't about to say no to some quiet time. Plus, there was the sunset.

"I'd love to see more of the area," Angel said, standing up from his chair before I could answer.

"There might even be two horses already saddled in the barn for you," Dad said with a wink, laughing when Angel reached out to clap him on the shoulder.

"Minnie and Stud?" I asked even though I already knew the answer.

"She won't let anyone else ride her," Dad said.

I took Angel's hand and led him back to the pool. I took a shortcut out the side gate and instead of heading left to the big barn, I started for the stables. We had lots of horses, but we kept the family favorites in the old barn away from the others. Ours were old and gentle, not good for more than short rides or petting zoos. Dad wasn't kidding about Minnie.

She chuffed and moved to the front of her stall when she saw me. Her coat was salt and pepper and her mane was a gray color. She was the first horse to really be mine and only mine. As she got older, she preferred me more and more until the day she refused to move when my mom tried riding her.

"This is Minnie," I said and reached for her muzzle. She pressed her nose into my hand, the door rattling against the lock. "She's an old lady, but she's *my* old lady."

"Clearly," Angel said after Minnie completely ignored him when he approached. I took his hand and pressed it to Minnie's muzzle. She froze under his touch. The annoyance was obvious in her eyes.

I turned away from the stall, ignoring Minnie's chuffs when I clicked my tongue at the black horse standing in the middle of his stall. Stud was an old, retired racehorse that my dad liked too much to leave in the main stable. He was never a high-ranking horse, but he did well during his time. Just like my dad said, a saddle was already strapped to his back.

"This is Stud," I told Angel as I opened the door. Stud moved just out of his stall, waiting as I gathered a bridle for him. He took the bit obediently and waited for his rider without a sound. "He's gentle and takes commands well. He's my dad's favorite, but he's the horse we always have friends ride."

"Hello, Stud," Angel said and took the reins from my hands. He stroked the dark horse's muzzle while I opened Minnie's stall and placed a bridle on her. She was excited, happily trotting to the end of the stable with me in tow.

"Minnie, wait," I said, grabbing onto the bridle around her muzzle. I looked back at Angel as he brushed his fingers along Stud's neck. I opened my mouth to tell him where to put his foot, but my instructions weren't necessary. Angel slipped his foot into the stirrup and swung his leg over Stud's back, easily seating himself in the saddle with the reigns in his right hand. He made a clicking sound with his mouth, urging Stud forward until he was standing next to me at the entrance.

Angel patted Stud's neck and smiled down at me.

"I know my way around a horse," he said.

I guess when you grew up during a time when a horse was the only way to get anywhere, you would.

"All right then," I said and mounted Minnie. "I guess, I'll skip the lesson."

I led the way from the stable, but it became obvious where we were headed in minutes. Angel urged Stud ahead so he could ride next to me as we started down the dirt path. The trees were thick through here, the road carved between them just wide enough for work trucks to make it through. There were two different sections of the vineyard. This side was the only one I ever went to. The road led all the way to the end of our property where an open field was past the vineyard. It was raised on a hill that provided the perfect view of the sunset and the stars.

"You told me that there are other things out there," I said. I wasn't sure how to explain it without using his signature word: monsters.

"Yes," he said as he adjusted his hold on the reigns, so they were in his right hand. "Vampires aren't the only supernatural creatures out there. I can't be sure what else there is. It's a big world."

"What have you run into?"

He thought for a moment before glancing my way. He sent me a small smile that eased my nerves.

"Witches. I run into witches the most. I met a werewolf in a bar in Texas. I've run into a few guardians, but I don't usually stick around for a conversation," he said.

"What's a guardian?" I asked, imagining some kind of robed figure with glowing hands.

He studied me for a moment. It was the curious look he always sent me right before revealing something. I'd seen it a few times before and was starting to piece together what it meant. At first, I thought he was worried about me. Now, it seemed more like he was trying to judge how much I knew. Why he thought I might know anything about guardians was weird, but still, he looked over me with that gaze before speaking.

"They are kind of a higher being. The only reason demons exist in this world is because there are gates that open up from the Shadowlands. It's a kind of afterlife for supernatural beings. The guardians try closing those gates. They are human, but they are frozen in time and gifted powers to help them work as a unit to close their gate," he explained.

"Okay..." I said. I hadn't expected the answer to be so complicated. "How do you become a guardian?"

He shook his head.

"It's not like being a werewolf or a vampire. You can't become one. Most people don't know that they are a guardian until they change. They call it waking. It's when you survive something that should've killed you and you wake up with powers and immortality instead. Once they meet their match, kind of like a guardian soulmate, they become mortal again and start aging. It makes them stronger, but they are easier to kill since they are mortal."

Weird.

"How do you know all of this?"

He hesitated for a moment, switched the reigns to his other hand.

"I met one before I moved to New York City."

He said it as though it was different. Whoever he met, it was a different encounter than just any guardian.

"Oh," I said, unable to hide the sting from my voice.

Angel snorted and sent me a smile.

"It wasn't *that*," he said. "Not my type."

"Not blonde?"

"Not blonde and," he said with a laugh, "she found her match. He didn't know it yet, but she did, and she watched him love another. At least, that's what it seemed like to me. I don't know if they were a match, but there's a kind of buzz that surrounds all things supernatural that I think only we can sense. It's how I know when we're around someone that's more than they seem. It's how I keep you safe."

My heart warmed at the last part. He smirked when he caught my eye, probably because I was blushing. I was sure of it. I was easily embarrassed, but this man had an entirely different effect on me.

"Have you ever loved someone?" I asked, staring down at Minnie's mane.

"No," he said without a pause. "Not until you."

I exhaled and looked at him. Centuries and he'd never been in love? He kept his eyes on the road ahead.

"What's in that barn behind the pool house? It's the only place we haven't explored," he said. The trees opened up to the vineyard. We continued down the dirt road next to the fence, a truck whizzing past on the main road to the right.

"Um, it's not that great," I said, trying to think of something to say about the barn while also trying my best to push the images away. "It's mostly an entertaining space for events, wine tastings, sometimes weddings... It's empty."

"Your mom said they host a wine tasting for their country club friends a week after the summer social every year. I guess I'll just have to wait until then to see it."

Angel smiled at me, but it didn't fully touch his eyes and I knew that it was because he could sense my discomfort. He knew. How much he knew, I wasn't sure.

I urged Minnie into a trot and Angel kept up pace as we made our way past the vineyard and to the open field. The horses climbed to the top of the hill. The sky ahead was a mix of orange and purple as the sun slowly vanished along the horizon. Angel must've dismounted with vampire speed because he stood next to Minnie with both hands extended toward me. I swung my leg over and he placed his hands on my waist, slowly lowering me to the grass.

We walked to the other side of the hill and sat on the slope. He slipped his hand into mine as the sun disappeared and the sky darkened.

"I love you," I said, the words a meek whisper. I kept my eyes on our fingers, letting out a deep breath. I felt his hand under my chin, raising my eyes to his. Why did he have to be so handsome? It made me more nervous, but it shouldn't. He'd just told me he loved me. It didn't matter. My heart beat fast in my chest at the small voice at the back of my head urging him to say it again, confirming what I already knew.

"Your heart sounds like a jackhammer," he said with a small laugh, moving his hand from my chin to my cheek. "Take a deep breath, Mouse."

I did, an awkward laugh slipping past my lips at how stupid it all was.

"That's a good girl," he said with a devious smile. "If I kiss you, is that heart of yours going to be able to handle it?"

I slapped his chest with the hand not entwined in his. With speed only he possessed, he'd moved his hand from my cheek to catch the offending hand. He held it tight in his grip, a smirk pulling on his lips. He leaned toward me, so slowly that my entire body tensed in anticipation. I wanted to launch myself at him, but I was rooted to the spot as I felt his breath tickle the skin below my ear. He let out a deep hum at my earlobe that vibrated through his lips when he pressed them lightly against my neck.

"I love this," he said. His hands gripped the back of my leggings, lifting me by my butt so I was straddling him. He slid his hands over my hips and to my stomach, sliding upward until both tightened over my breasts. "And this," he said with a squeeze before his hands continued their climb. One moved to my cheek while the other wound tightly in the hair at the base of my neck, holding me in place so I had no choice but to stare into his gentle expression.

"I love this the most," he said and ran the pad of his thumb across my cheek. "And no monster, human, or even your deepest fears will hurt you as long as I'm yours."

I took his face between my hands, intending to pull his lips to mine and press my body to his. Instead, he held me in place with the hand in my hair and rested his forehead against mine. After a moment, I noticed my heart rate slowing. My muscles relaxed and I lowered my hands to his chest, rubbing the fabric of his shirt between my fingers.

"I love you," I said again, this time without any worry.

"I love you," he said, finally bringing his lips to mine.

# CHAPTER 18

"I think Angel's the only one here under the age of forty," Mom said.

I turned from the list of participants in the golf tournament. We rode to the club in two cars, Angel and Dad in Angel's SUV and Mom and I in the BMW. We only came this early to show support for Angel and Dad. We planned on going to the club for breakfast and then moving to the pool over lunch before the young couples brought their kids for the afternoon.

"I don't recognize most of the names," I said, relieved. It was the only reason I came to look at the list posted on the bulletin board.

"You know Dr. Yadav," Mom said.

She was right. I knew a handful of the names listed on the page, not personally, but I knew they were club members. Dad tried hard to impress a few of them for the sake of business.

"I don't know that I'm really hungry yet," I said. My stomach ached. I knew I should eat. Angel would've told me to at least nibble on something and that the feeling would go away after a few sips of water. Angel was also not here right now.

"Do you feel okay?" Mom asked, turning from the bulletin board.

"I think maybe I'm still waking up."

"Well, we'll just order you a muffin and some fruit. Maybe you'll feel better after a little coffee. That always helps me get the day started." Mom led the way down the hall to the restaurant.

The room was busier than usual this early with people preparing for the day of tournament events. We got a small table near the windows that overlooked the garden. The waitress asked for our orders, writing down my complicated coffee order before scooting away and giving me a glimpse of Olivia Saxon.

She was beautiful but in a severe way, the kind of woman who never smiled and wore her hair pulled back a smidge too tight. She had red hair that was piled into a thick bun at the top of her head. She was dressed in her signature black: black T-shirt and dark-wash jeans with red lipstick. She stared down at her mug looking bored, turning the porcelain in a slow circle on the saucer. As if on cue, her eyes flicked to mine, and my heart stopped dead in my chest before I could rip my gaze away.

"So, what classes are you taking in the fall? You have enrolled already, right?" Mom asked.

"Um, yeah. I enrolled," I said, struggling to switch my attention to my course schedule. "I don't remember exactly. I know I have a Music in Film class in the fall."

"Lily," Mom started, hesitating a moment with that look of concern on her face. "Are you happy there?"

"Yeah. I love NYU," I blurted.

She shook her head, waving away my comment before she said, "Okay, but I feel like you're not enjoying your music classes like you did before."

Like I did before. Like I did before I started Wilted Rose Strings.

I sucked in a deep breath and prepared myself, blurting out the words before I could second-guess them.

"I have this YouTube channel that's doing really well, like I'm making a good amount of money, and I want to keep writing and performing music like this even though it's not traditional or normal at all."

My mom stared back at me in surprise, sitting so still that I worried about how long she was taking to process it all. Before either of us could say a word, our waitress returned with our drinks. She took our food order and slipped away. As she did, I noticed that Olivia Saxon wasn't sitting at her table anymore.

"Wow," Mom said under her breath. "That's like something you hear on the news."

"I know it's not..." I bit down on my bottom lip and turned my mug between my hands, staring at the little leaf design over the surface.

"It sounds revolutionary," Mom said with a gasp. "You're an entrepreneur just like your dad and me. We always thought you'd have the family's first normal career."

I couldn't believe it. I didn't expect her to be so supportive. I thought that maybe she'd accept it, but I hadn't considered she would be excited about it.

"It's not like I'm famous or anything," I said.

"What's this channel called?" she asked, her phone already in her hand.

I directed her to YouTube, and she started with my first-ever video, working her way through my entire backlist while we ate. I tried nibbling at the muffin she'd ordered for me, but I couldn't get my stomach to settle enough to take any real bites. While she was busy staring at the screen, I pulled off hunks of the muffin and tossed them into the potted plant just behind my chair.

"This is really good," Mom said after finishing a video. An ad played for a few seconds before I recognized the opening sounds of my newest song, the first video I ever appeared in. Mom looked down at the screen as my stomach churned, making it to the chorus before she glanced up at me and then down at her phone again.

"Everything good?" the waitress asked, a pitcher of water in her hand.

"Great. Can we get the check?" I asked, sending her away before my mom could ask for a refill of coffee and keep me staring at all this food with my stomach in knots.

"You look..." she started, pausing a moment before she looked up at me. "You really are all grown up and onto new things. I'm proud of you."

"Mom," I started, my chest tightening.

"I mean that. You're making a name for yourself. You found a wonderful man."

"You said he's rude to you," I reminded her, getting a laugh in response.

"Rude doesn't mean wrong," she said with an eye roll. "I admire his honesty."

The waitress returned with the check and my mom handed over her credit card before she could take more than two steps away from our table.

"The pool?" Mom asked as she finished signing the receipt.

I rose from the table.

"The pool."

We met up with Angel and Dad back at the house. I changed into the blue chiffon dress and climbed into Angel's SUV, him sitting beside me in a button-up shirt and slacks. I noticed that he took the long way to the main road, avoiding the road over the bridge. He never said a word about the route and there was no way I was bringing it up.

"So, how was the tournament?" I asked as we pulled into the parking lot of the country club.

He put the car in park, and switched off the engine.

"It was fun," he said and opened his door. "Your dad's not as good as he thinks he is though."

I laughed, opening my own door and stepping onto the pavement. By the time I'd shut the door and smoothed my dress down, Angel was at my side. He'd trimmed his facial hair, leaving it just scruffy enough that I could feel the prick of it under my fingers. I rose onto my tiptoes to adjust the bun at the crown of his head. He bent a little to help my reach.

"How was your day?" he asked when we straightened up and followed the rest of the partygoers into the building.

"Good. We had breakfast here after we wished you both luck," I said.

"What's their breakfast like? What did you have?" he asked.

I paused, thinking about telling him I'd eaten waffles or something. I'd already hesitated too long.

"Just a muffin, a little fruit," I said, noticing the way his smile dimmed a little with concern. "We got lunch to go. The restaurant makes a great chicken sandwich."

I wasn't about to tell him that I let that sandwich go cold on a plate in the pool house.

"What should I expect from this party?" he asked, turning his attention to the open door on the left. The ballroom opened onto the back patio where the garden was. It was filled with older couples when we entered, all sitting around tables and a few dancing to the jazz band playing music in the corner.

"Lots of people making business deals, gossiping, and pretending to like each other mostly," I said as we moved through the room.

We didn't stay inside long. We moved to the patio where the crowd got significantly younger. On the other side of the patio was an outdoor grill where two men in country club polo shirts were flipping burgers and tending to shish kebabs. Angel slipped his hand in mine, giving it a squeeze with a smile as he started toward the grill. We were already in the line before I could muster the courage to speak.

"I'm not hungry yet."

"You should eat before the line gets long," Angel said. "Besides, the food is always better at the start of a party than at the end."

"I just don't want to eat right now. That sandwich was huge. Let's get a drink first."

"You shouldn't drink on an empty stomach," he said, eyebrows raised.

"I only ate a few hours ago," I said, reluctantly letting Angel guide me forward as the line moved.

"And you didn't eat that much today and it's getting crowded and it's hot out," he said, stepping behind me and playing with the end of my ponytail.

"How could you know that?" I challenged as the man in front of me waited on a hamburger with double the meat.

"I'm older than you," Angel said in my ear with a laugh.

I reached behind and poked his stomach.

"Doesn't mean you know everything."

"No, but I know a lot and I know you," he said, pulling my back to his chest with one arm. The other tugged gently on the end of my ponytail before moving down my spine. "And you let your anxiety get the best of you and that makes things worse."

I was prepared with a rebuttal, ready to point out how long it had been since my last panic attack, but his fingertips spread apart along my lower back until he was cupping the right side of my butt in one hand between us.

"Maybe you forgot about that lecture though," he whispered in my ear.

I spun around, mouth open to say I wasn't sure what in response. He smiled knowingly before looking past me.

"What would you like, ma'am?" the waiter asked.

I whirled around, cheeks flaming.

"Shish kebab," I said, the words sounding almost slurred.

"Just one?" the man asked as he pulled one from the grill by its skewer.

"Two, please," Angel spoke up, sliding his hand into mine. "And a water."

The man added another skewer to the plate and handed it to me before filling a cup with water from the glass dispenser. Angel carried the water as we walked toward the stairs of the patio.

"Not fair," I told him, making a point to raise one of the skewers to my lips. I pulled a piece of pineapple from the end while Angel laughed.

"Anyone I should meet?" he asked as we made our way down the stairs to the garden.

It was shaded from the sun thanks to the main building. In just another hour, the sky would grow dark enough for the string lights to illuminate the flowers. A few more and the fireworks show would start.

"Not really," I answered, spotting my parents near the closest outdoor bar. My dad was laughing with a large man holding a beer while my mom took a glass of white wine, probably chardonnay, from the bartender.

"How's the food?" Angel asked, pulling my attention away from the crowd.

"I'm not hungry. My stomach is all mixed up, actually. Maybe I'm sick."

"You're not sick," Angel said gently, letting go of my hand so he could take the plate in exchange for the plastic water cup. "You're just nervous."

"I mean it, Angel. I feel like I might throw up," I said as my stomach twisted.

"If you do, we'll go home," he said simply, nodding to the cup.

I raised it to my lips and took a cautious sip, taking another as I noticed my parents walking our way. I relaxed a little just as my mom reached past me, hand extended.

"I'm so glad to see you back at the club," she said.

"Pleasure," a woman's velvety voice said. I turned around to face Olivia Saxon. Her eyes moved from my mom to me, staring so intently that it felt like they saw all the way through me.

"You know our daughter, Lily. This is her boyfriend, Angel Ramírez," Mom said.

Olivia looked at Angel next, frozen for a moment before I saw the brief hint of a smile on her tight lips. She extended her hand to him, and Angel gave it a curt shake.

"Angel," he said. Olivia seemed almost amused by his reaction.

"The Saxons live on our street. I'm sure you know the one. It's the only one you'll pass to get to ours," Mom said, patting Angel's shoulder.

"Their family has been around longer than ours. They've owned their home over a hundred years, isn't that right?" Dad asked Olivia.

She didn't take her eyes off Angel when she agreed.

"Longer," she said with a laugh and glanced my way for a moment. "What is it you do, Angel? You seem like you work hard."

"It's not that interesting," Angel said with a scoff.

"Oh, I'd disagree. You can learn a lot about a person from their handshake," Olivia said with a smirk. "Yours says you take your work seriously and work well into the night."

Angel let out a single laugh.

"Thank you," he said with a nod. "If we're judging people based on their handshake then I'd say you are a very observant person. It takes a very detail-oriented person to notice the small things."

She smiled, a sweet expression that faded fast when she extended her hand to me. Angel pulled me to his side as she took my hand before I was prepared. If Angel had the firm handshake of a businessman, I was sure mine was like cold spaghetti. Olivia withdrew her hand almost as soon as she'd taken mine. She looked me over for a moment, her expression curious before a smile tugged at one side of her face.

"Is that Paul?" my dad called out, pulling my attention away from the strange woman and sending ice through my veins.

"Do you know any other gingers in this county?" Paul asked, holding both arms open beside him in greeting.

"Only your sister," Dad said and pointed to Olivia.

Paul shook his hand before leaning in to place a kiss on my mom's cheek. I froze when his eyes landed on me. If I turned away... If I refused... If I stomped on his toe or screamed in his face my parents would be furious. The entire club would shun us. Olivia would do whatever it was she did best and air out all our family secrets, not that I knew of any.

Paul Saxon leaned in and pressed his lips to my temple, his hand taking mine for just a second long enough so that he could slide his thumb across the back of my hand the way he always did.

"Lovely," he said, my chest tightening and head spinning at the nickname.

*"Easy now, Lovely," he said.*

I was tossed so far into the past that I wasn't rescued by reality until I heard Angel speak.

"I'm Angel," he said and extended his hand. "Lily's boyfriend."

Paul smiled even wider at the news, accepting Angel's hand and giving it a few shakes.

"You don't say?" he said, looking from Angel to my parents. "He's a proper man, isn't he? I always knew Lily would find someone like him," he said to my mom who laughed at the comment. "I always said that the good girls always attract the men who are a little rough around the edges. I think a real lady softens them up, takes the bite out of them." Paul said and eyed Angel before adding, "Maybe not all the bite though, am I right, man?"

Paul clapped Angel on the shoulder, sliding himself between Angel and me before I could do anything about it. Olivia smiled in a way that was unnatural for her, the corners of her red lips forced upward.

"Don't worry," she said, keeping her voice low. She took a step closer, making sure my parents were too busy being amazed by Paul's charisma to notice us. "He'll tell you when he figures it out."

"Figures what out?" I said, the words not as forceful as I wanted.

"What he's looking for. It's the entire reason he's here," she said with a shrug. When I didn't respond, her smile only grew. It was like she knew some big secret and it only worsened the sick feeling in my stomach. "He's not from around here. He adores you, that's obvious. But he hasn't been honest with you. Just think about it. Has he told you why he left home? Men only keep that out of the standard get-to-know-me spiel when they're hiding something. He's either on the run from his past or he's looking for something and it's not you. He just found you along the way. I'd think about what he was doing when you found him."

What was she talking about? If Angel hadn't found me when he did, I wouldn't be here. I didn't know everything about him, but how could I when he'd lived several hundred years?

"Do you feel okay?" Olivia asked, stepping back from me with a worried look on her face. My vision blurred and I thought I might pass out. No. I couldn't pass out here. My stomach rolled and I nearly vomited right there, but I managed to control the feeling as I hurried up the steps. I tried not to look too obvious as I crossed the patio. I burst into a run when I saw that the ballroom had cleared out, and even the band had packed up. My heels clicked along the hardwood as I ran to the end of the hall for the bathroom, glad for a brief second that it was empty before I doubled over the trash can just inside the door.

Part of me was glad I hadn't eaten much, but the dry heaving made my head hurt as I struggled to get a breath in. Just as I finished and pushed myself up by the edge of the trash can, I felt a pair of arms on mine. I sucked in a deep breath, but the sick feeling stole my scream as I fought against the arms. It felt like I'd been zapped by lightning, my entire body flailing weakly against the arms that tightened around me.

"It's me, Mouse. It's me. It's me," Angel said, pinning me against his chest with a grip so tight that it was both comforting and panic inducing. My mind went to the moment I'd buried as soon as it was over, the way he'd wrapped his arms around me from behind the same way Angel had now, the way he whispered in my ear, the feel of him against my leggings...

"Let go. Please, let go," I sobbed, stumbling forward when he did.

My hands found the edge of the marble counter and I whirled around to face him, my body instantly relaxing as I looked back at him. It was like the floor crumbled beneath me. My knees shook as the adrenaline drained from my veins. It was exhausting. It was embarrassing. I felt sick. I could barely get a full breath in before it was forced out in a panic. I wanted to be alone, to curl up on the floor, and to sink through the tile. I wanted him more.

I'd barely raised my hand.

We were out the side door of the country club and halfway across the parking lot before I realized it, never lifting my head from where I'd buried it against Angel's chest.

# CHAPTER 19

I felt a little better after we left the country club, but not by much. Instead of everything feeling sped up, it was like I was stuck in slow motion. I stared at my hands in my lap as we drove, the car silent. It wasn't until we'd been driving for a long time that I looked up and realized we weren't anywhere near my small hometown.

I looked at Angel and noticed how tight his hands were on the steering wheel. I'd never seen him so mad. It made my heart skip in my chest. Was he mad at me? Had something happened when I was talking with Olivia?

"Angel," I said softly.

The seat belt tightened over my shoulder and across my lap as he slowed the car back to the speed limit. He turned onto the dirt road and stopped, putting the car in park and sitting back in his seat.

"They live down the road from your parents, down that road you didn't want to drive on," Angel said. His voice was low. It was primal, the intimidating side of him that took over whenever he allowed the vampire within out. It sent chills over my skin.

I couldn't speak. I didn't want to admit it, even if he already pieced it together. I couldn't.

"What did he do?" Angel asked. He looked at me. His eyes were dark the way they always were when he was like this, but they weren't angry. He wasn't *just* mad, anyway. He looked back at me like he'd just been given the worst news.

I struggled to speak. My every attempt was nearly swallowed by my sobs. I hugged my arms around my chest like they could keep me from falling apart. Everything sped up when I was pressed back into my seat by the lurch of the SUV. Angel turned the car around and we were back on the pavement, speeding back the way we came.

He didn't speak as we drove, and I didn't bother filling the silence. I focused instead of taking deep breaths and slowing my heart rate. My efforts were smashed apart when I saw the bridge ahead. Angel barely slowed as he turned down the road. I sucked in a gasp as we drove over the cement bridge, and I could see the Saxon estate just ahead on the right.

"Angel," I said between breaths. "Angel, please."

My body iced over, and I was frozen in place as he turned onto the long driveway. The concrete was cracked in several places as we drove. A white Range Rover was parked in the circle drive and Olivia got out of the driver's seat as we pulled to a stop halfway down the driveway.

Angel got out of the car, moving to the hood as I scrambled to free myself from the seat belt. When I rounded the front of the SUV, he surged forward with supernatural speed, and I found myself standing behind him. When I peered around him, Paul Saxon was slowly walking around the back of the white car with a welcoming smile on his face.

"I didn't think I'd see you again so soon," he said with a laugh. "I thought I'd have time to change into something more comfortable at least."

"You're lucky you're still standing," Angel growled.

"Am I?" Paul asked. His eyes flicked to me. I wanted to move farther behind Angel, but I was frozen in place. I stared back at him as his smile spread. He licked his lips and inclined his head to me. "Always a pleasure, Lovely."

There was a bang and Angel had Paul pinned to the back bumper of the Range Rover, the body of the car crinkled around them like it was a mere sheet of tin foil. Paul let out a groan as Angel sank his teeth into his shoulders, gripping both of his biceps. Angel ripped away from Paul with a sickening pop. I nearly keeled over as blood sprayed over the white of the car before seeping down the front of Paul's dress shirt. Angel took a step back. He turned to Olivia and spat a mouthful of scarlet at her feet before wiping the blood from his chin with the sleeve of his shirt.

"Angel!"

I was halfway to him before I remembered why we were there. My brain filled with images of fall leaves. I could hear him breathing in my ear, hands pulling me against him... He smiled back at me in the same way now, despite the bloody mess at his shoulder.

"Go back to the car," Angel said gently, standing in front of me again. He cupped my cheek, guiding my eyes to his. "Get in the car."

"Someone is feeling possessive," Paul said with a laugh. The pain from the bite was evident in his face as he took another step forward, so he was standing next to his sister. He held out his right hand, palm flat, and a block of ice grew from his palm.

"Paul," Olivia said with an exasperated sigh.

"Don't let him tell you what to do, Lovely," Paul said and took another step forward, running his left index finger over the ice like a sculptor with a chisel. "Especially not a vampire. They'll do anything for blood. The rat bastards of the sky."

"You touch a hair on her head and I'll separate you from yours, guardian piece of shit," Angel snarled, placing himself in front of me again. I could hear Paul laugh. I glanced around Angel's shoulder to see that he'd carved the block of ice with his powers so that it was in the shape of a human. It was a woman. It was me.

"You're just mad that I had her first," Paul said, raising his eyes from the block to Angel as he slid his index finger over the curve of my icy hip.

I felt the bile rise at the back of my throat, my vision blurring before I realized Angel was gone. Paul only laughed harder now and when I got my bearings, Angel had Olivia's back against his chest. He pulled her head back by her red hair, his knife stretched across her neck.

"You've really done it now, mate," Paul said and tossed the sculpture aside where it shattered.

Olivia raised her hand to Angel's forearm, a smile pulling across her lips as her eyes met mine.

"He carried you across the apartment. You were in a black dress, barely awake, drugged. He tucked you into bed. How sweet," she told me, ignoring the way Angel pulled her head back farther so she was looking straight at the sky. "Does she know that she talks in her sleep? Have you told her what she said that night? Of course not. It scared you just as much as it intrigued you. She saw you before she ever met you. You knew that night what she was. Why not tell her?"

"W-What? Tell me what?" I asked, looking at Angel.

The anger in his face melted when his eyes met mine.

"Lily," he said, begging me to stop.

"Afraid she won't fuck you again if she knows?" Olivia asked, her and Paul both laughing.

Angel pressed the knife to her throat, a line of red leaking across her skin.

"Lies," he said.

"Fine. I lie." Olivia smirked. "But you do worry she won't love you the same if she finds out your secrets, why you were in New York, the real reason you watch her sleep and hope she sees the thing you've been looking for since the beginning."

I gasped when Angel drew the knife across Olivia's neck in a single, quick move. He let her fall to the ground at his feet, raising his eyes to mine. I could see the apology in his expression, eyes full of hurt that I struggled to find sympathy for. I wanted to. In some ways I did. My chest ached. I wanted to forget everything Olivia had said so badly.

"Lily," Angel said and took a step toward me.

I took a step back, right into the side of the SUV. Paul laughed, the sound echoing around the driveway until it was cut off by Angel pinning him against the Range Rover again.

"Stay. Away," Angel said, gripping the front of his shirt.

"Gut me. I know you want to. What's one more body?" Paul asked with a smile on his face. "Show her the monster you really are."

Angel let go of him and was at my side a second later, guiding me toward the passenger door as Paul laughed in the background. Angel lifted me into the seat and buckled me in. No sooner had my door shut than his opened and he was behind the wheel with the car in reverse moments later.

"I'm sorry. I'm so sorry, Mouse," Angel said, throwing the car in drive and speeding toward the vineyard.

I didn't say a word as he turned into the driveway, parking the car behind the house. I hopped down from the SUV and started across the back lawn for the pool house, glad that he didn't do anything vampiric to keep up. He never once called out to me. He didn't even try keeping pace with me as I strode to the front door of the two-story house. I threw the door open and took the stairs two at a time until I was standing in the living room with my arms wrapped around my middle.

Moments later, the door to the apartment shut quietly. Angel didn't move from the door. He didn't attempt to comfort me as I cried. I didn't want him to. I did, but I didn't. I wanted things to go back in time before the social at the country club. I wanted to snuggle against his chest under the moonlight while the horses grazed. I wanted to wake up to his smiling face and the smell of those scrambled eggs.

Several minutes had passed before I mustered the courage to speak.

"You killed her," I said past a sob. Angel took a step forward, eyes full of concern, but stopped when I raised my hand.

"They're both guardians. They're immortal. She'll be awake and healed soon enough."

"How did she do that?" I asked and pointed to the door. "How did she know all of that?"

Angel looked away from me. I noticed the anger cross his face for a moment.

"Guardians all have powers. Olivia's is accessing the thoughts of others, by touch apparently," he said with a groan. A second later, he cast a nervous look at me, and Olivia's words replaced all the images of the attack. I didn't want to go there. When she told me to think about what Angel was doing when he found me, I assumed she was trying to mess with me. Angel just admitted that her power allowed her into the thoughts of others. She probably was playing games with me, but she was likely right about him.

"What did I say that first night, after you saved me at the club?"

Angel nodded as though he'd expected the question. He let out a deep breath and looked back at me with sad eyes.

"Angel Ramírez," he said just loud enough for me to hear. "You said my name."

More silence.

The beginning of our relationship had been such a whirlwind that it took me a while to remember all the details of that night. The next day was the first time he'd made those amazing eggs. He'd convinced me to eat them and then told me off for being rich and not being more concerned that he was still in my apartment. I didn't remember everything about the fight, but I know he never introduced himself and I never asked for his name. I knew that because it was part of the reason he was so mad. I was naïve. I chose bad friends to go out with, friends that left me alone with a stranger overnight. I let him stay the next morning.

I didn't even know his name.

"H-How… I said that in my sleep?"

Angel nodded.

"You talk about the future when you sleep. It doesn't all make sense, but what does has all been true."

I didn't know what to do. I wasn't even sure what to ask anymore.

"I don't understand," I said.

"That night, I tucked you into bed. I was deciding if I should leave or stay when you said my name. I thought you were awake, but you weren't. I was stunned. I stayed because I thought you might explain in the morning, but when you didn't understand what happened, who I really was… I wasn't sure what to think."

"Why didn't you tell me?"

The tears were salty on my lips. Angel tugged at the bun at the crown of his head.

"I still wasn't sure how much you knew in the beginning. When you had that first panic attack, I couldn't add anything else. I didn't want to ask unless I was sure you knew. It became pretty clear after you were attacked in the garden that you had no idea that anything supernatural existed at all, much less your own abilities. It took another few nights of watching you sleep to understand it and be sure myself. By that point, I wasn't there to figure it out. I swear. I asked you out because I couldn't stay away from you. I didn't want to. I had no other intentions."

"But she said that you are looking for something and that you hoped I might know what that is. How could I… I don't get it. What did you figure out about me? Are you saying I'm some supernatural thing too? How?"

I fought to inhale fully. I could tell from the twitch in his hands that Angel wanted to pull me closer.

"You're a seer, Lily," he said.

"What does that mean?" I breathed.

"Have you ever had déjà vu?" Angel asked, taking a small step forward. This time, I didn't move.

I nodded. "Of course."

Angel scoffed, a small smile pulling at the corners of his mouth.

"That's not normal not like that anyway. Coincidence is one thing, but people don't have that experience often enough for it to seem like a casual thing. I think that you have visions when you sleep because you let your guard down and you can relax."

"So, I'm like, seeing the future?" I asked, a headache forming at my temples. I tried thinking about a time when I had a recurring dream that came true. It was hard to tell the difference between what was a dream and what was just a memory. I couldn't remember a specific dream, but I remembered feelings. I remember feeling paranoid that something bad was going to happen and I'd started avoiding the trees on the other side of the vineyard. I remember feeling on edge being in the barn at my parent's annual party. It was the reason I left to begin with. It was how I ended up running through the trees...

"Lily," Angel said softly.

I looked back at him. He was just feet away now, his body tense as though ready to spring to action. His expression was soft, the same look on his face from the café at the student union. It was the entire reason I sat across from him. It was the reason I stumbled into his chest now.

I let out a howling sound against his shirt that made my entire body cringe with embarrassment. Why was I like this? Most people didn't crumble at the slightest worry. Lots of people had been through what I had or much worse without bursting into tears at the mere thought of someone being upset with you or that you might do the wrong thing.

"I'm sorry," I sobbed as he led me to the living room. I barely made it that far before I plopped down on the edge of the coffee table.

Angel knelt down in front of me, pushing my hair away from my face before he began swiping at the moisture.

"It's not your fault," he said, voice firm. "None of it is your fault."

I nodded. I knew that, but I didn't feel that way all the time. I had to remind myself.

"I get these feelings before something happens," I started, sucking in a few deep breaths before I continued. "I've felt that almost all the time since..."

Angel scooted closer so his ribs were pressed to the edge of the table between me. I was so tired. I wanted to curl up in bed and forget it had all happened. I didn't want to face yet another vision or dream or whatever it was that would send me into another spiral of anxiety. I lowered my head until it found his. He placed one hand against my cheek, not at all fazed when more tears wet his fingers. His other hand wrapped around mine as I pressed my nails into the back of my hands until I felt the sting of it. He gently separated my fingers, rubbing his thumb back and forth over the half-moons indented on the skin.

"You don't have to carry it alone," he said.

"It happened at my parent's party last summer. I had one of those feelings when I was in the barn. I had to leave. I knew I shouldn't go through the vineyard, because I'd had a bad feeling about it, too. I should've gone to the house, but the trees were closer, and I knew someone was behind me. I just felt it." I paused when Angel adjusted his hand on mine.

I hadn't realized it, but I started to scratch the side of my index finger with my thumb. He eased his hand between the fingers, giving my palm a soft squeeze and raising it so it rested against his cheek.

"It was in the trees," I said. "It wasn't... He didn't go further. It could've... He came from behind and just held me."

"Who?"

I didn't have to tell him. He already knew.

"Paul Saxon."

I exhaled. It felt like I'd been holding my breath all year.

Angel stood up, turning his back on me and giving me the perfect view of the shredded back of his dress shirt and the wings that were protruding from it now. My breath caught in my throat, a grip like steel around my chest that made it hard to think about anything but that night. What I hadn't said was the way Paul's hands felt on my skin. He smelled like cigar smoke and bourbon. He held me tight from behind,

breathing in my ear and giving a chuckle that made the hairs on the back
of my neck stand up straight even now.

*"So beautiful, lovely. Lovely Lily."*

Angel pulled his shirt free from his pants, withdrawing the dagger
he told me was always concealed at his lower back. He'd taken a single
step away from me when I felt the dam finally burst. I wasn't sure what I
yelled. I didn't recognize the sounds I knew had to be coming from my
own mouth, but I knew that Angel understood their meaning and he
was there inches from me again. He brushed my hair away from my face
and wiped away the tears with his fingers, taking purposeful breaths as
he coached me to do the same.

Angel moved his hand from my face to my chin, raising my eyes to
his with a finger. He looked at me with a serious expression.

"I swear that no one will hurt you again," he said. "I'm going to
make sure that he's forced to endure his immortality, locked away, and
never encounters another soul again."

We moved to the couch. I snuggled against his side, and he wrapped
his arms around me, leaning back against the pillows. I noticed after a
long while that it was quiet. Too quiet. I glanced up at him to make sure
he was still awake before remembering that he never slept. He smiled at
me before I lowered my head to his chest again. It rose and fell with slow
breaths he didn't require. His heart had not beaten for centuries. His
skin was cool to the touch, cooler than I remembered it being.

My stomach growled and Angel laughed in response.

"Any special requests for the chef?" he asked and sat up.

I stood up, taking his hand.

"Grilled cheese."

Angel's smile widened and he nodded.

"You got it."

# CHAPTER 20

I was lying on a lounge chair next to the pool, listening to pieces of a new song I was working on when the phone call interrupted me. I raised my phone to look at the screen, the sunlight from above making me see spots.

"All good?" Dad asked, glancing my way for just a second as I sat up and tried blinking away the spots before he went back to the latest James Patterson book propped on his lap.

"Just Anne," I said and disconnected the phone from my headphones.

"Tell her I said hi," Dad said as I stood up and pressed the phone to my ear.

"I just wanted to say congrats," she said. "I didn't want to interrupt your family time. I'm sure it's been... Your parents should be getting to know Angel and I'm sure you guys are enjoying the alone time. Your parents aren't taking the whole time off that you're there, right? You're there half the summer, aren't you?"

"No. They, um, didn't take that much time off. Well, they both got a week off. It's Saturday." I looked back at my dad when I reached the end of the pool. My mom came from the house with a pitcher of mojitos, Angel right behind her with four glasses.

"I know it's Saturday. Jazz and I are driving to meet her family for dinner. We've been so busy all week that I didn't get a chance to call before. I didn't want to tell you over text. Going viral isn't something you congratulate someone for in a text."

I turned toward the pool house when Angel looked up at me. What was she calling about?

"Can you— Hang on. Why are you calling?"

I heard Jazz laugh in the background and I wondered if I was on speaker.

"You haven't checked Wilted Rose Strings since you left, have you?"

I had checked YouTube since I left. I remember sitting in the passenger seat of the SUV listening to every song on my channel as Angel drove us here. I showed my mom my channel over brunch. I remembered the moments so vividly, but I only now thought about how long ago that had been. It had been a week since the social at the country club. Angel and I had spent most of the week relaxing around the house and riding horses. I even got brave one day while we were out and we walked to the big barn. We didn't go inside. I'd be brave enough for that on another day.

"What happened with my channel?" I asked. I could've looked, but I was too nervous. My brain immediately imagined that I'd be overwhelmed with comments, or someone had figured out who I really was from my half-naked video. I felt the heat rush to my face as I remembered the way I danced in my underwear. Oh, God.

"Lily, your channel blew up! 'Lion Inside' has millions of views and people are using your song on TikTok. I don't know which platform it went viral on first, but it's all over. I can't believe you don't know. Do you not get notifications about this stuff?" Anne asked. I heard Jazz yelling her congratulations in the background.

I could've told her that I turned off notifications a long time ago when my channel first started to gain subscribers consistently. Watching the numbers made me anxious, so I avoided it. Instead of replying, I opened the YouTube app on my phone and went to my channel. My heart stopped. I felt lightheaded looking at the subscriber count. When I refreshed the page, it shot up even more.

"Lily?" I heard Anne call through the receiver.

I pressed the phone to my ear and blurted, "What do I do?"

Anne and Jazz both started laughing. I wanted to yell at them, but I knew Angel was already listening in. I wasn't exactly sure how good his hearing was. He may already know the news.

"Enjoy it!" Anne called back. "You're a great musician. I know you don't consider yourself one, but you're a really good singer, too. Just bask in your success and take a vacation. I just wanted to call and say congrats."

"Okay," I said, not sure what to do. "Thanks."

"I'll see you when you get back," Anne said and hung up.

I lowered my phone, staring at the app for YouTube and wondering just how high the number of likes and subscribers had climbed during our short conversation. I couldn't look again. I was excited about the success, I was. But it meant a lot of questions that I wasn't ready to answer. I liked exploring what felt comfortable and challenging my confidence with my channel. I put some personal emotions into those songs, especially 'Lion Inside,' and having it blow up and be liked by so many people was both a little too intimate and also hugely flattering. I wasn't sure which made me the most uneasy.

I shut my phone down entirely before I turned to join the group. Dad was still busy reading his book. Mom sipped on her mojito in a chair she'd pulled across the patio and Angel sat at the end of my lounge chair with two drinks in his hands.

"Who was that?" Mom asked as Angel handed me the glass, eyeing me in that way that told me he could sense my nerves.

"She said it was Anne," Dad said, finally tucking his bookmark into the page and looking up. "How is she? Is she coming home for the summer?"

"Oh, invite her over, Lily. We could have a dinner party," Mom said.

"You know she doesn't come home anymore," I said and took a long drink from the glass. It was refreshing. My mom made the best cocktails. She used fresh mint from the garden.

"They'll come around eventually." Dad shrugged.

"It's just a shame. How can you just ignore your own child like that over a little difference? You know, it takes some balls to argue that it's against God's plan to be gay when it's also against God's plan to get a divorce, which May did," Mom said, wagging her finger like she'd just won the argument.

"May did?" Dad sounding more impressed than appalled.

Mom nodded with a dramatic gasp.

"She did. She was married to some man before she moved to New York and met Huy. She got a divorce. The rumor is that she was still married when she met Huy."

"What? How do you know?" Dad asked.

Angel placed a hand on my thigh and leaned close.

"How do you feel?"

"Better now," I said and took another drink.

He smiled as I lowered my glass, already halfway into the mojito.

"You should be proud."

"I am," I said, noticing the awkward inflection at the end. I cleared my throat and raised the glass to my lips again.

"What are you two whispering about over there?" Dad asked.

I turned from Angel. Both my parents were staring at me, my mom looking a little too excited.

*Be brave.*

"My YouTube channel has gone kind of big," I said, forcing myself to keep my eyes on them despite the urge to look away.

My mom gasped and reached for her phone on my dad's lounge chair.

"YouTube channel?" Dad asked, looking from me to my mom when she slapped his shoulder.

"I told you about it. It's Wilted Rose Strings. That's the YouTube channel. I played you all those songs the other night," she said as she scrolled through her phone.

"That was a YouTube channel?" he asked, looking at me.

"What did you think it was?" Mom's mouth parted in shock as she stared at the screen. I hoped to God that she didn't tell me how many subscribers I had.

"I thought she just posted it online. I didn't know you meant that there was a whole channel," he defended, looking at the phone when my mom turned it to him. He studied the screen for a moment before his serious expression changed. He looked up from the phone at me, eyebrows raised before he looked down again.

"Is this a job now, Lilypad?" he asked.

Oh, God. Was it? I'd gotten monetized a few months ago. I didn't make a lot, but it was mine and it was a good amount considering the amount of work I had put in between all my classes.

"You should start a band," Mom said.

"I don't know about that." I thought about what little time I already had. I couldn't manage more rehearsals than I already did for school.

"Surely you know enough musicians," she said and plucked her phone from my dad's hands.

"It's not that," I started, not sure what it was. I had college and what little social life I had with Anne and Angel. I also managed to post videos to the channel fairly regularly and was always working on new songs. Having at least one other member of the team would only spread my work out, not add to it.

"Well, how are you getting all the instrumentals now?" Dad asked.

"I do most of it myself," I said with a shrug. Not many people knew how much I'd taught myself. I wasn't great at piano, but I could play what I needed with some practice. I added percussion with my software. For 'Lion Inside,' I hired a guitarist.

"I think you should expand your work and add to your team, whatever that means," Angel said. "You love creating and performing music, *this* kind of music."

I sat my glass on my leg, the condensation cold against my skin.

"I can't just quit school," I said.

They all started at once with their protests.

"Don't quit," Dad said.

"That's not what I meant," Mom said.

Angel took my hand and gave it a squeeze.

"I didn't mean to leave college," he said with an encouraging smile. "I think that you should see how far this goes. Expand as you need to. Let yourself do something just for the fun of it."

My shoulders relaxed in a way that made me wonder how long I'd been living all tensed up like that. I felt a little burst of energy. I shouldn't need my parents' approval to be on YouTube or decide how my music degree would translate to the rest of my life. Still though, having them so excited about seeing what would come next made me feel better about the projects I wanted to take on. It made me want to push the boundaries just a little more the way I had always imagined, maybe even show my face in my own videos.

"You don't have to dance half-naked in front of a camera to do all this though," Dad said, not phased when Mom slapped his shoulder. He shrugged, cheeks turning red. "You have a birthmark on your thigh. Otherwise, I wouldn't have known."

"Thanks, Dad," I said, my face heating.

Angel wrapped an arm around my shoulders and clinked his glass against my nearly empty one.

Mom raised her glass and said, "To new adventures in music and new family members!"

I saw the way her eyes met Angel's, a knowing look passing between them as the four of us pressed our glasses together and drank.

There was a tiny café in town that Anne and I used to frequent. We liked it because it sat off the highway and all kinds of people would stop in. We saw lots of biker clubs, a few cute guys I watched from afar, a few cute girls that Anne always approached, and even the governor once. He bought our drinks. That's where Angel and I were today, spending mid-morning sitting in a corner of the empty café. The employees were too busy preparing pastries and looking at their phones to pay attention to us.

"Why did you come to New York City?" I asked.

My intentions must have shown on my face because Angel's smile dimmed a little at the memory of the fight with the Saxons. He glanced at the counter across the room and then scooted his black armchair around the table, so he was sitting closer to me.

"I understand that you must feel a little confused about me," he said, taking my hand. "I want you to know that I will be nothing but honest with you, now and forever."

My heart skipped in my chest at his words. I forced myself to sit still despite my squirming insides.

"I never thought you were lying to me," I said slowly. "I just wasn't sure if you'd told me everything."

"I've told you more than I've ever told anyone," he said, and I was sure he had. "Whatever is bothering you, because I can tell something is, just ask."

I nodded. There was so much I'd wondered. A lot of my questions hadn't come to me until after we'd first talked about vampires, and we'd put a label on our relationship.

"Okay. Well, um…" I looked at the counter. It was abandoned, all the employees in the back room from the sound of it. I turned back to Angel, slipping my hand from his to cup my coffee. "You said that things were a lot like Dracula. There are the wings and not having a reflection. The sun doesn't bother you, though."

Angel reached within the collar of his shirt and pulled out a silver chain. A pendant hung on the chain, a tapered vessel about two inches long that contained what looked like dirt.

"I like to think of it in terms of the old phrase: ashes to ashes, dust to dust," he said, leaning closer so I could hold the pendant. "We are undead, cursed with eternal darkness."

"But you can walk under the sun because of, er, this?" I asked, starting to worry about whatever the dark dust inside the pendant was.

"Dirt," he answered simply. "More specifically, dirt from my home, where I was turned."

I nodded. That made sense with the story of Dracula. He slept in a coffin of dirt.

"Can I ask you a question?" he asked.

I finished the last of my coffee and sat the cup aside, a little nervous about what he might ask.

"What do you see in your visions?"

I stared back in stunned silence. I almost replied that I hadn't had any visions, just dreams, but that's not true. The dreams were visions. It was my first dream the night he saved me from the club that told him we had a future together.

"It's been the same one and only flashes of things," I said.

"What kind of things?"

"Well, colors, I guess. There's red writing on a wall like someone smeared it in paint. I think it's on brick. I can't tell what it says. I'm not even sure it's words. It could be a painting or something."

His brow furrowed like he was thinking hard.

"Does that mean anything to you?" I asked. He was the one who heard me talking in my sleep. I wouldn't have known I'd said his name that first night if it hadn't been for Olivia Saxon.

He shook his head.

"What do I say when I'm asleep?"

He shook his head again. His body went rigid, the same way it had when he talked about being locked in the tomb.

"Not very much," he said. "It's always the same."

"What do I say?" I repeated, taking his hand. At first, he didn't react to my touch. It took a moment before his fingers laced with mine; the coolness was nice compared to the warmth of the summer rays through the window.

"That it hurts," he breathed, keeping his eyes ahead.

Chills raced up my spine. My thoughts went to the red smeared on the wall in my dreams.

"We should go," Angel said, pressing his lips to the back of my hand and breaking my trance.

# CHAPTER 21

The first time I stepped into the barn was because Angel volunteered to hang lights along the rafters. I expected to be nervous and was surprised when I wasn't. I held the end of the blub lights as he flew to the top of the barn, black wings stretched so wide that I was amazed they didn't brush the walls on his ascent.

"We'll be done a lot quicker than your dad would've been," Angel called down to me, perched on one of the many boards stretching halfway to the ceiling. He walked effortlessly from one beam to the next, looping the lights into hooks already screwed to the bottom of the beams.

"Did you bring another pair of slacks, different from what you wore to the club?" I asked.

"I brought two. Is that what I should wear?" he asked, looking down from the beam.

My parents hosted a yearly wine tasting in the barn. All their country club friends were invited along with anyone else my parents were trying to impress. It was a mix of business and pleasure, though usually more business though.

"The barn gets a little warm, so it's a more casual event. You can wear a nice pair of slacks and a button-up, no tie."

Angel hung the last of the row of lights and stepped from the beam, his wings cushioning his fall as he swooped to the ground. It was so fluid a movement that he landed lightly on one foot and continued walking the length of the barn toward me.

"What are you wearing?" he asked, arms extended toward the next roll of bulb lights in my arms.

The truth was that I didn't know. I brought two dresses: the blue, backless dress I wore to the club and a white, short A-line dress with spaghetti straps. I brought a pair of tight-fitting spandex shorts to wear underneath whatever I chose, but I realized now that the black shorts wouldn't work under the white dress. My heart skipped in my chest. I couldn't wear the blue one again; my mom wouldn't let me anyway. A lot of the same people would be at this event as at the country club. Did it matter? My mind was replaying the ambush over and over. It definitely didn't matter. I wouldn't be without an extra layer at least. Maybe I could pretend to be sick or slip away with Angel to the guest house and just crawl into bed.

My thoughts came to an abrupt stop when Angel put a finger under my chin. He lifted my eyes to his, a smile spreading across his face.

"You're safe with me. Always. I swear it," he said and kissed my lips. "And you're beautiful no matter the day, whatever you wear, whatever you're *not* wearing..."

I tossed the lights at his chest, resisting the urge to kiss him again. He laughed and kept his eyes on me until the last second as he turned, black wings spread wide, and he flew toward the rafters again. The air whooshed past, tossing my hair behind me and chilling my skin.

"Can I help with anything?" I asked from my barstool.

Mom insisted that homemade pasta was the only way to eat pasta. She'd spent most of the afternoon rolling dough into noodles. She tended to a pot of boiling water, making sure the noodles didn't clump together.

"You can make the salad. Angel has a handle on the meat and veggies," Mom said.

I slid off my stool and moved to the long section of countertop that Angel had cleared for his work. He sat a baking tray next to me as I pulled a large bowl and cutting board from the cabinets at our feet.

"I am so glad we don't make dinner for the party in this kitchen anymore and we just hire caterers," Mom said as she finished placing the last noodle in the pot.

"We have too many guests to make enough food here," I said.

"We could manage." Angel bumped his hip into mine playfully.

"Only because of Angel," Mom said. "I don't know how you do it, but I swear you were a five-star chef in another life. Gordon Ramsey who?" She laughed as she lifted her wine glass from the counter and turned from the pot. "If I could keep you, Angel, I would."

"You're too kind," Angel chuckled, tossing a pound of ground beef into a mixing bowl.

"I mean it. You have professional skills. How did you learn?" Mom asked.

Angel had premixed his spices into a separate bowl so he could toss them into the meat, which he did now. He used his hands to toss the raw beef.

"My grandfather sent me to a man in our village as an apprentice," he said. I was surprised for a moment by the honesty. It was the same story he'd told me on the way here weeks ago.

"Well, whoever taught you must have been very successful," Mom said and took a sip from her glass.

I turned back to my cutting board, positioning the knife over the carrot and slicing it before I thought about how thick I should make each cut.

"Move your pointer finger," Angel said.

"What?" I asked, coming out of my thoughts.

He smiled back at me, forming a ball of meat and placing it on the baking tray.

"Keep your fingers together," he said, showing me his own hand as though he was wrapping it around the hilt of a knife. "Don't rest your pointer finger on top like that. Keep it around the handle."

"Oh. Okay," I said and adjusted my grip. I focused on making my second slice the same thickness as the last before deciding two was enough. The others would be a more normal size.

We worked in silence. It took a lot of attention to make sure the carrots were uniform. Normally, I wouldn't care. But I knew that Angel would've been perfect and I didn't want my poor cooking skills to put his five-star abilities to shame. I finished cutting the carrots and added them to the romaine before I looked at him. He'd finished forming the beef into meatballs, all the same size and perfectly separated on the baking sheet. Despite having finishing, his hands were resting in the mixing bowl and his dark eyes were focused on them, remnants of oregano and beef clinging to his ruddy fingers.

"What is your favorite thing to make?" Mom asked.

Angel didn't react, his gaze focused on his fingers. He lowered his hands to the bottom of the bowl, spreading his fingers so the blood ran over his skin.

"Angel?" I pressed myself to his side, breaking his trance.

He immediately shoved his hands on the rag at the back of the counter, quickly rubbing the blood from his skin.

"What was that?" he asked, moving to the sink where he began lathering up with soap.

"Nothing," I answered. I pushed my concerns aside despite the anxiety churning in my stomach.

---

Dinner was amazing, thanks to Angel manning the kitchen. I ate more than I should have, my stomach full and my head a little fuzzy from the wine we enjoyed as the sky grew dark and one game of cards became two.

"Are you sure you ate enough, Angel? You barely touched your dinner," Mom said as Dad finished gathering the cards in his hands.

The humor in Angel's face dimmed a little, more than I was used to seeing.

"I like to cook more than eat, believe it or not," he said and took a sip from his wine.

"I'd think if you made the meal you'd like the largest helping though," Dad said, shuffling the cards. "Another round?"

"I think I should get some sleep. We have the party tomorrow." I glanced at Angel who looked indifferent.

"No one will arrive until seven at least," Mom said with a wave.

"I'm an early riser," Angel said before I got a chance to deliver my poor attempt at a lie.

"Ah," Dad said with a knowing nod. He raised his right arm beside his head, flexing like a bodybuilder. "Gotta keep in shape."

"My body isn't used to all the late nights," Angel laughed.

"Well, the barn is all set up. It should be a relaxing day," Mom said as Angel and I stood up from the table.

"You can get your workout in plus a nap, Angel." Dad winked.

"That's the plan," Angel said, clapping my dad on the shoulder before following me into the hall. We went out the back door, past the pool, and through the pool house as usual. Once we were upstairs, I closed the door behind us and locked it before bracing myself for whatever might come next. A fight? An agreement?

"You should go hunt," I said.

Angel pulled his shirt off and balled it up between his hands before looking at me. After a moment, he nodded.

"After tomorrow's party," he said and went into the bedroom. I followed him, watching as he slipped out of his jeans.

"I meant, like, tonight," I said.

Angel finished dressing in his loose sweatpants and took a white T-shirt from the dresser before he turned to look at me.

"I don't know the area well enough. We leave a week from tomorrow. I already have a criminal in mind back in New York City," he said, adjusting the sweatpants at his hips. He'd left his shirt off, looking back at me in a way that made my muscles contract. I could feel my face flush. I also knew it was intentional.

"We've been here over a month."

"I'll survive," he said, leaving the bed to join me in the doorway. He kissed my forehead, the gesture and the smell of him nearly enough to crumble my resolve.

"You told me a month was the limit," I reminded him.

"I've survived worse," he said, slinking his hands around my waist. "We leave Saturday. The man I have in mind frequents bars on Saturdays. He likes Black women with colored hair. I know his MO. He won't have a chance to begin the night. I can make it until then."

"I don't want you…" I tried hard to find a word that was softer than "hungry" or "thirsty."

Angel was standing in front of me a second later, his bare chest inches away before I noticed him move. It made my heart stop. He rarely used his vampire speed around me like that and for a moment, I saw a brief look of desire cross his face. My stomach clenched at the thought of his touch.

He smiled, his shoulders relaxing, and he took my hands in his. He pressed a kiss to my forehead.

"Feeding once a month is just my routine," he said. "I'm not hungry. I promise."

I let myself be distracted by his closeness, reaching out to touch his chest before he captured my hand. He raised my gaze to his with a gentle finger under my chin. He smiled.

"You're still worrying about me, aren't you?" he asked.

I bit my lower lip, trying to decide how to impress upon him how important it was that he took care of himself. I could stay alone tonight. I was fine. Instead, his hands slid from my face to my waist and then over my hips until they were sliding over the back of my jeans.

"Let me take your mind off of things," he said, pulling me against him.

As much as I wanted to, especially now with his hands going from soft caresses to more firm squeezes, I couldn't get rid of the pit in my stomach. It only got worse now that I was aware of it, making my chest tighten and my breath catch.

"Mouse," Angel said, moving his hands from my jeans to my lower back.

My brain was filled with flashes of the dream that had plagued me for months. The brick wall. The red smeared across it. I realized now that the reason I couldn't make out what the red said was because there was a single bulb in the dark room. It was the flickering of the bulb that made the vision come in flashes, not my memory. It was all promptly cut off by a flash of red. The feel of something soft across my eyelids and a pair of hands grabbing me from behind. I felt the ghost of an exhale at my left ear and shoved hard at the arms closing around me, a small squeal escaping before the arms released and I backed into something hard.

I stared back at Angel, his hands held up in surrender.

"Lily," he said calmly. "It's just a panic attack."

"I saw... I could feel it..."

He shook his head. "You're having a panic attack."

"No. No."

He hesitated with his hands raised toward me before he took the last step forward to cup my face. He slowly stroked my cheeks, thumbs moving back and forth as he took exaggerated breaths.

"Breath for me, Mouse. Just once. That's it. And again. Good girl," he coached, continuing the steady rhythm of his thumbs across my skin until I realized I was mirroring his efforts, my chest easing and lungs filling completely.

"I had a vision," I said between breaths.

His thumbs continued to move back and forth over my cheeks. He nodded.

"The same one or different?"

"There's more," I said. "I don't know. There was a single bulb, flickering. It was like a shed or a basement or something. I don't know. I couldn't see what was on the wall. I couldn't tell."

"Okay. It's okay," he said, taking a step closer when I extended my hands toward him. I moved to grip the front of his shirt but remembered he was shirtless when my fingers met bare skin.

"You should go hunt," I said, the coolness of his skin stranger than normal.

"Saturday," he said, shaking his head.

"No. You shouldn't wait. You should go now."

"Lily, I won't."

"*Please*. I can't explain it, but I just have a really bad feeling about this, and I can't... I need you to go. I need you to go, Angel. Just go hunt, please," A sob choked the last of my words.

"Lily," he said and pulled me closer, a hand at the small of my back and another brushing my hair from my face. What would normally have been a comforting gesture was just annoying now. Maybe I was just having a panic attack. Maybe the panic attack triggered a false vision?

Whatever it was, I needed him to understand. I was fine on my own. I wanted to know that he would be, too.

"You need to hunt," I said past the tears.

"I can't," he groaned, the pain in his voice making me pause.

"W-Why? Why can't you just go for a few hours?" I asked.

His jaw tightening and the blackness in his eyes should've been enough of a sign. Still, his eyes had grown darker throughout the day from the hunger he tried to deny. My stomach twisted as I remembered the fight at the Saxon estate.

"If anything happened while I was gone"

"I'll lock all the doors. Please," I said, wishing he was wearing his shirt so I could bury myself in the fabric, breathe in the smell of him, and hold on tight.

"It's just a few days," he said, brushing away a tear from my cheek.

"You're distracted. All those people at the party tomorrow... I need you with me then. I don't want you hurting, especially not tomorrow. Please." I moved my hands to his face. My muscles relaxed when his expression did, making me suddenly feel tired. He paused for a long moment before looking down at me and tightening his arm around my back.

"You call me for anything, okay? Swear that you'll answer my calls, texts, all of it. Promise?" he asked, tone urgent.

"Yes. I will," I said, tightening my grip on the hair at the base of his neck and pulling a few strands free from his bun by accident.

"Swear to me. I need you to swear, Lily."

"I swear."

He let out a deep breath and stopped stroking my hair. He brought his forehead to mine, taking another deep breath before kissing the spot between my brows.

"I love you," he said and pressed his forehead to mine again. "I won't let anything happen to you. No one will ever hurt you again."

"I love you too," I said.

"Don't make me go," Angel said in a whisper. A shiver shot up my spine. The words nearly melted me, nearly had my fingers tighten around his hair. I moved them over his shoulders and let my palms rest against his chest instead.

"Please," I said, forcing the words past my lips.

I was prepared to shove him away, but he was gone. I stared at the bed, turning around the room as though I'd see him as he darted through the door. I walked back into the living room and found it exactly as we'd left it.

He left. It was just like I'd asked.

I made sure the first-floor door to the pool house was locked and checked all the windows before making my way upstairs to the apartment, locking that door behind me too. I did a final check of the living room before I went to the bedroom, locked that door, and crawled under the sheets all alone.

It didn't take long to fall asleep, but it was far from restful.

# CHAPTER 22

I couldn't escape the dream, not even when I knew it was only a dream. It was last summer all over again, me in the barn at my parents' party, leaving when the pit formed in my stomach, and finding myself facing Paul Saxon at the edge of the vineyard.

I was finally pulled out of my morning stupor when I reached across the mattress only to find it empty. I worried for a moment before I remembered the night before. Angel was gone and that was a good thing.

I took a long, hot shower and slowly got ready for the day. Without Angel to lead the way, breakfast was nothing but an assortment of fruit and cereal.

"Where's Angel?" Dad asked when I joined him and Mom in the dining room.

"Um, working out," I said, surprised at how quickly the lie fell from my lips. Maybe being around Angel and the secret world of magic had finally rubbed off on me.

"I thought he got up early for that," Mom said, patting the seat next to her.

"It's his long workout day," I said, not even sure what that meant. It was something I'd heard someone say somewhere sometime. My dad seemed to understand. He let out a low moan of understanding and nodded.

"I didn't take him for the running type," he said and lowered his iPad to the table. "Runners don't usually have that much muscle mass."

I shrugged and busied myself with the coffee carafe, filling half my mug with cream before topping it off with the dark liquid. The smell alone was invigorating. My therapist made me give up caffeine when I first started seeing her, she said it could make anxiety worse. I glanced down at the cup and wondered if setting the mug aside would ease the sick feeling in my stomach.

"When do you leave? Tomorrow?" Mom asked, pulling my thoughts away from my churning stomach.

"Um, yeah. We have to get to the city," I said. I sat the coffee in front of my seat before I settled in, regretting that I'd made a cup at all.

"Will you at least stay for brunch?" Mom asked.

"Probably not. I think Angel needs to be back kind of early. We'll probably be gone before you guys wake up," I said, not sure why I wanted to avoid them so much. It wasn't like they'd have anything to say. There was really no rush to get home. Anne was gone with Jazz, so other than having the apartment to myself for a few days, I had no reason to tell them we were leaving so quickly.

"Do you need to do any laundry today?" Dad asked, looking up from his iPad.

"I don't think so. I'll have to check our things. I should probably go and pack." I stood up, lifting the mug from the table and snatching a banana from the fruit bowl just to avoid suspicion. My parents exchanged curious looks before they glanced at me. I averted my eyes just before I could risk adding any questions to the mix.

"I'm going to miss Angel's cooking," Dad said with a laugh, raising the iPad again.

My mom let out a moan of satisfaction and said, "Thanksgiving will be top-notch."

My heart picked up pace as I made my way across the yard to the pool house. I pulled the door shut behind me and took a deep breath, hoping to see Angel at the top of the stairs. I sloshed hot coffee over my hand on the way up, gasping and assessing the glistening drops on the hardwood floor on the top step.

No Angel.

I went to the kitchen and set the mug on the counter. With a rag that was balled in my right hand, I dropped to my knees in the doorway and wiped up the coffee.

Angel left late last night. He hunted through the night. He was on his way back now. It took us a whole day to get here by car. It would likely take him that long in his true vampire form. He would be here in time for the party.

The floor was dry by the time I remembered the towel I dragged across the surface. I stood up and tossed the tag toward the kitchen, missing the counter and watching as it dropped to the tile. I knew I should at least eat the banana sitting next to my coffee. I could practically hear Angel in my ear telling me I'd need the energy, and that not eating wouldn't make my anxiety better.

I needed to do something.

I went to the bedroom and began gathering our things from the dresser and bathroom. It would be a late night anyway; I wouldn't want to pack in the morning. I packed every item with more care than I'd done in the first place, zipping the entire room in our suitcases before I remembered my dress for the party was still buried in the suitcase. I sat only the necessities for the night on the dresser beside the dress and left the rest packed away in our suitcases that sat upright in the living room.

You would have thought we were leaving in minutes instead of hours.

---

There were already dozens of people at the barn. The sun had set, and the lights Angel and I had strung from the rafters cast warm light onto the grass outside where several people were standing as they talked about things I didn't care to listen in on. I'd waited an hour longer than I would have to go to the party. I waited hours longer than I thought I would have to go on my date.

I went to the party alone.

I scanned the expanse of the barn when I got to the entrance, hoping I'd spot him among the crowd. My parents stood to the left where the bar was. At least a dozen of the vineyard employees were working tonight, all dressed in black slacks and white button-ups and carrying bottles of wine or trays of glasses. One of them saw me lingering, a woman with braids, and came over with a tray of red wine.

"Would you like a cabernet or a merlot?" she offered, gesturing between the glasses. I could see now that they were all labeled with little plastic tags around the stem of the glasses.

"Cabernet," I said.

She handed me a glass and told me to enjoy myself before moving back toward the crowd. There were more people than I thought there would be. Normally, the Nortons waited until the party was half-over to arrive and I realized a moment later why. Their daughter came with a handsome man by her side who Mr. and Mrs. Norton proceeded to introduce to a group of my dad's business friends.

"Lily?"

I turned toward the voice, recognizing a girl from high school.

"H-Hi. How have you been, Shawna?" I asked, awkwardly patting her back when she pulled me into a hug. I got a whiff of her sweet perfume before she pulled away and flashed me a smile. I was a little surprised by her enthusiasm. It wasn't like we were friends in high school. We had a few classes together, but I had a lot of the same people in my classes. It was a small school.

"I'm a pre-med major," she said.

"That's great," I said, looking past her where my parents had been. They'd since moved, and I couldn't spot them before she asked her next question.

"I heard you were at NYU. Orchestra. Your mom told my mom at the club that you have a boyfriend," she said, pulling my attention back on her. She gave me a sly look, leaning in a little closer. "My mom said he's the kind of guy that stands out at the country club, you know? I haven't seen anyone here that doesn't, well, fit."

The implication was there in her voice.

"He's around here somewhere," I said and waved my hand toward the room as casually as I could. "He came early to help set up. I wasn't feeling that great, so I stayed back to pack. We have to leave pretty early in the morning, I probably won't be here very long."

Shawna let out a low hum of understanding as she lifted her glass to her lips.

"I should probably go find him, just check in and stuff," I said and backed my way toward the crowd. I nearly spilled wine on my dress when I bumped into an elderly man. I had only taken a few steps before my dad called my name. His hand came down on my shoulder and he steered me toward a group of well-dressed men and women. I didn't recognize a single one of them, which meant only one thing: he was trying to seal a business deal.

"Have you all met my daughter?" he asked. He barely gave any of them time to respond before he introduced me. "This is my Lily. She's a student at NYU, on a music scholarship. She just played in a spring showcase and was the youngest student they had invited to play in years."

"What do you play?" a woman asked.

"Cello mostly," I replied, wishing I'd left off the last word when she straightened up and took a step closer. She grabbed the man behind her by the wrist and pulled him closer. He was at least half her age and had the same dark-brown hair and dimpled smile.

"Luka, this is Lily. She goes to NYU. She plays the cello," the woman said before looking back at me. "You play other instruments, right?"

"Um, not very well. I can play lots of stringed instruments, but I'm not... I play cello mostly, well, only really."

Luka smiled, but not just any smile. He was impressed. He clearly thought my stuttering was cute and I knew before he opened his mouth that he would make a move. I knew I'd be stuck either embarrassing myself by running away, embarrassing him by rejecting him, or jeopardizing my dad's business deal.

Luka opened his mouth to speak just as my dad pulled me close to his side.

"She's seeing a businessman in NYC. Mary, do you know an Angel Ramírez?" he asked. Luka closed his mouth and took a step back, taking a sip of his wine.

"I don't think I do. Which company is he with?" Mary asked, patting her son's forearm sympathetically despite the thoughtful look she sent my dad.

"He never told me the name, actually," Dad said and glanced at me.

"I'll go and find him," I said and stepped away from him. "I bet he'd like to be included in the conversation."

No one gave me a second look as I stepped away. The crowd was so tight where we were that I decided to move toward the wall of the barn. I finished my wine and sat the empty glass on the bar and pulled my phone from my clutch. My fingers found Angel's contact in seconds. I pressed the phone to my ear and turned the volume up as it rang, waiting until it went to voicemail to hang up.

The phone buzzed in my hand and my heart leaped in my chest only to sink again when I opened my mom's text.

> Are you here?

I felt something close to a sob build in my chest. I took a deep breath and typed my response.

> Have you seen Angel?

I only had to wait seconds for her message.

> He was looking for you. I think he went to the pool house.

Thank God.

I skirted the room and suddenly felt like I could get a deep breath when I made it to the lawn. It grew darker as I walked toward the pool house. I took the stairs inside the door two at a time and fumbled with the key at the top. My phone buzzed once in my hand as I opened the apartment door. I looked down at the screen and my entire body went cold. I froze in place, sure I wasn't reading it right. She had to mean someone else. That couldn't be who told her.



I looked up, directly at Paul Saxon. He leaned against the bedroom doorframe with a smirk on his face.

"Didn't expect to find me in your bedroom, did you?" he asked with a laugh. He straightened up and moved closer, looking over me in a way that sent chills up my spine.

"Forgive my manners. I should've told you how beautiful you look first. You're absolutely gorgeous," he said and took another step closer as his eyes roved over me. "That dress... What you must have on under it..."

My heart suddenly came alive as he raised a hand toward me. My eyes found the closet object, the coffee mug from this morning and the banana on the counter. A second later, I closed the gap between the door and the kitchen, my right hand grasping the handle of the mug the same moment I felt his hand snag the back of my dress.

I swung around, slinging coffee over his white dress shirt. The mug whooshed past his chest and before I could take another swing, his wrist captured mine. I threw the banana at his face just as I felt my foot slip from under me. The banana flew past his shoulder like a boomerang, and I slipped on the rag I had dropped on the floor earlier.

Paul went down with me, hovering over me for just a second before lowering his body to mine and pinning my hands to the floor next to my head. I was paralyzed, my heart hammering in my chest and my lungs fighting for air. I should scream. I knew I should, but I could barely take a breath at all, each one shallow and leaving my lips before it had fully passed them.

"Shh. Easy now, Lovely," he whispered into my ear.

Something like a squeal escaped me and I tried to pull farther away from him. I sucked in my stomach to keep it from his chest. I tried sliding my legs from under his.

"You're shaking, Lily," Paul said in awe. He pulled back, sitting up and pulling me with him. He held my wrists tight, keeping them on my thighs as he stared at me.

"I'm not going to hurt you. I would never hurt you. Well," he said with a snort and a sly grin. "I won't hurt you as long as you're a good girl. Can you do that for me? Can you come along quietly so I don't have to get mean?"

He tightened his grip on my wrists for a moment until they went numb. My eyes stung and the sob building in my chest kept me from speaking. He stood up, pulling me to my feet where my knees nearly buckled. I looked at the living room and realized it was empty. Our suitcases were gone. The apartment looked clean as though we were never there. My heart skipped in my chest as I put the pieces together.

If I left with him now, no one would think to look for me. My parents would think I'd gone home.

When Paul relaxed his grip, I ran for the door. I could feel him after me, feet pounding against each step and hands brushing my back as he reached for me. I let out a shriek when he shoved me near the bottom of the staircase. The air shot from my chest when I braced myself against the floor. I rolled to my back just as he crouched over me. His hands went past mine and gripped my throat, cutting off my frantic breaths as I clawed at his hands. My lungs burned and black spots clouded my vision before I felt myself fading in a dark haze.

"I told you to be a good girl, Lovely."

# CHAPTER 23

My throat ached. I couldn't see. I realized my hands were tied together when I moved to raise them to my face. They were bound behind my back. I could tell that there was fabric tied over my eyes now that I was awake. The floor hummed beneath me and then there was a crunching sound. Gravel.

The engine turned off and a door opened. Moments after it shut, another opened, and I felt the cool air tickle my ankles. I whimpered when his hands pulled me to the door by my legs, thankful when I was pulled upright. The gravel under my bare feet hurt and it must have been obvious because he scooped me up a moment later.

"We'll get you nice and warm. There's a fireplace and a hot meal waiting for you," Paul said.

I opened my mouth to speak, ready to beg him to let me go, but my throat was so sore that the words came out hoarse and painful.

"Not so nice, is it? Should've done as you were told," he said with a small laugh.

The temperature was the biggest difference when we moved inside. The sound of crickets cut off abruptly and warmth greeted me. The room grew warmer the farther he walked until I was lowered onto something soft. My eyes burned at the sudden light, only able to make out Paul's shape in front of me holding a long piece of red fabric.

"I won't make another trip like this for you," Olivia said. I thought she was talking to me until my vision came back and her glare was directed at Paul. She held a cardboard to-go container and my stomach growled when the smell reached me. I knew it anywhere. I grew up with that pizza.

"You give it to her," Olivia sneered and nearly tossed the pizza box to her brother. Paul took it and sat it on the coffee table. He lifted a thick blanket from the back of the couch and draped it over my lap before turning to the meal.

I already knew from the smell that it was pizza, but I hadn't expected it to be Mario's supreme pizza, the entire pie covered with more olives than usual. *My* usual.

Paul stepped away from the open box and motioned to it.

"All yours, Lovely," he said. He reached a hand toward my cheek, and I turned away, catching sight of the rest of the room. My heart skipped in my chest at his sudden inhale and I turned to look at him again, expecting a slap or a punch. Something. His piercing gaze held mine, furious for a moment, before he replaced it with a forced smile before he sat next to me.

"Where are my manners?" he said with an awkward laugh. "You need your hands to eat."

I didn't realize I was holding my breath as he removed the ties around my wrists. He kissed my shoulder and as he pulled away, I felt the tension release and the air escape my lungs.

"You must be starving," Paul said as he sat my restraints next to the pizza, a pair of black leather cuffs that sat next to a red silk scarf I was sure had served as my blindfold moments before. The sight of them lying so simply next to my favorite local meal made my throat tighten and my eyes burn.

"Bitch," Paul said under his breath. "If I kept my hands around your throat a few seconds longer... You realize that, right? You're alive because I allowed it. Do you know that?" His tone grew darker as he stood up.

I nodded my head when words failed me.

"Then you will respect me," he said, towering over me for a moment before he leaned in. I shrank away, fading deeper into the couch cushion as he drew closer. "Got it?"

"Y-Yes," I whispered.

"What are we doing with him?" Olivia asked with a bored sigh.

Paul straightened up and I felt my muscles relax. I felt better as he rounded the coffee table, rubbing the back of his neck with one hand as he stood before the fireplace.

"I thought we agreed to let him desecrate," he said.

"Then what are we doing with her?" Olivia asked and pointed toward me.

"Whatever I say," Paul shot back, shooting his sister such a challenging look that even she stood frozen. After a moment, a smile pulled at the corner of his lips, and he turned back to the fire and continued to rub the back of his head.

"W-Where's Angel?" I asked.

I knew something was wrong. Maybe it was my fault. I should never have forced him to leave. Maybe I misinterpreted my bad feelings for his hunger when they were really a warning. Maybe my visions were trying to warn me about this.

Olivia and Paul looked at me at the same time. Olivia looked annoyed at my question, but Paul's expression softened, and he moved toward me. He knelt to the ground in front of me, taking my hands in his.

"His soul is black, cursed with wings and eternal darkness," he said and pressed his lips to the knuckles on both of my hands. "You are so pure, light... You have power, more ability than any darkness can offer. Don't let it consume you. Don't let *him* consume you."

My heart hammered against my chest with each gentle kiss on my hands. He stood up and moved to Oliva, guiding her to the other side of the room where they began whispering. I tried to listen in. All I could tell was that Olivia was pissed, practically hissing her frustrations back at Paul. He remained calm the entire time, untouched by her anger the same way I left the cardboard box of pizza despite my rumbling stomach.

Paul led me through the winding halls of the estate to a guest room. A button-up shirt was laid across the bed, clean clothes for me to dress in he said. He left and closed the door behind me. I heard the lock click into place, the simple sound bringing on panic like I'd never felt before.

I curled up in the sheets of the bed, my back pressed to the headboard and eyes locked on the door. I didn't sleep the first night. I tried to stay awake into the second but awoke to the turning of the door handle the next morning. I was on my feet before my brain had caught up with my body, facing the doorway where Paul was standing with a tray of bacon and eggs.

"Eat, Lovely," he said with a smile as he moved into the room.

He left the tray on the corner of the bed before moving back into the hallway. He shut the door and the lock clicked back into place.

The next time I woke, I was lying on the floor and instead of Paul, it was Olivia Saxon in the doorway. She tossed a dress on the floor before me.

"Put that on," she said with a tired sigh.

"W-why?" I asked, sitting up and pulling the dress toward me.

"Just do it and come downstairs," she groaned before pulling the door shut with a snap. I realized as I heard her feet padding away that she didn't lock the door.

The dress was a soft blue with flowy chiffon that stretched to my knees when I stood up. I quickly stripped off my white dress and exchanged it for the new blue one. Barefoot, I stepped into the hallway. I half-expected to see Olivia waiting for me, but no one was down the long hall. I took deep breaths as I walked, trying to keep myself from scurrying down the stairs and running for the first exit I could find.

I followed the smell. Turkey. I was hungry enough that my head swam at the thought of devouring the meal. Olivia and Paul stood in the dining room just off the foyer. The table was set for the three of us, fine China and polished silverware glittering at the closest end of the table. A turkey sat on a platter between the plates, sides of potatoes, green beans, and a Caesar salad positioned around the bird.

"Beautiful," Paul said. His eyes roved over me for a moment before he went to the head of the table and pulled the chair out, motioning for me to sit. His smile dimmed when I didn't move right away and something in the tightness of his face sent a chill down my spine and willed my feet forward.

"You must be famished," he said as I sat.

"Not eating for a few days will do that to a person," Olivia said under her breath as she took her seat, proceeding to fill her plate with potatoes.

"Why?" I asked. I hardly recognized my own voice. The pain had faded from his grip around my throat, but the words still came out hoarse.

"Why not?" Paul returned with a shrug and lifted a butcher knife from the table. My body tensed in response even as he positioned it above the turkey and began carving off slices of the golden meat. He moved the first slice to the plate in front of me before cutting away pieces for himself and Olivia.

"Why?" I asked again, sounding much more like myself than before.

"Do you know what Stockholm Syndrome is?" Paul asked, setting the knife down and reaching for the salad.

"Yes," I said. Was that the goal? Kidnap me and make me fall in love with him?

"You must have it or else you would see him for what he is," Paul said with a snort.

"What? Wait. You mean Angel?" I asked as he filled his plate with salad.

"He's a vampire. They feast on human blood. They are driven mad by it. There's no substitute. They cheat death."

"You cheated death," I said, the words sounding small as they came out.

Paul and Olivia both laughed.

"There's no such thing as a moral vampire," Paul said.

"How is what you do any better?" I said, surprised by how loud I was. The words carried through the room and grabbed their attention. My heart fluttered as they glared back at me. I looked down at my place setting. Of course, they'd left me without a knife.

"Don't forget, Lovely," Paul said through his teeth. He slowly moved closer as he spoke, closing the distance between us and stealing the air from the room with every inch. "You sit here in my house before a feast I prepared just for you, rejecting my hospitality. You're on the wrong side. You aren't thinking rationally and why would you? A naïve thing like you." He was just inches away now. He rested his hands on the arms of my chair and drew in close, lowering his lips to my ear. "Is it the way he looks? Is it the things he whispers in your ear, all the ways he promises to give you everything you want? Is it the way he touches you in the dark?"

I tried to push him away, but his hand gripped mine before I could reach his chest. He squeezed my fingers so tightly that it hurt, but the shock of what he did next overtook the pain.

Paul slapped me across the face.

Hard.

A strange squeal slipped through my lips and my hand was pressed to my cheek before I realized exactly what had happened. He pushed my hand away and turned my face back to his with a rough hand, holding my chin in place so I was staring into his intense gaze.

"I could whisper those words in your ear. Believe me, I know the same tricks," Paul said, spit flying from his lips.

"Paul," Olivia said, clearly tired of the conversation. She let out a groan and sat her utensils next to her plate before looking up at her brother. "You need to decide what you want to do."

I felt dizzy.

What did that mean? What was the plan? They'd obviously talked about it before.

"Thank you," I whispered. The entire room was so quiet, quieter than I'd ever heard. "For the meal."

Paul's expression turned from surprise to satisfaction as he released his grip on my face. I speared my hunk of turkey with my fork and bit off a piece. He slowly sat on the edge of his seat; a smile pulled at his lips as he relaxed against the chairback.

"You underestimate me," he said to Olivia, pointing at her with his fork before spearing a potato.

I gagged with every mouthful, every bite like ash. I thought about Angel with each forkful I lifted to my lips, wondering where he was and trying not to imagine if he was alive or not. I created a new scene instead, one where Angel burst through the glass windows to rescue me. He would stand, bat-like wings spread wide, and rip Olivia and Paul apart. I imagined that stupid butcher knife Paul held before. I replayed the way it would look plunging into his chest as Angel held him against the wall, saying the same words he'd told me so many times before.

*No one will ever hurt you.*
*No one will ever hurt you.*

# CHAPTER 24

I'd worn the same clothes long enough that they'd grown stiff under my arms and itchy along my back. Despite donning the beautiful blue dress for dinner, I changed back into the same dress I'd been captured in. It was short, shorter than I wished for now, but it provided more coverage than the button-up Paul provided me and hoped I would change into.

I knew it was his shirt. I saw the way his eyes lingered on me, and I tried not to think about the number of times he'd imagined me wearing it. I didn't care how stiff the fabric got; I would wear my party dress forever. I knew just based on the time elapsed that something had happened to Angel. I had tried ignoring all the realities, but the more days passed, the more I had to consider all the options.

He was either captured or dead.

I chose to believe he was captured and being held somewhere close.

I wanted to believe he was captured and being held somewhere close.

I would believe he was captured and being held somewhere close.

He was captured and being held somewhere close.

I let my mind go to that place, imagining that he was just behind a door down the hall, and he had slipped his restraints, breaking down the door with his vampire strength, and swooped into my room like the hero I needed. He'd been the hero I needed so far, the man I wanted, the one person in the entire world who could talk me down from a panic attack without making me feel small. My throat swelled just thinking about it.

When I was left alone behind my locked door, I let myself relax. I let the tears stream down my face and the horror of it all flowed freely. I screamed into my pillow so loudly that it grew painful. I was sure my throat would never recover from the night I was strangled. I hadn't heard my true voice in so long that I wondered if I was remembering it correctly.

I barely flinched when the lock clicked on the door. A second later, it swung open, and Olivia stood between the frames with the annoyed look I'd grown accustomed to.

"Follow," she said before turning and starting down the hall.

I did as I was told. I kept just close enough to her that she couldn't question my intentions. She led me down the hallway and toward the first floor where I'd learned the kitchen and dining room were. I was so used to eating in my bedroom that the sight of all the food on the dining room table seemed strange.

There were platters of sliced ham, a bowl of scrambled eggs, and several assortments of fruit and pastries that seemed like overkill considering that there were only three of us. My mind went back to the last meal I ate in this room, the Thanksgiving-like feast that still made my stomach turn.

This was a test.

"Please, sit," Paul said kindly, motioning to the long table before us.

"Thank you," I said, hoping my hoarse tone would come off remorseful enough that he wouldn't suspect anything nefarious.

"I should've asked," Paul said as he scooped scrambled eggs onto his plate. "Do you prefer your eggs scrambled or sunny-side up?"

My chest ached.

"Sunnyside-up, actually," I said, holding my breath as I waited for his and Olivia's reactions.

Thankfully, neither of them reacted to my comment. I accepted the bowl of scrambled eggs, scooping a helping onto my plate that I knew I'd have to stomach. I forced the breakfast down without alerting either of them to my feelings. Paul led me back upstairs and I focused on the path we took instead. My feet were used to the carpet runner down the hall and the soft way the stairs squished under my feet. I hadn't taken in my surroundings much before.

We passed a grant foyer when we left the dining room. Across the way was another hallway with a door at the end and several hooks along the wall that held a coat for every season and footwear to match neatly lining the wall beneath. The stairs to the second floor curved slightly to the right on the way up, the photos along the wall all of Olivia or Paul and were from different decades based on their looks. Paul led the way down the hall and to the guest room at the end that I'd grown to know so well. He held the door open for me and I slipped by him quickly, keeping quiet when Paul complimented my hair before he locked my bedroom door.

I was so used to crying after they locked the door behind me that my eyes burned at the sound. I clutched the pillow to my chest, and it was the most grounded I'd felt in days. After sliding the dresser in front of the door, I was relaxed enough to let my mind go to the real places, the scenes that would unfold if my parents knew the truth. I clung to those moments, the only moments of the day that kept me from slipping into compliance and kept me from doing everything Paul and Olivia asked.

They couldn't win.

I wouldn't let them, no matter how terrified I was.

---

The bedroom door unlocked like it had several times before, the dresser protesting as it was slowly pushed back by the door. Olivia stood in the doorway looking bored as always. She didn't even give me a command before turning and starting down the hall. I followed. I had no other choice. I could resist, but it wasn't like I had anything over the Saxons. Even if I could predict the future, what good would that do in a fight?

I followed Olivia in her skinny jeans and a black T-shirt to the same dining room I'd spent every day in. It was the only room I was allowed in other than the guest room. The only difference this time was that I had pulled on Paul's dress shirt over my stiff party dress. He noticed immediately, eyes lingering on me more than usual as I entered the room. I pulled the front of his shirt closer together to hide the little bit of cleavage that was visible.

"Beautiful," he said under his breath as he moved from the table to greet me. I allowed him to take my hand, holding my breath when he pressed his lips to my knuckles. He released my hand, but instead of lowering his fingers, they went to my face. He brushed his index and middle fingers along my cheek, and I felt the subtle throb from his slap a day ago. He ran his fingers down my jaw and to the bruises around my neck. He tutted and let out a sigh.

"Such a shame to mark such beautiful skin," he whispered and continued to trace the marks from one side of my throat to the other.

"Does it ruin your image of me?" I asked.

My heart was in my throat. It felt like I would choke on it. My stomach twisted so tightly that I thought I would throw up. The words didn't even sound like my own; it was something Angel might say. It was something he would *definitely* say and realizing it made something swell in my chest, something that took a slight edge off of my panic.

Pride.

Paul stood frozen, his fingers gently lingering just under my chin. His expression was hollow, like he'd receded inwards. His gaze met mine and made shivers shoot up my spine. His eyes were curious, but the sinister smile that spread across his lips brought my panic back in full force. Part of me wanted to apologize, but I couldn't find the words. My mouth went dry.

"You will melt at my feet soon enough," he whispered.

He turned his back on me, adjusting the front of his jacket before walking to his seat at the table.

"How about a bottle of wine?" Paul suggested, looking at his sister who reluctantly got up and moved to the liquor cabinet at the back of the dining room.

I thought it was breakfast time. A glance at the table would've been enough to tell me otherwise. There was a bowl of green beans, a salad, a basket of rolls, and a platter of chicken breasts. Who was doing the cooking this entire time? The Saxons didn't eat like this all the time, right? This was part of the show. It had to be.

"Red or white?" Olivia asked in a careless tone. She stood at my side with a bottle of each, the label of my parents' vineyard embossed around the neck.

"Red," I said hoarsely.

She lifted the wine glass from the table and filled it more than what made for a standard pour. I watched the dark liquid swirl around the glass when she put it in front of me and made her way around the table. It shimmered under the warm light, growing still in moments. That's when something else caught my attention.

The stems of the glasses were silver, a beautiful filigree holding the glass aloft. It was in one of those detailed sections that I saw my reflection for the first time. I'd been avoiding the bathroom in the guest room, afraid of the moment Paul would return. I made my trips to the toilet as few and as fast as I could, and my heart raced faster and faster with every minute I was in the room.

Dark marks encircled my throat, marks I knew matched Paul's fingers. An oblong bruise marred my left cheek as well, that side of my face slightly swollen from the slap. Strangely, I didn't feel small. I didn't feel as abused as I'm sure I looked. I was angry. I was mad that I had allowed people to push me around my entire life, even when they didn't mean to. I allowed friends and family members to assume things about me because it was easier than risking rejection or worrying about starting an argument. I put up with people who weren't always that nice to me because I wanted to avoid a confrontation.

"Why am I here?" I asked.

Paul paused with his glass to his lips before lowering it to the table.

"Because I want you here," he said like it should've been obvious.

"For fuck's sake," Olivia said, her chair scraping across the floor when she stood. I pushed myself to the back of my own chair when she charged. She grabbed my arm and shoved the sleeve of Paul's shirt back before wrapping her hand around my bare wrist. She stared at me angrily, the room going silent for a whole minute while her frown deepened, and her hand tightened around mine. For a moment, I thought she might hit me too. Instead, she groaned and tossed my hand into my lap before turning her back and walking to the back of the dining room for the cabinet. She pulled down a bottle of vodka and pulled out the stopper before taking a swig.

"What kind of witch are you?" Paul asked, looking across the table at me with admiration.

"She's a damn seer," Olivia said, looking down at the bottle with a grimace. "Not a witch."

I had to be careful what I said next. I didn't want to piss them off, but I didn't want to end the conversation either. I barely knew what I was. Maybe they could give something away that might help.

"How would you know? Have you met one before?" I asked.

Olivia snorted and raised the bottle to her lips again.

Paul laughed and stood up. He took his wine with him as he made his way around the table to me.

"Seers are rare. All the more reason to keep you around." He raised his glass in a toast to me.

"Paul," Olivia said, her tone warning.

"My sister doesn't see the point."

"I'm tired of your damn games, Paul! You always make a meal of them."

Paul whirled around to face her, red wine trickling down his glass and onto the floor. They looked at each other for a long moment before Olivia let out an annoyed sigh and reached for the cabinet. So much for a swig of the bottle. She needed a whole glass.

Paul turned back to me with a smile and closed the space between us in a few steps. He took a drink from his glass before motioning toward me with his index finger.

"Come here, Lovely," he said softly.

The tone made the hair on my arms stand up. It held a darker meaning, I knew. I was back in the forest, his arms wrapped around me from behind, that same tone whispering in my ear...

"COME HERE!"

I stood a few feet away from him before I realized I'd moved. My heart was quick in my chest. I tried slowing my breathing, focusing on what Angel would do instead of letting the panic take over.

"I shouldn't have raised my voice. Forgive me," Paul said, his soft voice so different than moments ago. He reached out and brushed a piece of my hair away from my face, hooking it behind my ear. "My sister would have me hurt you, do what I must, as with so many other pretty girls. No. You're different. The *seer*. Lovely Lily. You're different. Perfect. So damn beautiful."

He took a step closer and moved his hand to my face. I closed my eyes when I realized what he was doing. He brushed a stray tear from my cheek. I bit down on my bottom lip as it quivered, seconds away from every bit of resolve collapsing.

"Shh," he said and brushed another tear away.

I opened my eyes and found his piercing blue ones, so close. He raised his glass and this time instead of lifting it to his lips, he held it to mine. He tipped it upward and I let the wine flow over my trembling lip. He didn't stop, raising the glass until I was forced to swallow and accept the final mouthful.

He smirked.

"I'm not so bad after all, am I, Lovely?"

I spat the final drink back at him, red splattering across his face and seeping into his shirt. He took a step backward in surprise and I ran for the hall, thinking only about the floorplan I'd forced myself to memorize from all the walks to the dining room and back. I ran past the foyer and past the curved stairs, nearly tripping on a pair of boots along the wall of hooks as I reached for the handle of the door.

I pulled it open and let out a shriek when I heard his feet just behind. I tried pulling the door shut, hearing him groan as the wood bashed against him. It was enough of a distraction that my foot missed two steps to the lawn, and I fell. I tried scrambling to my feet, a scream bursting from my lips when I felt his hands push me to the ground.

He flipped me onto my back and pinned me down by my throat, straddling my chest.

"I don't like it when you fight me," he said with a growl.

I tried kneeing him between the legs but missed his most sensitive spot. I'd used enough force that it knocked him off balance and enabled me to roll to my stomach.

"Just tie her up already!" Olivia yelled.

The air rushed from my lungs when he pressed me to the ground. I tasted grass before a new sensation grabbed my attention. My wrists started to grow cold, fast. They were so cold that my fingers started to go numb. When Paul let go, my hands were bound behind me at the wrists. I remembered his powers from the fight a few days ago. Ice. I was frozen.

"Forget your damn theatrics!" Olivia yelled as my vision went dark. I recognized the feel of the silk against my eyelids. It wasn't tight, as he tied it hurriedly. A second later I was tugged roughly to my feet, light peeking out from the bottom of the scarf.

"I have a final game," Paul said, forcing me to walk ahead. We must have turned a corner because the wind caught the back of the dress shirt and tugged at the blindfold. I nearly tripped when my feet met something hard. Paul guided me to step onto the path as another gust ripped through and the scarf was pulled from my face. The red silk fluttered through the air like a streamer until it got caught against a statue of a woman with angel wings spread wide behind her. She looked far too seductive to be an angel. If she was an angel, she was a fallen one and that fit the rest of the yard perfectly. Everything in the surrounding garden was wilting or dead, the only color from the red scarf still fluttering behind the statue.

On the opposite side of the garden was a door that was set into the side of the hill. It was made of iron, the kind that looked original to the house. It was padlocked near the top and near the bottom. Olivia hurried ahead of us to reach the door, pulling a set of keys from her pocket.

"Not yet," Paul told her.

She groaned, spinning the keyring around her index finger before catching both keys against her palm.

Paul held me in place before moving from behind me. He stood inches away, staring at me for a long moment before a sinister smirk pulled across his face and the rest of my body went as cold as the ice binding my wrists.

"Don't make me do this, Lovely," he said and reached out to cup my face.

Tears of fear blurred my vision, and I was kept from letting a sob escape when I felt his finger brush the tender bruise on my cheek. I had very few options left. I could only control so much, but making myself as undesirable to him as I could was still within my power.

"I would rather spend my life locked behind that door than

anywhere near you," I said, my voice shaky. Still, I meant what I said and the rejection sealed my fate as Paul Saxon's expression fell.

I was prepared to take another hit. I was sure he'd lash out again.

He raised his hands to the top of his head and sucked in a deep breath. He turned away from me and I could tell this was different than before. He wasn't just angry. I hit a nerve. I wasn't sure how, but his resolve cracked under my insult, and he wasn't sure how to handle it.

"Unlock it. Unlock it. Fucking unlock it!" he said as Olivia turned toward the door with the keyring in her hand.

The first lock pulled away with a loud clank and she passed it off to Paul before moving to the bottom lock. It had just opened when Paul lunged. I felt the sting first, my body going tingly as I realized what he'd done. The knife in his hand dripped blood onto the cement path. Olivia pulled the lock from the door as I felt the deep burn from the slash across my right bicep. I caught a glimpse of the red seeping into the button-up shirt before he grabbed me again. His hands went to my wrists as he urged me forward. I heard a crack and my stomach turned in panic before it became clear that he had broken my icy restraints so my hands weren't bound behind me.

The door opened to a room of darkness and Paul shoved me inside.

"See you later, Lovely," Paul said as though the whole event had been a joke. "Or not."

The door shut behind me and I heard the first padlock snap into place. The second was drowned out by a hiss. My head snapped up and after a moment of panic, I realized the room wasn't as dark as it seemed.

There was a single, exposed bulb halfway through the long room and at the very back, was a black mass. Another blink and I could make out that it was a body, a kind of creature, something with wings...

My body went limp when I realized what I was staring at.

Angel's face looked longer than normal. His ears were tapered to points. His hands went to his shoulders, fingers long, so long that I knew the tips had to be razor-like talons. They clenched into fists, claws digging into his shoulders until I saw blood seep into the white fabric of his dress shirt. He closed his eyes and looked up to the ceiling, letting out a hiss of anger mixed with what sounded like a frustrated groan. He let out a single yell toward the ceiling and his claws cut through the fabric of his shirt, shredding it so it clung to his chest by thin ribbons.

It wasn't until he pressed his back against the wall behind him that I saw the worst of it. His wings stayed spread wide from one end of the room to the other. A thick chain was threaded through the center of each wing. They had healed around the wounds, leaving him bound to the far side of the room. He'd have to rip through his own wings to free himself. From the look of the holes, he'd tried several times.

Angel lowered her gaze from the ceiling. His deep, red eyes met mine.

# CHAPTER 25

"**S**tay there!"

Angel's words cut through the room when I took a step forward. I froze. His chest rose and fell with each deep breath. A sound halfway between a groan and a growl filled the space between us as he pressed himself closer to the back wall. He sucked in a deep breath and held it for a long moment before exhaling.

"Tie off that cut," he said. With a single pull, he ripped what was left of his shirt from his chest. He balled it up and threw it as far as he could. It landed five feet in front of me. I hesitated a moment before slowly walking forward to take it, noticing that he kept his worried gaze on me.

"Are you okay?" I asked as I picked up the shirt.

"Lily," he said, his words almost a plea.

I pulled off the button-up and started assessing the scrap of Angel's shirt. My stomach turned when I saw the cut across my right bicep. It was deep enough that it would probably scar without stitches. I began wrapping the fabric around the wound as tightly as I could bear, tying the ends together to create a crude bandage before I reluctantly pulled the shirt back on to help mask the smell.

"Okay," I whispered, looking over myself for any other marks. "It's covered."

"I know," he said roughly.

"You can probably smell"

"I see," Angel corrected.

I looked up at him and noticed the way he stared at me. His eyes were trained on my face, his expression full of concern despite his piercing red eyes.

"Are you okay?" I asked again.

"Just stay there," he said with a curt nod.

"They... What did they do?"

"Nothing I can't withstand," he said, trying to keep his voice calm. "What I can't endure is you any closer. Seeing you here, knowing you're with me... It helps the urge."

Oh.

"D-Did you feed?" I asked, taking a few steps back so he might relax. Thankfully, it worked, and his wings relaxed a fraction against their restraints.

Angel shook his head.

"They ambushed me. They told me they had you. He had your..." He sucked in a deep breath, his body tensing. "He showed me your clothing. I did everything they said because I thought you needed me. I didn't want anything to happen to you and you weren't even here. It was a trick to separate us."

He slammed his fist against the wall behind him and I felt the bricks under my feet vibrate from the force. I started walking toward him, getting three steps ahead before he snapped again.

"STAY BACK!"

My heart skipped in my chest. That tone... Even though I knew he wasn't mad, it made me nervous. Panic began tightening around my chest as I thought about how long he'd been down here, how much longer we both would be, the position that might put him in. Angel's expression softened when it met mine.

"Stay there, Mouse," he said. "Please."

My entire body ached more than before to reach him, despite his fear. He wouldn't hurt me. He said that looking at me helped ease the urge. Seeing my face made it easier. So, I kept my eyes on him and started to walk forward despite his silent pleading.

"Mouse," he whispered as I reached the lightbulb overhead. "Lily," he said, this time more forceful.

I stopped just a few feet in front of him, far enough away that I knew the chains would keep him away, but almost close enough to touch him. I kept my eyes on his face, and he didn't look away from me.

"You won't hurt me," I said.

"I don't want to."

"You won't."

"Lily, if I do—"

"You won't," I said and took another step forward. I was just a foot away from him now. He kept his hands by his sides. "You told me you won't. You told me no one would ever hurt me again."

"If I move even an inch toward you"

"Is that knife still at your hip?" I asked.

His lip curved upward in a smile that made my eyes burn. I saw that his were glistening. He took a deep breath and then a slow step forward so his bare chest was nearly against mine. After a long moment, I raised my hand and lightly touched his skin. I waited in case it was too much, but he didn't react. I slid my hand over his stomach and to his chest, pressing firmly against him.

He exhaled.

"I won't hurt you," he whispered, so quietly that I knew the words were meant for him.

"You won't hurt me," I echoed.

He nodded and his gaze moved from mine for the first time. My stomach twisted when I saw the fear cross his expression again. He raised a hand to my face, gently touching the bruise on my cheek. I could feel his eyes roving over me now, stopping halfway down my face. A growl rumbled in his chest as he raised both his hands to my neck, running gentle fingers over the marks around my throat.

"I'm okay," I said, glad I got the words out when I did. A tear slipped down Angel's cheek, and I brushed it away with my thumb. He captured my hand in his, giving it a tight squeeze before lowering it from his face.

He brushed the hair from my face, a hand lingering at the base of my neck. I could feel the pressure building in my chest. His other hand slid around my waist, pulling me close just as everything fell apart.

---

The room behind the iron door in the hill was a wine cellar. I was so focused on Angel that I didn't get a good look at the space until after my eyes were puffy and sore from crying. Metal racks full of glass bottles stretched the length of the room. The chains threaded through Angel's wings were attached to the metal racks. They were tethered high enough that Angel couldn't lie down. The most he could do was kneel on the brick floor. He didn't need to sleep, but I could tell that being forced to stand most of the time exhausted him in different ways and annoyed him more than anything.

The first night, I slept with my head propped on his knees with his arms around me. I woke from my nightmare, my skin slick with sweat.

"Just a dream," he said, brushing his hand across my brow.

I nodded, but his words didn't calm my nerves. A rumble from my stomach distracted me for a moment. I didn't regret anything about how I had acted the previous night in the Saxon house. I did wish I had eaten more though.

"I'll get us out," Angel said. "The next time that door opens, I'll get us out. I'll rip my own wings off to get to him."

I knew he meant it. I also knew that he wasn't the same. He tried to hide it from me, but his body wasn't strong the way it normally was. His eyes were a deep red now, even when he looked back at me and kissed me softly. There was a tense moment that came with each touch, a brief second when my fingers would meet his, and by the end of the second day, he shied away when I shifted forward to kiss him.

"You won't hurt me," I told him. "You won't."

He shook his head, opening his mouth before pausing. He lowered his hands from mine, letting them rest by his sides.

"I need to get you out of here," he said.

"The next time the door opens, I can attack. Maybe I can hit him with a wine bottle"

"No," Angel said and shook his head. "*Now*. I'm going to get you out now."

"How? You're chained and the door is locked."

"Somehow. I have to get you out of here," he said.

The chains rattled as his wings flexed. I noticed the way his body tensed, and I took a step back to give him space. He looked at the chain attached to his left wing, reaching for the chain where it was stuck through the webbing.

"We have to be smart about this. Angel, we can't use all our energy without a solid plan."

"You don't understand," he said, tone sharp enough to send a jolt through my stomach. He looked back at me with those piercing red eyes, his expression intense. "The smell of you..."

"You won't hurt me."

He shook his head and looked back at the chain.

"It's not the hunger," he said and tugged hard on the chain. It groaned but remained firmly latched to the metal wine rack built into the wall. "You need a doctor."

My eyes followed his gaze to my right arm. It was sore and a little warm. I'd never had an injury like this before, so I didn't know what was normal. Maybe it wasn't supposed to feel this way.

"I-I'm all right," I said meekly.

"No," he said, voice firm. "You're at risk of an infection. You need stitches. I'm going to get you out now."

He looked back at the chains, this time focusing on the length attached to his right wing. He pulled hard again and when that didn't work, his breathing picked up pace. He looked taller, more muscular and I noticed when he turned toward me again that his face was longer. His ears were tapered. He adjusted his stance, bracing his feet beneath him.

"Angel," I said. My heart was a hummingbird in my chest.

"Stand back, Mouse," he said gruffly.

My legs felt like lead and no amount of reason could spur them to action right away. Angel's deep breaths started to sound more like growls and his expression was less like him than ever. It was chilling, eyes locked on the ceiling above me.

"STAND BACK!"

His voice ripped through the room and seemed to echo forever. Every nerve in my body activated and I tossed myself against the wine rack on the left before I realized I had even moved. Angel let out another roar and launched forward in a blur of dark wings and bare flesh. His scream echoed off the bricks for a long second; I was sure I would never forget it. My stomach turned at the sound that came next. Two rips, a thick sound that only made Angel scream louder. Then, he stumbled forward and landed on his hands and knees against the floor.

He caught himself, pausing for a moment as the silence sucked all the air from the cellar. He lowered his forehead to the bricks and let out a deep roar into the floor, every muscle along his back tensing. His black wings draped around him and obscured him, giving me a clear look at the mess of shredded webbing.

I nearly threw up.

The chains had pulled and stretched the dark webbing until Angel had ripped himself free from the restraints. Dark blood dripped from the tips of his bat-like wings and onto the bricks. He would heal. Vampires healed faster than humans. Still, they were immune to death, but not pain.

"Don't," he said.

I'd barely taken a step forward. Of course, he'd heard me.

"Your wings..."

"They'll heal," Angel said. He let out a deep breath and lifted his head from the floor. "I'll be able to retract them in an hour."

He sat back on his heels, running a hand to the top of his head and pulling the elastic from his hair. He shook his head, dark hair stretching toward his shoulders. He combed his hands through the tendrils and began gathering it again at the top of his head, using the elastic to tie it into his signature topknot.

My chest was tight. I tried blinking away the tears, but they fell hot over my cheeks anyway. I couldn't move, couldn't pull my gaze from his tattered wings.

"Shh, Mouse," Angel said, back to his calm voice as though he hadn't just ripped himself from a wall. "Deep breaths."

"I'm trying. I'm trying," I said, the dizziness so disorienting that I lowered myself to the floor just in case I collapsed.

"You're safe. I'm free. I'll be healed soon, and I'll get you out of here," he said.

A sob burst from my chest. My vision blurred and I was sure I'd black out. I was seconds away, I was sure. Everything felt hot, like I'd been running instead of trying to keep my feet under me. When I lifted my hand from the floor, Angel's was there. He lifted my hands to his chest before holding my face between his hands. His wings draped around us, sending a rush of air over me to match the coolness of his touch.

"Big breath in," he said, his chest swelling under my hands. I kept my eyes on him and pulled air into my lungs until I felt his chest sinking. I followed the rise and fall of his chest, my body relaxing with each breath. I noticed more about him as my muscles eased.

There was a subtle darkness beneath his eyes. I found myself inches from his chest before I realized I'd reacted to how good he smelled. That deep, almost floral smell was stronger than normal, and desire contracted in my center when a deep sound rumbled in his throat. His hands slid around my waist, and he pulled my hips against his. I could feel his need rise to meet mine, the pressure just enough that I tipped my head back just as he let out a groan of pleasure, lips parted enough that I could see the length of his fangs.

The next growl that came was of frustration and it sent a jolt through my body. I was alone. My hands were still suspended in the air in front of me, but Angel was kneeling at the back of the room again next to the discarded chains.

My body was still buzzing with lust. I could still feel him between my legs...

"I just need a moment to heal, and get my bearings," Angel said.

I was still recovering from the heated moment.

"Okay," I said. "Time."

"A little time," he agreed with a nod.

Time was not something we could afford.

Time was something we had very little of.

I would've held him tighter if I had known.

# CHAPTER 26

I was startled awake. My neck tensed painfully as I pushed myself from the brick floor. I massaged the sore spot as I reminded myself that I had been dreaming. I looked at the opposite side of the room and saw Angel kneeling at the end, crimson eyes watching me with concern. His wings were still stretched wide and though they weren't in tatters like before, they were only partially healed. There was still a large slit in each where the chains had pierced, though the smaller cuts had healed.

"I should be healed soon," he said.

I glanced around the room out of habit. There wasn't a clock or a window in the place. From the relaxed way my muscles felt, I had to have been asleep for a while. It felt like hours, long past the amount of time it should've taken him to heal.

"You need to feed," I said, a pang of worry shooting through my gut as I accepted what that would mean.

"No," he said firmly.

"You need to be strong when we escape."

"Absolutely not."

"You said it earlier. You need to be focused. You need to heal, and you will much faster if you've fed."

"I won't use you that way," he said, standing up.

I rose the same time he did, taking several steps toward him until he raised a hand toward me.

"You won't hurt me," I said, knowing he would have to for this to work.

"I don't *feed*, Lily," he said. "I always kill. I've never tried to stop once I've started. I let the urge take over until I've had what's left. I won't risk you."

"We might be dead either way. Why not try?"

"I won't be!"

The words came out almost like a snarl. He looked away as soon as they flew from his lips, his hands going to the top of his head. He took a sobering breath before looking at me again.

"Whatever happens, I'll still be here. I can't... I already despise what I am. I won't suffer another minute of my existence if it means ending yours."

His eyes were glazed, full of so much emotion that it made my chest hurt. I didn't want to do this. I didn't want to pressure him, but it was already killing me inside to watch him struggle the way he was. He told me before what happened the last time he was locked away like this. He told me how he starved and desecrated, withering away into something barely human. He was out of his mind with hunger, unable to stop himself.

The risk would be less if we tried now.

"It's been decades since the tomb," I said, slowly making my way toward him. I pushed Paul's button-up from my shoulders and let it fall to the ground behind me. "You can do this. You won't hurt me."

With two final steps, I reached him and pressed my fingers against his palms. Instead of lacing his hands with mine, he raised one to my cheek.

"I love you," he said and pressed his lips to my forehead.

"I love you," I replied.

He backed away, turning toward the metal rack along the long wall behind us. He lifted a dusty bottle from the rack by the neck and tapped it against the metal hard enough that it shattered and sent red wine splattering across the brick floor. What was left of the bottle in his hand was a jagged piece of glass. He walked back to me with that bottle, held by the neck like a dagger, and I prepared to feel the sting of the sharp edge when he took my right hand.

Instead, he pressed the neck into my palm. He moved his hand to my forearm and tugged me forward. I gasped as the point of the bottle grazed the spot just under his ribcage, a thin line of blood trickling down his stomach.

"Keep it right here," he said in my ear, reminding me of the words he'd told me days ago.

I wanted to shrink away. I wanted to put another inch between the sharpness of the bottle and his skin, at least. Angel held my arm just a moment longer, giving me a second to calm my breathing. I nodded and his grip loosened.

"You can do it, Mouse," he whispered.

"I won't have to," I replied.

He didn't say a word in response. It sent chills over my skin.

He stood perfectly still for a moment. I worried that I would have to promise it would be all right again before he would move. I flinched when he finally did.

"It will only hurt for a second, Mouse, just a second." His hand moved to the back of my neck, cradling my head. The other hand brushed my hair from my shoulder. He rubbed his thumb back and forth along the space of skin that stretched between my neck and shoulder. I knew he was doing it for my benefit, preparing me for what would follow.

He moved his hand to my shoulder and lowered his lips toward me. I sucked in a deep breath, a whimper escaping my lips when I felt the pinch. It stung, making my eyes water for just a second before the sensation changed. It dulled to a throb, warmth spreading in my core as his lips pressed tighter against my skin.

I arched against him, remembering the bottle in my hand when the glass slipped a little between my fingers. I focused on holding it steady, but the warmth was spreading, and my heart picked up pace. My free hand went to the front of his pants, pulling him flush against me as the smell of him made me squirm.

The pain in my shoulder was growing to a burn, fueling the need deep within me and leaving me wanting more at the same time. I wanted him to hold me tighter. I wanted to feel the sweet pain alongside soft touches, feel his hard body melt against mine.

The sound of glass shattering pulled me from the moment just long enough that I remembered the reason for what I was feeling.

My right hand was empty now, my only weapon in pieces on the floor. It crunched under Angel's feet as he turned us, my back pressed to the wall. He groaned at my shoulder, the sound almost a plea before he ripped himself away from me. His head tipped back as he let out a loud gasp, blood dripping from his lower lip and down his chin. He wiped his mouth on his forearm, looking back at me with amber eyes that made everything within me clench. His hands went to the bandage on my right arm, pulling the fabric away from the wound. He lowered his lips to the cut. I could feel the skin grow warm. The soreness melted away with every stroke of his tongue.

He straightened up, cradling my head again before he pressed his lips back to the bite at my neck. The burning faded as he used his vampire powers to accelerate the healing. I felt such a mix of emotions that it was exhausting. I wanted to sleep. I wanted to curl up in a warm bed with his arms around me and drift into a dreamless sleep. More than rest, I wanted his body against mine. I wanted his hands on me, his lips on mine...

"Damn it, Mouse," Angel said, breathless when he pulled away.

I opened my mouth to beg for more, but his attention rose to a spot above me on the wall. As curiosity replaced the desire, his wings began to shrink until they were gone entirely. I stepped away, turning to see what he'd noticed. The bricks were splattered with my blood, a few smears across the wall from where he'd pressed his hands. My stomach dropped.

"My dream," I said as it all fell into place. My reoccurring dream. Everything Angel and the Saxons' had said about me being a seer.

I moved closer to the wall to get a better look. Blood dripped over the bricks and into the grout between them. I followed one drop as it rolled down the wall until it slipped between a brick and vanished. There was a crack in the wall. It was a long crack that stretched several feet.

Not a crack. It was a door. At least, it once had been.

"No way," I said, excitement building in my chest.

Angel gently pulled me to one side and moved to the wall, running his hand over the spot and tracing all the way around, following where the jamb on a door would go. Then, he stepped back and with a single kick, the bricks smashed apart. The light from the bulb stretched just far enough into the space to make out where it went.

The floor sloped upward. It was a concrete ramp, the kind you might use to move wine barrels into the cellar or move large amounts of bottles. I followed Angel into the hall, taking the ramp up to the wooden door at the top. Dirt cascaded down on us when he tapped his fist against it.

"I bet the grass grew over it," I said.

"Not anymore," Angel said and motioned for me to back up. "Let's get out of here."

I moved out of the way. He went to the end of the ramp where he had to crouch to keep his head from bashing the wooden door. He placed both of his hands against it and with a push, it flew from the ground, and we were blinded by sunlight.

Once my eyes adjusted, I stepped through the hole in the ground and onto the grass. We were on the backside of the hill. I could see the top floor of the house.

"The car might still be parked out front," I said, looking back at Angel.

He studied our surroundings, eyes lingering on the back door to the estate for a moment before he looked at me.

"I can hotwire the car. You can drive to the nearest hospital. I'll meet you there," he said.

"What? Without you? I can't"

"I need to get you to safety first," Angel said, cupping the side of my face.

I shook my head as my stomach twisted.

"I can't leave without you," I said.

My anxiety must have shown because he softened against me. He pulled me to his chest and kissed my forehead.

"All right. We go together," he said and pulled back, moving his hand to mine. I laced my fingers between his and followed him to the side of the hill.

The garden was empty. The concrete path split between four quadrants; the angel statue was positioned in the center ahead of us. The four flower beds were mostly brown and wilted, but the far-right section looked different than before. The ground was disturbed, fresh dirt replacing the dead flowers I remembered being there.

Angel led the way past the statue, slowing as we got closer to the flower bed. He pulled me closer by our entwined hands, moving so he was standing on my right. He didn't move in time, and I caught sight of what he intended to hide from me.

The dirt looked fresh because it was. A shovel laid on the concrete path. There was a hole in the middle of the flower bed, a deep rectangle deep enough that it must have taken someone several hours to create it. Lying farther away from the shovel were several wooden stakes and next to the pile of dirt in the flower bed was a spear with a wooden tip. My stomach twisted and I froze.

"Not here," Angel said and pulled me to his hip. "Deep breaths. Focus on the way ahead."

I kept my eyes on the spot ahead, remembering how Paul had pinned me to the grass. A shiver shot up my spine and I was sure I could still feel the icy shackles around my wrists.

"You can do this," Angel said beside me, urging me forward again after I'd stopped.

I nearly jumped out of my skin when the gunshot echoed through the yard.

I was pressed to Angel's cool chest seconds later, cradled snugly in his arms as we rose into the air so fast that it made my stomach churn. Another gunshot rang out and Angel let out a groan. I rocked in his arms like a plane in turbulence before he righted himself, rising another yard toward the sky when a third shot pierced the air and Angel let out a sound between a yell and a growl.

I screamed when my legs tipped toward the garden. He adjusted his grip on me, arms wrapped around my middle as we fell toward the ground. The lawn rushed toward us and he roared again, using his wings to slow us enough that instead of smashing to the earth, we slid several feet across the grass.

The shock of the fall left me so stunned that it wasn't until Angel knelt in front of me with his wings shielding me from view that I even considered the possibility of being injured.

"Shit," Angel said.

I followed his gaze to my leg where the swelling had already started around my ankle. I thought the darkness on top of my foot was just dirt from sliding along the ground, but I could see now that it was my swollen and bruised skin. Just when I thought I would for sure throw up, the pain came. It shot through my foot and up my shin and I whimpered at the same time as the gunshot came, much closer this time than before.

Angel leaned closer, his scream echoing in my left ear.

"Let's go. We have to go!" I cried, feeling my hands shake as I debated if touching my leg would help or make things worse. I knew trying to stand on it would be disastrous. I could tell just from the look of it alone that I couldn't withstand the pain.

"I can't fly," Angel said.

The gunshot came from the other side of the garden. Angel nearly fell against me, his scream of pain sounding more animalistic than before. When he raised himself again, spreading his wings wide around us, I could see that he was angry. His ears were pointed, his fangs bared and his eyes dark. His wings even looked different, larger than I remembered.

"You're shot. We have to go," I said, slapping the front of his chest in hopes that it would pull him out of predator mode. It did for a moment, his eyes falling on mine below him.

"Two more," Angel said just as another shot rang out.

He let out another yell. The next shot sounded close enough to make me feel faint, Angel's scream of pain mixing with my own plea for help. The air went silent. Then, I heard a click. A strong wind struck me full in the face and Angel's dark wings were no longer wrapped around me.

They were stretched high, Angel standing yards away from me now as he faced Olivia Saxon. She swung the butt of the rifle at his head. Instead of making contact, there was a blur of movement. Angel stood in front of her with the rifle in his hands. It sliced through the air, warping when it made contact with Olivia's skull.

She collapsed limply to the ground.

Angel turned to look at me, starting forward when a strange crackle echoed through the garden. He slipped, falling on a sheet of ice that had developed on the grass separating us.

"Angel!"

I saw Paul to my left. He lowered his arm from where it was pointed at Angel and he burst into a sprint, heading straight for me. I tried scrambling to my feet, the pain shooting hot through my right leg and sending every thought of escape from my mind.

It had to be broken. Shattered. Damn, this hurt!

Angel's scream pierced the air and made my skin go cold. I looked up from the grass and straight into his painted expression. Paul stood next to me; he held a spear of ice between both hands. The end jabbed through the webbing of Angel's left wing. Angel let out a hiss and backed away, blood flecking onto the grass as he prepared to fight.

"Hello, Lovely," Paul said and winked at me before moving his gaze to my injured ankle. He made a tutting sound. "What's this, a little bump?"

I screamed when he smacked my ankle with the end of the spear. His laughter was cut off when Angel launched at him, both men falling over my shoulder and skidding along the concrete. They broke apart when they hit the angel statue.

Paul had scrapes along his right arm and across his face when he stood up. His spear was shattered around them. Angel rose to his feet without a wince despite the long tear in his wing and the bullet holes that marred the other. Before he could make a move, Paul iced the path beneath them. I could feel the chill settle in the air from his powers and a deranged smirk replaced what little bit of fear had been in his expression before.

"Before we do this little number," Paul said and motioned between himself and Angel, "I'd like to know how you managed to escape."

"I'd like to put your head on that spear," Angel said with a growl.

"Ooh," Paul said with a laugh. He relaxed his stance, crossing his arms. "You don't have to get defensive. I'm just impressed. I must say, I've never met a vampire who is so... controlled when it comes to his powers."

Angel stretched his wings as though preparing to use them to launch himself at Paul before he caught a look at them. They would heal, but not fast enough to be useful during this fight. Paul had his powers, the ability to navigate the ice like no one else could. He had the advantage.

I caught Angel's gaze, his eyes lingering on me long enough that Paul noticed.

"Did you feed?" Paul asked, amused as he looked from Angel to me and then at Angel again. "How did you do it? Did you lure her close, maybe even seduce her?"

Movement from the left caught my attention. Olivia had healed. She was disheveled but ran at Angel with a shovel held above her. Before I could alert him, Angel turned and caught the shovel by the head with both hands. They froze for a second before a crack rang out and the shovel split in two.

Olivia lunged with the splintered wood pointed at Angel's stomach. He stepped aside at the last second, the end of the broken shovel bashing Paul in the gut as he moved to intervene. He staggered backward, slipping on the icy path and falling into a flowerbed of dead tulips. As Olivia pulled the wooden pole back for another attack, Angel swiped the head of the shovel across his body with such immense force that it cut through the air like an airplane propeller.

A line of scarlet blossomed across Olivia's throat. Her lips parted in shock and eyes widened. I heard Paul gasp, insults flying from his lips as Olivia staggered toward the angel statue. Fear replaced the shock on her face, and she took another step to place the statue between her and Angel. Angel tossed the shovel aside and turned to face her. She tripped, bracing herself on the pedestal of the statue.

Before she could move, Angel grabbed her arms and pulled her chest flush against the statue. He turned to face me with Olivia's arms pulled tight around his chest like she was hugging him from behind.

"Don't look," he told me, voice breaking with emotion.

I didn't.

I winced at the pain in my leg as I shifted on the grass, closing my eyes and then covering my ears when I heard a series of pops and cracks. I stayed like that until Paul started screaming again. He scooted farther away from the garden, off the icy path and now lying in the grass as he yelled at Angel, his face red and spit flying from his lips.

Angel took slow steps toward him, stopping as he reached the grass.

Paul stopped screaming and scrambled to his feet, shaking as he continued to back away. His eyes were wide with fear, no longer the charismatic gentleman he was known as at the country club. He slowed his steps until he was standing still, his body relaxed and his eyes darting toward the house and then the trees several yards to his right.

"Run," Angel said in a calm, deep tone.

Paul didn't hesitate. It was eerily silent in the garden as his feet padded against the grass. Angel watched for a long moment, his eyes trained on the man as he ran so hard that he nearly tripped several times on the uneven ground. He was halfway to the trees when Angel vanished a dark blur across the lawn. I didn't think to look away, too transfixed with horror at what was unfolding.

Angel's wings spread wide behind him as he rose into the air, landing in a crouch on Paul Saxon's shoulders like a wolf attacking a deer. As they went tumbling, Angel pushed away from him and used his wings to glide to the ground where he landed easily on his feet. He turned from the trees and there was no mistaking even from yards away what he held between his hands.

As Angel tossed Paul's head to the ground, my vision blurred and I felt my own sinking into the grass beneath me.

# CHAPTER 27

When I regained consciousness, Angel was buckling me into the passenger seat of the SUV. My stomach twisted and every bump in the road toward the highway made my ankle ache.

"Almost there," Angel said, reaching over the center console for my hand.

I didn't realize what he meant until we pulled into the hospital parking lot. The little bit of control I had left crumbled, and the sob slipped past my lips. I couldn't get a full breath. My head throbbed and I felt dizzy. My chest hurt. My stomach hurt. My leg hurt. Everything hurt and the last thing I wanted was to be here.

"It only gets better from here," Angel said when he opened my door and scooped me into his arms.

"I can't... I've never been..." I said into his neck.

He held me close and hurried toward the front entrance, barely jostling me.

"I'll stay with you," he promised as we passed through the sliding doors and into the lobby of the emergency room.

Part of me wanted to wait. I needed to prepare myself, to get a grip of the panic clawing at my chest. The rural hospital was empty, so a pair of women in scrubs were ready with a wheelchair before Angel could finish talking to the nurse at the counter.

"I got her," he told the nurse with the wheelchair when I tightened my grip around his neck.

"This way," the second woman said, leading the way through a double-wide door and down the quiet hallway.

The room was brightly lit and had light-blue wallpaper and posters about cleaning procedures near the sink in the corner. Angel sat me on the bed while the nurses talked to each other and milled about the room. A chair scraped against the tile floor as he dragged it away from the wall to sit next to me. He held my hand when I felt my pulse quicken.

"She's never been in a hospital before," Angel said, garnering the attention of the doctor as she entered the room. "She has panic attacks."

"What's your relationship to Lily?" the doctor asked as she snapped on a pair of latex gloves.

My stomach twisted. Angel gave my hand a gentle squeeze.

"I'm her boyfriend," he said.

One of the nurses approached me with a stretchy band that she began to wrap tightly around my bicep. My head swam when I saw the needle.

"Eyes on me, Mouse," Angel said just low enough for me to hear. He was close, his face inches from mine and brown eyes so warm I wanted to dive into them and never surface. He cupped the side of my face and brushed away a tear just as I felt the pinch at my elbow. Angel leaned in and kissed my forehead, relaxing me just enough so that the nurse could finish with the IV before moving to the computer screen in the corner.

"Sir, I'm going to ask you to step out for a moment," the doctor said.

My heart leaped in my throat and I opened my mouth to protest, gripping Angel's fingers as they slipped from my grasp.

"I'll be right outside," he said and pressed a kiss to my cheek. I bit hard on my lower lip and nodded as he stood up.

I'd forgotten until now that he was still shirtless. He'd healed since the attack, not a single mark marring the skin of his back as he left me alone in the room with the two nurses and the doctor.

———

The first thing they asked was if I felt safe with Angel. I was offended at first that anyone would think he was abusive before the doctor told me they were just following procedure. When they asked what happened, I told them about Paul Saxon attacking me at the pool house as if I'd rehearsed the words.

I felt numb. It didn't seem like my story, I felt so... It was like I was replaying the scene from above as I told it and not like it was me lying on the kitchen floor. I did cry when I reached the end where Angel and I were locked in the wine cellar together, leaving out all the parts about supernatural powers and vampires. It wasn't out of fear or panic like before. I felt angry. I was mad that it had happened, that I made Angel leave to hunt, and that I decided to go to the barn and face my anxiety that night without him.

I was glad when they let Angel come back in and they moved me to a less sterile room where they dimmed the lights and left us alone while they waited for my X-ray to come back. The pain meds in my IV made me relax and I noticed how sore my muscles were. It felt like I had run a marathon. Angel sat next to me, this time in an armchair that he'd pulled next to the bed, and I lay down and listened to the beep of the monitor while he stroked my hair.

Angel smiled back at me from his chair when I opened my eyes, feeling like I'd slept for days rather than just a few hours.

"You have a lateral malleolus fracture," he said with a comforting smile. "They're going to set you up with some medication and a boot. The police want to take a statement from you, but I encouraged them to wait until you woke up."

From the way he smiled, I knew that "encouraged" was putting it nicely.

"What about the Saxons?" I asked, a little surprised that I could even think about them without a jolt shooting through my chest. Whatever medication they had me on was doing its part.

Angel's smile dimmed and he took my hand, kissing the back of it.

239

"I wasn't going to leave you. I won't leave you," he said as I scooted into a sitting position against the pillows. "The police went to the Saxons and they were gone. There's proof of us being held there, but that's all."

He sent me a knowing look and it took a moment for it all to come together in my mind. Paul and Olivia were guardians. Guardians were immortal. Their broken bodies must have pieced themselves back together before they fled. The first thing I learned about the supernatural world was that it was extremely good at staying under the radar.

The police would never find Paul or Olivia Saxon.

"I shouldn't have made you go"

"Stop," Angel said, his tone firm. His hands were soft on mine, such a contrast to his serious expression that made my stomach clench. I wanted to look away. My cheeks burned with embarrassment. He lifted my chin gently, forcing me to look at him.

"You are not responsible for my decisions. You are not responsible for the way anyone behaves. You shouldn't apologize for how you feel, no matter how other people react when you express that. You are kind and empathetic. You are so damn considerate, and I love that about you, but it makes you question yourself and I wish you wouldn't."

"I'm sorry," I said, realizing as the words fell from my lips that I was doing exactly what he was trying to tell me I shouldn't. I didn't need to.

"Listen to me," he pleaded, drawing closer so he was inches from my face. "You need to know that it wasn't your fault. You were taken advantage of. Someone abused the kindness in your heart. You don't have to hide your feelings or your desires. I know that you're scared. You don't want to hurt people. You don't want your problems to be someone else's, but you are the brightest light I've ever encountered in my dark world, and I won't let anything dim that. Not fucking Paul Saxon. Not your parents' expectations. Not the world. Not even you, Mouse. You are worthy of exactly what you want in life. I won't let you settle for anything less, because you are worth it."

"Angel," I said, hating how petulant I sounded. I was past stomach-twisting awkwardness. I knew he was right, but it made me uncomfortable. It made me feel demanding when I knew it shouldn't. What was wrong with me?

"I can put you over my shoulder again if it helps," he said with a smile. "That seems to make you pretty assertive."

My cheeks heated at the memory.

"It's easier when..." I suddenly felt so embarrassed that I had to look away. I sat back against the pillows on the bed, my eyes burning. I wasn't sure if the tears were a reaction to the embarrassment or because I was trying not to acknowledge what I'd known the entire time.

"I won't love you any less if you tell me why," he said, sitting back in his chair. For once, I was glad that he didn't touch me. I needed the space, physically and mentally. I'd pinned the thoughts down for so long that saying the truth aloud sounded insane even though I knew it to be exactly that.

"I know it sounds stupid, but it makes me feel powerful when you're in control. I don't know what it is. It's stupid," I said.

"It's not stupid," Angel said with a small laugh. "And I'm not in control. It only seems like it because you allow it. You hold all the power. I've never been the man in charge, just the man trying to fit whatever you need. I'll hold you when you cry. I'll stand up for you when you need me to. I'll even tell you when you're selling yourself short, which is a lot of the time, Mouse."

I felt the smile tug at the corners of my lips. Angel took my hands in his, letting out a deep breath. His smile dimmed a little, making me nervous. I wanted to pull away from him and crawl into his lap all at the same time.

"Tell me if I'm wrong," he started and lowered his eyes to our hands. The pressure in my chest lessened. "All the panic attacks you've had when I'm around, they seem to come during times you're fighting to stay in control or when you worry that you might not be in control. Is that maybe why it feels empowering when I take charge? It's a kind of controlled release, a moment when you allow me to be in charge?"

A weird feeling came over me. I wanted to cry but also didn't feel like I could. It wasn't numbness, exactly. It was more like relief, like something fell into place that would normally have sent it all crashing around me.

"I think..." I said slowly, taking a moment to gather my thoughts. "I think that I need to let go. I want to. I really want to. I think I need to learn to let someone else take charge first before I can figure out how to take charge myself."

"Then we'll start there," Angel said, cutting off the panic as it built in my chest.

---

My parents were a mess. Dad spent most of the time on the phone with the various connections he had. Nothing came of any of those phone conversations. Paul and Olivia were long gone. Mom suggested that I spend more time at home while my fractured ankle healed. I knew it was her own way of helping, probably for the same reason I did the things I did. She just wanted to know that I was okay. It was that realization that made me feel good about my decision to go back to the city.

Angel and I left before I was fully ready, but I knew that I never would feel ready. I had to take the leap and accept that I could do this on my own, with Angel's help of course. The drive home was quiet, but not uncomfortable. I was surprised by how excited I felt when we reached my apartment building. My heart hammered in my chest on the elevator ride up and I could hardly get the key to turn in the door, I was so happy to be home.

I walked between every room, even looking over Anne's even though I knew she was still with Jazz visiting family. After I'd soaked in the familiar smell of the lavender candles we lit whenever we were home, I lay in bed and watched as Angel unpacked my suitcase and gathered dirty laundry.

I woke up slick with sweat. The room was dark. I never kept it this dark in my room. Was I in my room? I could smell the dusty cellar. I could feel the cold air on my arms, choking on the stuffy air. There was no way it was real, but I swore I could taste metal in my mouth

"You're home. It's a dream," Angel said in my ear.

"Lights," I managed to say between gasps.

He was gone and back in seconds, his weight settling onto the mattress next to me as my eyes adjusted to the purple light that filled the room. I forced myself to take a deep breath despite the ache in my chest telling me I'd suffocate. I knew he was right. It was just a dream. It was just a panic attack. I wouldn't pass out. *My heart is fine. It will pass.*

"The same dream?" he asked once my breathing slowed.

I hesitated.

This time was different. I knew it wasn't a vision, there was no question because it was something that had already happened. Everything that happened in the cellar replayed in my head, all the fear on Angel's face pierced my chest. Knowing how much it must have hurt for him to feed on me and how much harder it must've been to keep in control after being hungry for so long...

"No," I said, finally noticing the way he studied me.

"A new vision?" he asked.

I shook my head.

"No. It was more like a memory, well, it *was* a memory."

I was terrible at keeping secrets. I didn't have to see the way his body tensed to know he could read the hidden meaning in my expression.

"I hate that Paul wasn't the only man who hurt you there," he said, voice taking that rough edge he usually did when he was frustrated. "I fucking hate it."

"You didn't hurt me," I said, cupping his face. His jaw tightened and as intimidating as he looked when he was like this, his hands were soft when they took mine. He sat them on my lap and stood up. I was worried he would try brushing the conversation away like he usually did when we ventured into the darker parts of his reality. He didn't like to talk about being a vampire, not passed the surface anyway. I was too curious. He knew so many of the things that felt raw to me. It wasn't that I wanted to prod at a sore spot; I wanted to help bear the weight of whatever tormented him. I wanted to show him that he wasn't the monster he thought he was, he couldn't be when his humanity made him pull away from my neck in the cellar.

"If you hadn't been able to stop yourself..."

"Don't talk that way, Mouse," he said, his voice a soft plea.

"If I'd lost too much blood, would I be like you?"

"It doesn't work that way."

"Would you have made it work? would you have turned me?"

"Lily," Angel said, the break in his voice stealing the last of my questions. "Please, don't ask me. Please, don't ask me because I... I couldn't do that to you. I won't let you be cursed the way I am."

"You're not some demon from Hell," I said and patted his chest with both my hands.

"Yes, I am! That's exactly what I am!"

He'd never raised his voice at me. He removed his hand from the metal post of my bed. He'd bent the top so that it pointed toward the door. He groaned and used a single hand to bend the metal back in place again, the frame moaning as he forced it. He turned away from me. His hands went to the bun at the top of his head, and he pulled the elastic free, shaking his shoulder-length hair out before he began to gather it again at the crown of his head.

"What if you hadn't been able to stop?" I asked again, my heart skipping when he finished pulling his hair in a bun. He looked down at the metal bedpost and took a deep breath.

"You would have bled out and died," he said and looked up at me, expression serious.

"I wouldn't... I wouldn't be like you?"

"No," he said simply. "It doesn't work that way and I won't explain how it does. It wouldn't have happened back in that cellar, and it never will. I won't let it. I won't let you become what I am."

My eyes stung. This shouldn't hurt. Still, it felt like he'd rejected me somehow. I didn't want to be a vampire. I wasn't really sure what I expected him to say.

"It's that bad? You really think you're so cursed that you'd rather me die"

"I don't mean it to sound harsh. God, I hate when you cry."

He was sitting next to me again, taking both of my hands in his. He took a deep breath but didn't speak. He kept his eyes on our linked hands. He raised my right hand and used the back of it to brush a tear from his cheek. He let out another breath and looked up at me, back in control as his soft gaze held mine.

"I don't expect you to understand. No one should. Being a vampire, undying, makes it so easy to forget about the importance of every moment, how significant life is when it can come to an end. Over time, as you continue and never change or grow weak and the gravest of wounds heal in minutes... Life can so easily be trivial and it's not. I don't want to live forever and I want that even less now that I have you. That's what makes me cursed."

Cursed, like something out of a fairytale. This world was turning out to be more like a fairytale than I ever imagined. Vampires. Guardians. I thought about Olivia's mind-reading abilities. She said Angel wasn't being totally truthful about himself. She said he was looking for something.

"What have you been looking for?" I asked.

His hands tensed in mine. After a beat passed, he let go of me. He straightened up and slipped his hand into his jeans pocket. When he withdrew it, he had a small vial in his hand. He let it sit in the middle of his palm so I could see.

Blood.

My skin cooled as I looked at the vial.

"A long time ago, a witch told me a story about the origins of vampires. A woman was cursed with wings and darkness and left to endure the world, bound by the need for blood alone to remain sane," Angel said before replacing the vial in his pocket. "Blood of a guardian. It's one of the many things she said I needed to gather and bring back to her if I wanted to try undoing the curse. I nearly sucked out what little was in that vial to make the hunger more bearable in that cellar. I nearly did when you were locked in with me."

"Maybe you aren't the only one cursed," I said and adjusted on the bed. I tried sitting up more but stopped when my ankle ached. "If you were cursed by blood, then I'm cursed with sight."

Angel shook his head and took my hands again, opening his mouth to deny it like I knew he would.

"Everyone has something. We are all cursed by things. For most people it's their past decisions or something out of their control..."

My chest tightened and not because he looked up at me with those amber eyes. Angel sat next to me again and brushed the hair away from my face with one hand.

"I have never loved anyone the way I love you. No one," he said and let his hand move to the base of my neck.

"That's... a lot considering how old you are," I said, butterflies filling my stomach when he let out a laugh.

"Watch it," he said playfully, brushing my bottom lip with his thumb.

"You going to toss me over your shoulder again?" I asked, feeling the warmth spread to my face. You'd think after all this time I would stop feeling embarrassed whenever I took a chance on saying something sexy.

Angel smirked and shook his head.

"Not tonight, Mouse," he said and kissed my forehead before sitting back. "You should take some Tylenol and get some rest."

I groaned and grabbed the front of his shirt as he stood up. He easily could've pulled away, being vampire and all, but he didn't. He let me pull him toward me. He gave me a kiss before gently pulling my hands from his shirt and kissing my knuckles.

Angel brought a couple Tylenol capsules and a glass of water back from the kitchen. I downed them and lay down, feeling more comfortable than I had in weeks now that I was back in my own bed. Angel laid down beside me. I did my best to snuggle closer, wincing when my ankle caught in the sheets. He lay flat on his back and I propped my head on his shoulder, my ear pressed against his chest where everything was silent. No thump of a heart, though I knew it was still there.

# CHAPTER 28
## ANGEL

I didn't want to leave her alone after everything.

Call me paranoid.

I waited for another week until Anne returned from visiting her girlfriend's family to hunt. I should've taken care of this guy sooner. A man in his forties. Successful business owner. Father. Physically abusive to his wife. Emotionally abusive to his kids. Prostitute killer.

He's killed three women that I'm aware of, all drug addicts with no one to look for them. He's low on the police's priority list of criminals. For all they know, their deaths aren't connected in any way. That's how this guy works though.

I let my mind go to that dark place the closer I got to him. Once he was alone on the way to his next kill, I felt the shift from human to monster. I waited until he found his next victim, a skinny brunette that looked barely legal. He called her over from outside the club so blatantly that you'd think he was supposed to be there. Everyone on the street *did* think that it was planned, and the brunette leaned into the game.

"Dad! About time!"

She waved to the bouncer at the door and hurried to the passenger door of the BMW. I moved to the nearest alley as she climbed in, and he pulled from the curb. I used the rooftop as my highway, gliding from building to building until we got closer to the river, and I was forced to return to the ground.

I kept my eyes trained on the car as we moved farther and farther from the busy nightlife of the city and closer to the docks and abandoned sidewalks near the river. The car came to a stop under a bridge that stretched over the river, just far enough from the road that the streetlights didn't shine on the black BMW.

My senses were heightened, more so now that I gave in to my nature. I could hear him flirting, the way she giggled, the dirty things he said before they shifted in the front seats. I could see the passenger seat recline and he climbed on top of her. A single gasp of air and what was left of my control snapped.

I was next to the car in seconds.

I wrenched open the door, the lock snapping with a loud pop. The man looked up at me in shock with his hands still wrapped around the girl's neck and his pants hanging loose on his hips. I grabbed the back of his suit jacket and tugged him from the car and tossed him roughly onto the ground. I turned to check on the girl as she began to recover, panicked gasps sending the man into his bullshit story about how she liked it rough.

I froze. Like that, I was thrown out of my primal trance with a single look at her. Brown hair. Brown eyes. She even raised her hands to her hair when scared the way she did. I wondered if dimples would form on her cheeks when she smiled the same way hers did...

"Run," I told her. When she didn't move, I yelled the words. She didn't so much as scream as she ran toward the road.

I looked the opposite way where the man was yards ahead. I felt almost sick from the thoughts moments ago. I didn't want to go through with it. I never did but letting down the walls and releasing the beast within made doing it easier.

I needed to feed. I had to feed. I had Lily. I had to be in control with her. I needed to feed to be in control. This wouldn't be forever. I had the guardian blood. I didn't know what was next on that list, but if I could just find that witch...

If I let this man go, that was one more time he could go home and hit his wife.

My wings burst from my back, unfurling and carrying me yards at a time with each beat so that I was soaring above the man. I kicked the back of his head as I passed so that he tripped and rolled against the dirt. I swooped to the ground and quickly retracted my wings before turning to face him.

He groaned as he pushed himself from the ground. He'd just gotten a knee underneath him when I reached him. He opened his mouth to scream, but I clapped a hand over it and sank my fangs into his throat, feeling the warm gush from his carotid artery and instantly relaxing as I gave in to my thirst. They never made a sound when I latched on this way. The shock came first and then, once they realized the damage, it was too late. Just like those before him, the man's weight settled against me in seconds, his final breath tickling my ear as I fed.

I drank as much as I could, forcing myself to feed even as the disgust of what I'd done started to turn my stomach. When I couldn't stand it anymore, I lowered the man's body to the ground and looked over myself. I'd been clean as always. There wasn't even a drop of blood on the ground, not even now as the man lay mostly drained in the dirt.

"I'll take it from here."

I'd heard her sneak up behind me, but it was still unnerving to have her so close. I turned to face the witch with the blue braids. She wore leggings and a pullover zipped halfway. The silver pendant at her neck caught the moonlight, reflecting off the surface. The round pendant had a star in the middle of a circle of thorns, probably the sign of her coven.

"What did you find?" I asked and stepped away from the man, motioning for her to do her thing.

She hesitated, her eyes lingering on me in annoyance. I knew she didn't want to help, but she owed me after I took care of the blonde vampire that was bothering her coven. She would do the minimum and move on.

She lowered her eyes to the man on the ground, pointing a finger at him. His body began to shrink, his human body shifting until he was nothing but a piece of driftwood. The witch bent over to pick up the splintered piece of wood. She held it so I could see, turning it three-sixty before she tossed it toward the bank where it barely reached the tide. She looked back at me, eyebrow raised before extending her hand to me.

"Did you find anything?" I asked again.

"I just did you a favor," she said and nodded toward her palm.

We'd met only twice before, and I was already glad to be rid of her. I reached into my pocket and pulled out my wallet, counting out the bills until I had the five grand we'd agreed upon. I placed the bills in her hand and held back a growl as she counted the amount.

"I didn't find anything on her, but I found her coven," the woman said, pocketing the cash and pulling out an envelope. "It's all in there."

I almost pushed her hand away, but I decided to take the envelope at the last moment.

"I already know she's in Virginia," I said and checked the envelope. The photo I'd given her last time was still inside next to a folded piece of paper.

"She *was* in Virginia," the witch scoffed. "She's not now."

"Why would an entire coven move?" I asked, unable to keep the cutting edge from my voice.

"What's left of that coven is in New Orleans now."

"What's left?"

"You have a lot of questions and I don't see you handing over any more money for them," the witch said and started to back away. "I told you that it's all in that envelope. You're on your own from here. Whoever's left of that coven... Find some witch or warlock in New Orleans to explain. They'll have more answers than I can find."

She turned her back on me, starting into a jog and making it look like a normal midnight activity as she joined the sidewalk.

I took a different route back to the city streets, taking my time to walk until I caught a cab the rest of the way to my building. It was loud like always, music blaring from various floors on the way up and people yelling. I knew I couldn't be, but I was tired. Really, I was frustrated. It had been decades of searching and planning and I didn't want to spend a year longer than I had to searching for this damn cure.

I would find the cure and age with Lily, or I would let her find someone who could grow old with her. I'd stake myself and be done with it. She deserved a full life.

I wanted to shower, but I forgot about shutting off my service when I went to turn on the tap. I wasn't taking anything with me except the envelope. It was the last thing I needed in New York before I left for the next leg of my search.

I tossed it onto the old couch and sank into the cushions. I contemplated going back to Lily's apartment but found the envelope back in my hands seconds later. I opened the flap and pulled out the contents. The photo inside was the same one from that meeting that changed everything. The witch had long dark hair, tight curls framing her face. She smiled in the photo, a white woman with a short bob sitting on her right and a dark-haired man on her left. The three of them were meeting for coffee. The woman with the bob and the man brought a smiling baby that the three of them took turns holding like it was a prize.

I took the photo after days of following the witch, learning what she was capable of, the ways she was unlike the others in her coven. She didn't see other supernatural beings as abhorrent as so many witches did. She was also stronger, surprisingly strong for someone so young. I knew she was the one who could help me and likely already knew how. I met her the same day I took the photo, just moments after.

As soon as I snapped the photo, she looked up and right at me across the coffee shop patio.

I put the photo back in the envelope. The folded piece of paper wasn't a letter like I first thought. I'd imagined a snarky message from the woman with the blue braids, but instead it was a printout of a website. The photo at the top was of an old brick building with the street number above the double doors. The website specified the building as being a historic site that now served as an apartment complex. However, there was no phone number or page to look at listings. The website was just the single main page with a button labeled "click for more." Beneath the button on the website, the witch had handwritten a series of numbers.

I put the contents back in the envelope before folding it in half and putting it in the backpack by the door. I pulled it onto one shoulder and without a single look back, I went into the hall. Not one person stopped me as I walked toward the stairs. The elevator had never been functional and the trip down to the city street gave me time to think.

I'd parked the SUV on the street earlier today, telling Lily that I would move out of my apartment and into hers. There wasn't anything in that apartment I planned to take with me aside from what I'd already packed and left in a suitcase back at her place. I tossed the backpack into the passenger seat as I got behind the wheel, still deciding what I was going to tell her.

What I hadn't told her was that I had to leave. If I worked quick, I would be back before Anne even moved out of the apartment so she wouldn't have to be alone. By leaving, I could tie up loose ends and make sure Paul and Olivia couldn't find her again to hurt her anymore. If I found that witch, I was a step closer to putting an end to this curse.

One step closer.

# BONUS SCENE
## NIGHT SWIM

# ACKNOWLEDGMENTS

This book has lived in my brain since I wrote that very first scene featuring Angel in Shade of the Shadowlands. I hadn't planned on him being anything more than a character Tori worked with at the coffee shop, someone to interact with during scenes there. I knew the moment I wrote him that he needed to have a larger part and I knew by the end of writing that book that there was so much more to explore about Angel, and I couldn't help myself.

So, first, thank you to all of my amazing readers for picking up this book. This is a departure from my usual young adult style, and I understand that it may not be for everyone. I appreciate everyone who has given it a chance and I hope you fell in love with Lily and Angel the way I have. Thank you to my Patreon members for supporting me through the process and cheering me on when I shared sneak peeks and early drafts. You all have been invaluable, and I appreciate all the feedback you've given me.

A huge thank you goes to my husband. Alex, you have always been my biggest supporter in chasing my author dreams. Thank you so much for encouraging me and calming my worries. I love you. Thank you to Katie Stier for your many shoutouts and positive words. Thank you to Miranda Johnson for always being willing to listen to my ideas and always giving me constructive feedback. Thank you, Matt Johnson, for your many "when Amy's a famous author..." musings. Your comments always make me laugh and remind me why I continue to dream big. You never know what is possible. Dream big. Take a chance on yourself. You just might surprise yourself.

# About the Author

Amy Prokopis is a fiction author from Oklahoma who writes fantasy books. She loves writing everything from science fiction and fantasy to contemporary romance. She graduated from Oklahoma State University with a bachelor's degree in English and a minor in German before obtaining a master's degree in school counseling. Besides writing, Amy enjoys distance running and spending time with her husband, their son, and their Havanese, June.

# OTHER BOOKS BY AMY PROKOPIS